MOON LUCK

A Novel by

Wayne Scott Harral

outskirts
press

Contents

Preface

We will be on the Moon, living and working there, within our lifetimes. And for some of us, that is not so far away. And Mars is not that much further off. We will go there because, like our ancestors, we are never satisfied with where we are; we are always striving to be... there, somewhere else, and to be one of the first to do it.

I have enjoyed writing this story because it is a way for me to reach out there in my own way. It is the way I am. I am never just satisfied.

Enough about me. This book is for you, if you are like me. It's just enough in the future to be wholly fiction but premised upon current knowledge of the world (both the Earth and the Moon), science and technology. In fact, if you think I might have made something up, I encourage you to Google it. You might be pleasantly surprised at just how much of this story is laced in fact. Also, in the back of the book, you will find a "List of Characters and Other Names Used" where you will have a quick definition of some of the terms I did create and use in the story. And, if you are really so inclined, there is a map of the locations of the base stations as well as one of the ore mines.

Even if you do not fact-check it, and especially if you do, I hope you enjoy this story as much as I enjoyed telling it!

Acknowledgements

I wish to acknowledge and thank John Anselmo, an old friend and late-term author who inspired me to do the same. I also wish to acknowledge a few others who helped me when I needed it:

Jeff Vogler, sci-fi aficionado, whose, comments and edits made a discernable difference.

Tim Lawnicki, for when I needed some law enforcement and investigation concepts.

Mary Musgrave, plant physiologist, for her fascinating research on plant growth in space (regrettably, she passed away a few years ago)

Eleina Hancock, UConn, for help in my plant research

Prologue

28 March 2039, evening, New York, New York, USA, Earth

Breaking News. This is WNN – World News Network:

In an event that has shocked the nation and the world, NASA reported that an explosion occurred on the Moon Base Station Venturous late last night. One astronaut was reported killed in the explosion. No one else was killed or injured. The cause of the explosion is unknown at this time and is being investigated. The name of the astronaut that was killed has been withheld until the notification of the next of kin.

NASA, a member of the international joint venture Moon Exploratory Team or MET that operates the station, said that the explosion occurred in one of the maintenance modules of the Venturous resulting in a depressurization of that module. Standard safety measures in place at the time confined the loss of air pressure to just the one module. No other portion of the base station was affected.

MET's Mission Director, Kurt Vaughn, is reported as saying that it did not appear that the astronaut caused the explosion. Rather it was unfortunate that the one astronaut was in the module at the time. In response to questions, Vaughn stated that in its ten-year history of safe operation on the Moon, there had been no other incident – not even a bad scratch – prior to yesterday's explosion. MET implements extensive and redundant measures to keep its astronaut community safe and well. The loss of one of their own has been devastating to NASA; the European Space Agency, MET's other agency partner; and to SpaceX, Blue Origin and Lockheed Martin, MET's corporate partners.

News of this event has spread around the world as people from many countries express their sorrow. The White House said that later today the President will address…

Six days earlier:

Chapter 1
The Call Home

22 March 2039, 8:42 pm UTC,
MET Moon Base Station Venturous, Sea of Serenity, Moon

*T*his wait is ridiculous… six seconds… really…

Jim Sheppard was sitting up in his bunk in one of the base station's berthing areas. He could see his wife looking back at him via her video camera/monitor. Occasionally he could see her looking down at the virtual intelliboard of their home Skylake, or what used to be known as a personal computer. She was talking to him from their Murrieta, California, home. Sometimes she would look up directly at the camera lens, but mostly she was looking at the screen, looking at her astronaut-scientist husband, who was located somewhere on the Moon. Her auburn hair and deep blue eyes both glistening, or seemingly so, on his monitor. And he could see his two young children…

Six seconds had passed since he had last spoke.

"That must be exciting, Jim," Lori Sheppard is finally heard saying. "To be a part of that achievement. Growing plants on the Moon!" Hesitating, she added, "I think you are going to miss that the most, your work with the plants."

Jim responded proudly, "Oh, you know it! Our achievements here at the base station have been phenomenal! Breakthroughs are being made almost daily. Well, maybe not daily, but quite frequently. It's been great to be a productive part of so many advances here on the Moon. Current speculation is that in not too many more years there will be a full colony or two here."

Before he got too excited, Jim knew he must add the comment she really wanted to hear. "Still, I'm just glad that three and a half months from now I can turn over something great to my replacement." His time Moon-side, as some of the crewmembers liked to say, was coming to an end.

This was the part of the call he truly didn't like. Once he finished his sentence, there was the interminable wait for the transmission to not only make it's 2.6-second round trip from the Moon to the Earth and back, but the extra three and a half seconds it took to process the transmission signal before showing itself on his monitor.

In that waiting period, Jim could see his two children, Sarah and Sean, as they waited, not so patiently, for the transmission of their father's image and voice to get to them. Sarah, their 10-year old, and the older of the two, was making best efforts to stay focused on the conversation she really wasn't part of. And to be fair, Sarah also had to deal with her 4-year-old brother, who clearly had had enough of this conversation. His toys were waiting.

6 seconds.

Lori had heard his last words, that he would be coming home soon, and smiled. "I am sure that you will continue to be a vital part of the mission's continued success, even if you are here on Earth. Your knowledge and experience with the hydroponics… and the many other experiments you were a part of, make you a much-desired continuing member of the team."

Speaking a bit softer, Lori added, "You know the kids miss you and I miss you too. Very much. We can't wait to have you back home, hun."

"And I do miss you and the kids, too. Don't I know well

that Sean only knows me by these SpaceTime calls. To him, I am probably just someone on a screen. He was only one when I left for this mission." Jim hesitated and thought to himself, *stay upbeat. Don't falter now.* "Hey, three and a half months will fly by. I will be home before you know it." Jim was due to rotate back to Earth and be home in early July. "And, Sean..." Jim said looking to the son he had only held for eighteen months, "... I will be home for your Big 5 birthday party. We will get to do so much together very soon!"

SpaceTime.

You would think that in this day of modern technology, they could get the transmission speed down at least a few seconds. Jim knew, as did Lori, to talk to the other without hesitation or gaps and when you finished your thought, stop. Wait to let the other person respond. If you did not wait your turn, it was easy to talk over the other person, sometimes forcing that person to start over again. That only wasted valuable communication time.

On the other hand, the six-second delay gave a person the opportunity to think about what to say next. That was very important in these limited transmissions.

As a reflex. Jim looked at the base station's wall clock with its forest background, fancily displaying the Coordinated Universal Time date and time, under which the base station, Venturous, operated. The clock also displayed the times in New York, Los Angeles, Houston, Darmstadt, Dubai, Moscow and Beijing –Friday, March 22, 2039, 20:43 UTC for him, 1:43 pm PDT in California.

There on Earth, most clocks had moved forward an hour just a week ago for Daylight Saving Time, or as the Europeans called it, 'summertime,' but no such adjustment was made on the Venturous. It stayed with UTC year-round.

6 seconds.

Sean beamed. So did Sarah. And so did Lori when they heard his words. "That would be great daddy! Can we play together then?" asked Sean

"It's been so long since you've been home, dad," said Sarah with a big smile.

"Yes, it will be great to have you home and in time for Sean's birthday. That will be so wonderful," added Lori, "although I hope the weather improves here. It's not been the same California since you left." She was referring to the continual extreme weather patterns that had been plaguing the West Coast, seemingly dumping more rain than the state was used to or could manage.

"How are your folks doing?" directing his question to his wife. "Has your mother recovered from that flu bug?"

6 seconds.

"They are both fine and, yes, Mom recovered. They are still in the snow in Cincinnati, this late in March. All these extreme weather events must be attributed to the ongoing climate change no doubt." She added quickly, "They ask about you of course. I tell them you are fine."

"Dad, can you bring me back a Moon rock?" asked Sean.

"Yeah, one for me too," chimed in Sarah.

"I think that can be arranged. I'll see what I can do. Sarah, you can probably take a Moon rock to your fourth-grade class and share it I would think." To Lori, "And that's good news about your parents. I should SpaceTime them soon. I know they would like it."

Jim quickly asked, to keep his end of the conversation going, "How did the roof replacement go?" Jim was referring back to the constant heavy rains in Southern California that had not only devastated the wine production throughout the Temecula Valley, but, for his own family, they had led to an unplanned need to replace the roof on their 25-year-old house. Good thing his astronaut colleague Bruce Holmann came through with a solid recommendation for a repair comp…

6 seconds.

"They love that when you call from the Moon," Lori responded, cutting Jim's thoughts short. "As for the roof, it's done. The contractor did a great job. Tell Bruce thanks again for the recommendation. How's he doing?

Bruce Holmann was the senior astronaut and Executive Officer on Venturous. At 57 years old, and the mechanical engineer on board, he was also Jim's good friend for many years. Perhaps he was more like a mentor since Jim was only 38.

"He'll be glad to hear that. I think he'd appreciate some positive news for a change." Responded Jim. "He's still struggling – relationships remain a bit dicey right now between the SpaceX senior crew and the NASA and ESA leadership. Adding to that, it seems everyone is on edge with the Chinese trying to outdo us up here. I think they're still reeling from the fallout of the trade war of some 20 years ago."

Jim paused for Lori to take this in. He didn't want to share too much. Who knew what people were actually listening in – SpaceTime calls were anything but secure – and Lori didn't need to worry about onboard politics. He probably should not have mentioned the Chinese and the trade war. For all he knew, they too were listening in… hopefully! Ok he was rubbing it in. It took China nearly six years to fully recover and regain their commercial prominence – thanks to the support of the EU – but when they did, they were even more powerful and, frankly, more aggressive than in the early 2010 years. It was scary.

6 seconds.

Lori wanted to console Jim, reminding him that life on the Moon really is a good thing. "Ya know, I think Bruce has a tough job up there, keeping so many Type A's herded together, like cats as they used to say. But he's got you, and of course Dan Wedmond and all of NASA supporting him."

"Thank you for your kind support my dear, but in truth, this internal bickering between NASA and ESA, and the SpaceX consortium has been a bit debilitating. I know that the MET directors pretend it doesn't happen. I just wish Commander Wedmond would take a more active role in resolving the problem. Frankly, turning the matter of internal politics over to Jim only exacerbates the problem since some of the crew view his leadership as indifferent to the issues. And it's just stifling our real mission here – to study the Moon, make it habitable and make it a viable resource for our future. I think it's going to get worse before it gets better."

Moon Exploration Team! For some on the base station, team was not the optimal word.

In truth, thought Jim, the vast majority of the thirty MET astronauts, scientists and engineers here on the Venturous were truly dedicated to the mission and were wonderful to work with. Jim did not like to get down on MET. If they would only open their eyes to the egos at play.

But then, wasn't it inevitable? The concept of a public-private partnership of two continental governments and a global business consortium was bound to give rise to tensions due to the diverse goals of each partner.

Still, would we be here on the Moon without such joint efforts of government and business: NASA, Jim's employer and one-time leader of the space exploration race – ESA, the European Space Agency that had bloomed in later decades – and of course, there was Space Exploration Technologies Corporation, better known as SpaceX, and its small consortium of subcontracted firms; Blue Origin and Lockheed Martin. SpaceX was the world-renowned explorer of space and provider of many of the world's commercial satellite launch vehicles. Blue Origin and Lockheed Martin had equally impressive credentials in the space industry.

Then there was China. The China National Space Administration was also here on the Moon. In fact, their station preceded the Venturous by three years. And it was a leader in the technology to get humans to Mars as well. Add to the mix other countries such as Japan and Israel, that were following close on the heels of the two leaders. Jim knew, however, he was here on the Moon because of the joint effort…

6 seconds.

Lori, put on an obviously forced smile, "Hang in there, Jim," Lori said with a bit of a forced smile.

Shooing the kids away to go play, she added, "I am so proud of you. I know it's gotta be tough, but you and the M-E-T team have accomplished so much." She did not use the acronym like the Americans did, but spelled it out the way the Europeans tended to do. "The media are continually reporting your achievements. Sometimes, when I watch a 3DTV documentary, I feel like I am right there with you, hon."

"You are a wonderful wife and I miss you so much. You know that, right?" Jim smiled. "And you are right, there is so much that has been accomplished that we can be proud of."

With that, Jim's whole demeanor changed. His face glowed just a bit. But noticing the clock again, Jim said to his wife, "OK. You put me back on track. It's late for me, my love. I have to get going now. Hug the kids. We'll talk again next week. Love you."

Jim just stared at Lori, the person whom he, for all intents, lived for. As he waited that interminable six seconds, his daughter Sarah came back into view. He hadn't said good-bye to her and Sean.

He had been very fortunate. There was just a bit of remorse that went with his good fortune. But wasn't that supposed to make us stronger? He gave a slight wave to the women in his life.

6 seconds.

"Love you, too, Jim."

"I love you, too, daddy. Come home soon."

"I will soon enough, Sarah."

Jim ended the call, feeling both happy and sad at the same time, and not sure why. The call with his wife and two children gave him pause to reflect on his three plus years on the Moon serving on Joint Base Station Venturous.

He absolutely loved his work and would not have changed a thing. He had accomplished so much on the Moon and had shared in the accomplishments of his co-crewmembers. His focus had been on mechanical engineering, but when so many fascinating developments came out of the greenhouse, just going on its third year in operation, he found a whole new passion.

Still, three years in a confined space with 29 other crewmembers, men and women, tended to take its toll, even in a space as big as the 560 square meters of the Joint Base Station Venturous. He had to admit that he wouldn't mind living back on Earth, back in sunny Southern California and back with his very young family. He wouldn't mind not thinking of a closed-in berthing area that he shared with two others of his fellow astronauts.

OK, he would miss it here!

Alone for the moment, Jim reviewed his work plan for tomorrow as he prepared for bed. His fellow astronauts that he shared this berthing area with would be coming in shortly. Changing out of his workday jumpsuit and into a specially designed one-piece outfit that literally massaged the muscles and induced sleep, somewhat like the old vibrating beds of the past, he laid down on his small bed, feeling the suit starting to do its thing, tingling and stimulating his muscular system. He had adhered to a workout routine that kept him in good condition, but the massaging outfit acted on nearly every muscle in his body. Everyone on Venturous agreed that in its 10-year operation, this was one of the best, if not the most beneficial, innovations that could be found on the Moon. This was tech he would miss when back on Earth.

Within a matter of minutes, his body was fully relaxed; his mind on his family. He never did hear his astronaut roommates come in. He was… elsewhere.

Chapter 2
This Is Normal

Com'é interessante questa notizia!
Luca Barolo, senior ESA astronaut stationed on Joint Base Station Venturous, mumbled to himself in his native Italian as he walked gingerly along the corridor from his berthing area to the common area for the staff meeting waiting for him there. Luca was one of the new arrivals and had only been at the station a few weeks. Despite his intense low-grav training on earth, walking under the Moon's gravity still took some effort. After all, he was getting up there in age – 47 years old. It amazed him that his 86 kilograms of body mass was the equivalent of 14 kilograms on the Moon, but still took a full controlled physical effort to move about and not drift into walls, furnishings and the station's various conduits, ducts and pipework.

He practiced his conversions from kilograms to the American-preferred pounds, since many of the USA crewmembers still worked in that mindset. He thought to himself: Let's see, 86 kilos… that is about 190 pounds. But converting that to the Moon's acceleration of .166g was… about… $31^{1/2}$ pounds.

In his mind, saying 190 pounds just seemed to be heavy, but 31 pounds seemed so light! Maybe that was why it felt that it took so much effort to get momentum when moving or to stop the momentum when he needed to.

Luca grew up in Ivrea, Italy – in the Piemonte region near the old Olivetti factory. His thick dark hair contrasted with his light blue eyes, a common trait of the inhabitants of this part of Northern Italy. He studied physics at the University of Torino, not too far from his family home.

As a physicist back in Milan, but also as an experienced ESA astronaut with three tours on the International Space Station, he knew and understood very well the mechanics of gravity and momentum on the Moon. It was his life's work. Living it, however, was a different matter for the mind. He also knew from his space station experience that, given time, he'd be moving about with ease just like the others at the station that have been here, some for several years now!

Like the other corridors that the station comprised, the corridor he was passing through was short. The station corridors were intended primarily to connect the workspaces, laboratories, berthing areas, storage areas, and the Command Center with each other, but they also acted as safety barriers. In an emergency, such as a meteorite strike to some portion of the base station that penetrated both the outer structural shell and the inner insulated core, the corridors had quick-acting air-tight hatches at both ends that slid from the side. The purpose of these hatches, of course, were to rapidly isolate any compromised element of the station. In theory, if a crewmember were caught in a compromised room, reserve oxygen-nitrogen mix under high pressure would counter the rapidly decompressing space long enough for the crewmember to open a corridor hatch and pass through to one of the isolating corridors. Or if caught within one of the corridors, he or she could quickly enter the next sustainable space.

But that was theory, and everyone knew it be a matter of seconds within which a crewmember had to react. Among their various station safety drills, the crew practiced rapid compromised space exiting or RCSE, so that there would be no hesitation by a stranded crewmember should the real thing happen.

Six years ago, there had been a meteorite strike to one of the station's modules. It was of sufficient mass that the strike resulted in an air leak. The safety systems worked flawlessly, but there had been no one in the compartment at the time. A good thing, but the effectiveness of the system for saving lives was still... untested.

Entering the common area, Luca approached the large circular table and, with a bit of effort, sat down with the team already present. There waiting for him were Commander Dan Wedmond; Dr. Omoné Reisberg; SpaceX's Anna Kormendy; Executive Officer Bruce Holmann; and a member of the crew whose name he still had trouble remembering, but that he knew he was from SpaceX and from Canada.

"Sorry I'm late, but I was catching up on the news from the Middle East," reported Luca, his Italian accent emphasized in line with his elevated speech.

"Well, spill it," the Canadian said. "What are Iran and Saudi Arabia doing now?"

"Iran has definitely stirred the hornets' nest as you Westerners say. After Iran launched a few mid-range missiles at Saudi Arabia yesterday, Saudi wasted no time firing back. Who would have thought that neither side could actually hit their targets? So far, every one of the 16 missiles had been intercepted."

Bruce gave a wave-off gesture with his hand, "I have to believe that if both Saudi Arabia and Iran fire missiles at each other and could't land a single one, they never really intended to. You can't successfully intercept all 16 missiles. I just don't see that happening."

"Either way," chimed in Dr. Anna Kormendy, the Hungarian

from SpaceX and lead scientist on Venturous, "it will be a disaster for the people of the Middle East... and for Europe for that matter." Anna lifted her hands off the table in a gesture, illustrating her discontent to her colleagues.

"It will be a disaster for everybody," Dr. Omoné Reisberg offered in a conciliatory tone. Omoné, the base physician, was raised and educated in Berlin, but was born in Frankfurt to parents neither of whom were native German. Her mother, a doctor herself, had emigrated from Angola in 2002. While still living in Angola, she had suffered the loss of her family there. Despite the care and oversight, that, as a doctor, her mother had provided to her then-older sister and sister's father, her mother lost both to one of the many epidemics that plagued her homeland and so, alone, she came to Germany.

Her father, Alec Reisberg had escaped the fallout of the political upheaval in Poland. Once a country that looked favorably upon liberal ideals, or at least nurtured a population that was open-minded, Alec thrived as a journalist. But that started to change as Poland began to revert to the communist era mentality of one party dominating anyone or anything under its influence. Those powerful nationalists brought the communist mentality back under a central dictatorial control. Alec fled his beloved Warsaw, arriving within days of Omoné's mother, meeting in the same immigration services line. The two became friends; became husband and wife; and soon were starting a new family. Omoné was born a year later. She grew up in a home that nurtured diversity and a love of knowledge and in a city that, for the most part, offered the same.

Omoné always knew she was different but had worked it to her advantage as a means of helping others. Becoming a doctor, like her mother, was a given. Becoming a psychiatrist as well, that was Omoné going a step further.

Out of fascination and pure curiosity, she managed to get involved with the ESA astronaut corps and, in due course, was eventually selected to go to the Moon. That was two and a half years ago, when she travelled to the Moon along with Bruce Holmann and another astronaut by way of the Lunar Orbital Platform Gateway space station that orbited the Moon. It was not at all surprising that Dr. Reisberg became the medical doctor, psychiatrist and counselor on Venturous.

At present, however, the meeting discussion had digressed, or so thought the commanding officer of the Venturous. Asserting his dominance as both the station's commander and the apparent largest human on board, Commander Wedmond said to the team, "Let's defer this conversation until dinner. It's definitely a subject I do want to get into later. Right now, I need you to be focused on our rather important issues at hand, here on Venturous."

Accordingly, the crew members settled down, all eyes centered on the commander's.

Glancing at his agenda he paused, possibly for effect, and took a sip from his coffee cup that contained something that wasn't real coffee, but what the crew chose to call 'wannabe coffee.' He was one of a few who did not often drink from the MET-provided wholly enclosed drinking bottles. Commander Wedmond, having been in command of the Venturous for nearly two years, had long since mastered the art of drinking from an open cup.

"Housekeeping," he stated firmly. "I understand that our water generation and purification system is back up and working to expected norms." He glanced quickly at Anna Kormendy. "Our thanks go to you and Jim Sheppard for resolving that issue. That could have been a huge problem for us."

Anna Kormendy nodded, accepting the accolades. "That's what we at SpaceX do best – solve problems and make them go away."

"Yes, of course," says Dan, adding, "I am sure Jim will agree with you." Pause. "So, we can back off the rationing then?"

"Most definitely," asserted Anna. "We are still monitoring water output, but it's looking very good." She admitted though, "Jim's modifications to the osmosis pipe wheel motor were a contributing factor."

"No doubt," says Bruce Holmann, shaking his head ever so slightly.

Dan realized quickly he must maintain control. The first item on the agenda, and already he saw egos flaring. "I'll let the crew know restrictions will be lifted for now."

Luca Barolo smiled... big time. The plant people would be molti contenti, he thought to himself. The others took note of the newcomer's grin.

Commander Wedmond looked to his XO. "Bruce, I am not aware of any other system abnormalities. Anything to report?"

"No sir. Oxygen, CO2, waste disposal, and food consumption are all within parameters. All support systems are nominal. We are looking good."

"Good." Dan nodded thinking, Gotta love it when everything is operating like a Swiss watch! "Mr. Barolo, you've been here for three weeks. How are you adapting?"

"Very well, sir. Not too different from my assignments on ISS, but with a bit more room to move around."

"Are you getting up to speed on your assignments, experiments, living conditions?" queried Dan.

"Up to speed?" repeated Luca, hesitating on an American idiom. "Oh, yes. I am up to speed! I have been working with Mr. Holmann and Mr. Sheppard on the physics and mechanics of subterranean water storage systems. Pumping in low-grav has some very interesting effects."

Dan replied, "That's good to hear."

Anna interjected, "Luca, we tend to go by first names around here. It's just easier."

"All right, let's move on to our projects," says Dan, thinking that perhaps had they stayed with last names, there would be less disregard for seniority and the chain of command.

"Yeah, the fun stuff," said the Canadian from SpaceX. Luca still struggled to remember his name.

"Our iron ore mining continues well," stated the commander. "We are culling out about 50 kilograms of ore daily, varying depending upon the thickness and quality of the stratum we're chasing... Anna, please fill us in with some of the details?"

"Certainly. Our mining efforts, though temporarily on hold due to the breakdown of the rover, have been quite successful since the discovery of the ore two months ago," Anna asserted. "The location just inside Mare Serenitatis was unexpected..."

"Not so!" interrupted the Canadian. "I was able to deduce a probable location based upon our knowledge and research of the Moon's geology."

"Very true, Marc," chimed in Anna. "My faux pas. Which again supports my point that SpaceX should be leading this effort. We could be making much more progress if NASA and ESA would let us proceed with fewer restrictions."

Ah, that's his name. Marc Laboe, the SpaceX geophysicist. Luca just needed a reminder. Marc was the team's geology expert, credited for finding the iron ore veins about 10 kilometers from Venturous in Mare Serenitatis, or the Sea of Serenity as the Americans liked to call it. And he was also leading the effort in refining...

"Anna, we have discussed this at great length." The commander was clearly tired of Anna's grandiloquence. "MET has established the exploration protocol and we will adhere to it."

"But this is no longer 'exploration' as you say. At this stage, we are expanding and developing the available resources."

"More like exploitation as I see it," said Bruce.

"That's enough. We continue as per MET's directives," affirmed Dan, his voice not loud but clearly forceful. "Marc, please tell us about the refining experiments… succinctly if you will."

"Yes, sir. As you know, we have found that by operating in much lower pressures than on Earth, we can refine the iron ore at significantly lower temperatures. This was to be expected. The problem, of course, has been the lack of carbon molecules to complete the process. We have been experimenting with the use of our waste products. This has been successful, but our waste supply is limited."

"Who would have thought that to be a problem?" said Bruce.

"We continue our experiments with other Moon-based minerals. We think, because of the lower temperatures needed for the process, we can utilize what's available on the surface. But we're still in the experimental stage."

"Again, our hands are tied by your procedures," stated Anna. "We could be advancing this science much faster and stay at least at the same level of development as the Chinese, if we could loosen up the controls a bit."

The XO scowled at Anna. Won't she ever back off, he thought. "We'll that's just not gonna happen."

"Procedures are in place for many reasons, Dr. Kormendy. Not the least of which is for our safety. We cannot move ahead too rapidly nor disregard very well-considered protocols and risk the lives of our crew in the process. You know this." Dan began to lose his composure, but quickly settled back. "I would like to see us achieve great things with the iron ore refining project. It could mean accelerating our colonization of the Moon in the years to come. But we have to do it right and fully document the process. As a well-educated and experienced doctor, you know this."

Anna settled back, feeling that once again she has been unduly restrained and chastised for wanting to work faster. Beating the Chinese was a serious concern, but she knew that Dan was right. Safety was important.

"Having said that, I do have some good news for our geotechnical team. We received confirmation that the metallurgy lab expansion module will ship out in the next supply launch scheduled for this coming July. The MET directors are quite pleased with our success with the iron ore find and our research in refining it here on the Moon. They do want to support SpaceX's efforts in this area."

Priorities had changed back on Earth. The decision by MET management to move up the delivery of the module meant that Venturous would be deferring other projects that had been planned and awaiting crucial equipment and supplies. Some on the station would not be particularly thrilled with the delay of their life's work. These scientists and engineers had only so much time they could give to exploring the Moon before their time as an extra-lunar visitor was up and they rotated back to Earth!

"That's great!" said Marc elatedly.

"It is about time that M-E-T took our research seriously," said Anna, spelling out MET. The European crewmembers just did not get onboard with the acronym.

Few knew, of course, how much she had pushed MET director Jeff Fund, her boss and SpaceX's representative on the managing board, to get this done. Although it really did not take that much urging. Director Fund was of the mindset that SpaceX wasn't just in this for the notoriety of exploring the Moon. While their contribution to science was a function of its existence, as a private company, so was finding opportunities to make money. This was one of those ways.

The government agencies in this public-private partnership were aware of the SpaceX driving goal to turn a profit as well. The directors of NASA and ESA realized that if SpaceX could find a way to exploit whatever resources the Moon offered, then their governments' respective financial contributions of public funds would be reduced. Wasn't that the bottom-line goal of any P3, to share costs and reduce the public burden? If resources could be found and utilized on the Moon, the whole world benefited… in some fashion.

"Anna, I want you and Marc to work with Bruce on this. Review your plans and update them as necessary to accommodate the early arrival of the module."

"Will do," said Anna.

"Yes sir," said Marc, still beaming.

"Dr. Reisberg," said the commander, "I know this is out of your realm, but I would like you to assess the experiment schedules that will be impacted by this change up. I know some of our crew who were expecting equipment in July will be disappointed about this delay. I would like you to help me deal with this."

"I understand. I think the word has already been getting around, but we can structure an announcement that continues to stress the value of all our efforts."

Dan had to smile. He thought to himself, damn I am fortunate to have her on my crew.

"OK. Moving on. A few more items on the agenda." Looking down at it, Dan read, "Repair of the Moon Automated Rover/ Transport."

Apparently, over its eight-year operation on the Moon, the rover was one of the most overworked pieces of equipment at the base. It arrived, rather its parts arrived, two years after the establishment of the base and it had been operating nonstop since. Even the scheduled maintenance periods had to be accelerated to assure its continued operation. Still, the occasional break-down was inevitable. Thank goodness, a second rover was due to arrive in September.

Looking at the XO, "Can you give us a status update on that, Bruce?"

"Certainly," said Holmann. "The transportation of the iron ore has taken its toll. We lost a screw-drive gear on the left rear wheel due to surface rock damage to the gear cover and the resulting dust buildup. We had actually ordered a replace-ment for the drive gear assembly a few months back, but it's not due until the upcoming supply run. In the interim, I have worked with Jim Shepperd to fabricate a jury-rig until the re-placement parts arrive. I should have Martin up and running in a few days." 'Martin' was the unofficial name that the crew gave to the rover years ago, derived from M-A-R-T and tacking 'in' after that. The name just sort of stuck and everyone used it affectionately.

Anna said, "The sooner, the better. I need to get my team back out to the ore mine. We have so much more I'd like to do there."

"We will get all our teams back on their respective tasks," the XO emphasized. "There is a schedule for use by all our scientific and research teams and all have their priorities as well as you, Anna."

In an attempt to ease the obvious tension, Luca offered, "Perhaps I can assist you, Mr. Holmann. I was called upon to perform several makeshift repairs when I was on the ISS."

"Let's see if that will even be necessary, Luca," said Dan. "I think Bruce has it about wrapped up. But thank you for stepping up to the plate."

Another American idiom. Luca was amazed how many there were and how often they came up.

The discussion continued turning to the impressive results coming out of the greenhouse. The new base botanist, Eleni Dimopolous, had been on Venturous three weeks, having arrived the same time as Luca Barolo. She had picked up very quickly from her predecessor. It did help that Jim Sheppard, who had taken a strong interest in the program, could assist her in the transition. It also didn't hurt that she was one of the renowned plant physiologists in the world and had worked alongside Mary Musgrave, her American counterpart, and had been part of the Earth-based team supporting the program on the Moon.

Next up, Dr. Reisberg gave an update on several of her experiments, particularly the studies on the low-grav effects on body mass. Exercise was still proven to be the key to minimalizing the detriments to muscle mass – a common issue on Earth associated with age.

Experts have known for decades that from the age of 25 to 50 the decline in muscle mass is roughly 10%, subject only to the level of exercise. As a person reaches his or her 50's, the rate of decline slightly accelerates. Real decline usually begins at 60 years. Although no one on the station was in their sixties. The crew ranged in age from 32 to 57, giving her a good spread of specimens to work with. On the other hand, everyone here was considered in above average to excellent condition just to get into their respective space programs. That was also a factor to be considered in her studies.

Her experiments to date focused on combinations of isotonic and full extension physical exercises. Results were proving to be interesting.

Dan Wedmond adjourned the meeting and confirmed that the next meeting would be as planned, same time next week. The six crewmen stood to go about their duties, exiting through one of the five connecting corridors.

"Bruce, can I talk with you before you go?" asked the commander.

"Sure. What's up?" Anna gave them a quick look back but continued out one of the corridors.

"Listen. I know this is a tough bunch to work with. It's not like having the chain of command in place and giving orders as in the military. Managing them is not a simple task when you have so many Type A personalities." Dan knew that was very much a redundant statement. It was a given that nearly everyone selected to be in space was going to be more competitive, outgoing, ambitious, impatient and even aggressive – a classic Type A personality. More relaxed personalities, identified as Type B, would not make it to the space program.

Confirming the thought, Bruce said, "Aren't we all?"

"What I need from you as XO is to show a bit more restraint. I know Dr. Kormendy is aggressive and can be very challenging, but you are playing into her hands when you respond back the way you do. Don't give in to her."

"Yes, sir. I know you have cautioned me before on this." Perhaps more than a few times. "She just keeps pushing and I'm not Jell-O."

"I'm not saying you are, but you don't need to be a brick wall either. Let's face it, she would not be here and in her position if she wasn't considered by MET to be very capable and an expert in her field... just like the rest of us"

The commander's conciliatory approach, as always, set Bruce back on the right path. Though Bruce did feel that Dan should put his foot down just a little bit more. Anna and some of the lead SpaceX crew could be demanding and, sometimes, overwhelming. But when he thought about it, he realized that was exactly what their jobs were.

Throwing in a pat-on-the-back, Wedmond added, "You have

really been doing a great job with the crew. Keep it up. It frees me up to come in and make the tough decisions when needed."

"Yes, sir. Will do."

"Great. And thanks again for your efforts, Bruce. I truly appreciate it."

Chapter 3
Neighbors

At least we do not have to deal with the British anymore! They have no sense of humor.

Back at home in Shenzhen, his friends and family were fully aware of Commander Li's very humorous side. His own crew, however, had no idea. But his sense of humor was a factor in making him the type of leader he aspired to be and had attained.

He had tried attending post-graduate school in the University of Oxford's, Department of Engineering Science. But with the severe economic impact that overwhelmed the British Isle and the resentment he sometimes faced from the Brits – not necessarily from the student population, but from the local population where he resided – it was not comfortable for him to be there. At that station in his life, he deserved a bit more comfort.

He opted to attend Stanford for his post-graduate engineering studies. Back in China, this was frowned upon, given the animosity that lingered following the years of trade wars with the US. The fact that it all turned around in 2023 still didn't change the mindset of the older ruling generation. Li Yuen had not really been affected by it. Besides, he liked the Americans, especially the rather liberal types he encountered from San Francisco. Stanford was a top-rated engineering school and he could get to the nearby Jet Propulsion Laboratory, an aspiration he had always kept to himself.

Li was chosen by the Chinese National Space Agency very early after returning home. As a young man, he thrilled over the successes of the manned Shenzhou orbital launches and had even met Yaping Wang, only the second Chinese female to venture into space. Initially, he was assigned to the Tiangong-1 space station program in a ground support role. He was about to take his first mission into space aboard the "heavenly palace," but this was before the inevitable demise of the Tiangong-1 in April 2018, when it was unable to be kept in Earth orbit.

In due course, Li did get into space and served on one of China's later cislunar stations that was literally moved into orbit around the Moon in 2025. He had become what his American counterparts and fellow astronauts called a 'taikonaut.'

The purpose of this unnamed station was to support and co-function with the first base to be established on the Moon – Tiangong-3.

Now in its thirteenth year, Tiangong-3 was an impressive exploratory base located at the eastern rim of Mare Imbrium within the region known as Sinus Lunicus. Today, 40 Chinese yuháng yuan, or universe travelers, were currently serving on board, although two of the crew were actually Japanese. Commander Li was Tiangong-3's current commanding officer.

As fate would have it, or perhaps founded on scientific reasoning, the Gweilo, or Westerners, erected their base just 400 kilometers from Tiangong-3 in Mare Serenitatis. There were a few theories why the Venturous was established so close. Some thought it was so they could keep a close eye on Tiangong-3 and its crew and steal its discoveries and technical advances. But those less biased simply believed that, like the Chinese, this location had the greatest potential for finding refinable minerals, provided access to the always dark (and less known) side of the Moon, and was less likely to be bombarded by meteorite showers. This latter consideration was based solely on the observation that the mare had the fewest observed strikes and not for any ascertained reason.

But Commander Li was not concerned with the proximity of the Venturous. At the moment, he was examining the oxygen and water generation unit along with his chief engineer, Yang Junlong, making small talk as they conducted the examination.

"Yes, commander. It is true. My wife's family fared well by working with the European Union in the 2020's. Her father and uncle wanted to develop a business relationship with the British networking firm called Madge Networks. But they became concerned when the British hardline businessmen started talking about getting out from under the European Union's economic reign. They wanted to do business with a larger market base and the pending separation..."

"You mean 'Brexit?" interrupted Li.

"Yes, Brexit," said Yang. "This Brexit, as you know, devastated the British economy. European and Chinese businesses were leery of establishing business relationships with the Brits until their economy stabilized. Consequently, few companies would take the risk. Ultimately, the British economy collapsed. In the meantime, my wife's family went on to pursue business relationships with European Union countries. The other factor that fostered a pursuit with the European Union was the intense trade war between the Americans and us."

"Yes, I recall well. These situations in Europe, the US and with China in the early 20's was detrimental to the global economy in general."

"But what is detrimental to many, well, sometimes it creates opportunities for a small group of forward thinkers – like my wife's family."

The discussion diverted to the task at hand, the inspection of the oxygen and water generation system. Yang pointed to a portion of the osmosis system exposed to internal station atmosphere, noting, "Overall, the system shows no outward detrimental or deteriorating conditions. However, our maintenance protocol is to replace these interactive components."

While all systems on the Tiangong-3 were life supporting and, therefore, more than just critical, some were higher on the criticality list – such as the oxygen-water generation system. Scientists had long-since known that ice existed on the Moon, but in what quantities and where had been guesswork. Years ago, the discovery of ice by robotic rovers in sizable accessible quantities assured that life on the Moon could be sustained. Equipment was developed that was able to extract potable water, oxygen, and even some compounds suitable for fueling combustion systems.

There were backups to the life support systems and the raw materials they converted, but as everyone knew, reliance on the backup systems meant getting off the Moon very quickly if the primary system could not be fully supplied or rapidly repaired. Consequently, performing the maintenance protocol occurred without a second thought to assure that at least the equipment was working well and withing parameters.

"Very well. Continue with the replacement as planned." Li's direction was unnecessary because he knew it would happen, that the replacement work would be duly documented and reported back to the China National Space Administration, their ruling body. CNSA, in conjunction with the China Aerospace Corporation, the entity that actually manufactured and constructed or otherwise procured the parts and systems of the station, satellites and rockets that get here on the Moon, had strict procedures and they were in place to keep the station yuháng yuan alive and well.

Satisfied with the results of their inspection, Li and Yang headed back to their command module in the central part of the station.

From the inside, the interior corridors and passageways looked very similar to those found on the Venturous. But then, with limited space to work with and in which to house what amounted to nearly the same equipment as found on the Venturous, these spaces would be expected to be similar. Compartments, on the other hand, did vary. China's approach to laying out a workspace differed with how the Gweilo designed a workspace. In truth, China had the best of both worlds. They knew and, in some instances, participated in either the design or fabrication, of most of the elemental components of a workspace used in space programs worldwide. For their own facilities, China Aerospace Corporation built upon this knowledge and added a few innovations of their own, not shared with NASA or ESA.

Tiangong-3 was currently occupied by forty scientists, engineers and crewmen. The station layout resembled a wagon wheel with a large central hub with spokes as corridors to an outer ring that contained the station's labs, storage rooms and operating and maintenance rooms. Inside, however, was a second ring of living quarters and habitable personnel-focused spaces such as a gym, food storage, kitchen, showers, and of course, berthing areas.

The theory was that by placing the habitable spaces in the smaller inner ring, the design afforded maximum escape avenues to personnel in the event of a penetration of the exterior skin or a simple failure of one of the life supporting systems.

What was not contemplated, or perhaps not taken as a viable concern some fifteen years ago during the planning phases, was that the beautiful wagon wheel could not be expanded upon and still retain its concentric shape. Expansion required adding additional outward spokes and connecting to spaces that were now limited to one interior access.

The other consideration that might have been overlooked was expansion of the habitable spaces. As it was designed years ago, the initial crew size was only fifteen yuháng yuan with room to grow to twenty-eight. Now, thirteen years into operation at a crew of forty, there was some doubling up of berthing and the conversion of outer ring spaces to nonberthing but habitable use space. Living conditions were tight, even for space-based crewmen. It worked but there was degradation of the original plan for safe and habitable operation AND the conduct of its programs and research.

Future expansion was heavily weighed and evaluated by CAC, with a less-than-favorable assessment. But in view of the program's success, China was very strongly considering the creation of a wholly separate station, perhaps the Tiangong-4!

The central hub was the command module, from which the station was managed – not only the day-to-day activities but also the overall management of China's entire Moon-based program. It was also the core communications and master computing complex that supported the station's operations.

Entering the command module, Li noted that five of his crew were at their stations working on their respective tasks. Li looked back at Yang. "I have not had the honor of meeting your father, but I can only surmise that you are just like him."

"Thank you, sir, said Yang. "He was an excellent role model for me growing up. Then, with a smile on his face, Yang adds, "… when he was home that is!"

"I do understand. Your father served China well, but often from a place in orbit."

Yang's Junlong's father, Yang Liwei, was the first Chinese taikonaut to go solo into space, putting China as the third nation to do so. He was a pioneer of the Chinese space program and he did not hide the fact that he loved it, not even from his family. On October 15, 2003, he commenced his first Earth orbit. He did not spend a lot of time in orbit on the Shenzhou 5 spacecraft, but well before that he spent extensive periods in training and preparation for space away from his home, and certainly afterwards, training and preparing his fellow taikonauts for space missions.

Yang Liwei so loved the space program, he named his second son after one of his fellow taikonauts, Fei Junlong, commander of the first two-man crew on the Shenzhou-6 two years later. It was probably inevitable that Yang Junlong would, without hesitation, follow the path set out by his father.

"There will be time to talk more of him," said Li.

"I look forward to that, sir. With your permission, I will get on with the systems maintenance as discussed."

With that, Yang took a seat in front of one of the operations monitors and commenced documenting his inspection findings and scheduling the follow-on maintenance work accordingly.

Li approached two of his crew sitting in front of one of the many monitors in the command module. Xi Jian, his second in command, looked up and greeted Li, "Sir. We were just going over our resource extraction numbers. May I fill you in?"

"Please."

"I'll start with the essential needs," reported Xi. "Our ice recovery and extraction efforts remain on track with our primary supply coming from Eudoxus Crater. Our robotic transport rovers are no longer suffering from breakdowns now that we have an unencumbered path from near the crater to our storage site. Guan Nuan has reviewed the calculations; she currently estimates that we have barely tapped 0.3% of the available ice since starting our extraction operation in this crater. There should not be a supply issue as long as the transport rovers are kept operating. Stored supplies of ice to date will last for two months at the current rate of consumption of water. Oxygen, of course, not so much. Fuel derivatives at this point still only provide a marginal supplemental quantity."

"Future expansion of our base and to new bases is clearly supportable," interjected the other taikonaut working with Xi.

Li, wanting to sound formal without being demeaning to his crew, acknowledged both men stating, "That has been my understanding. Our colleagues are to be congratulated for their untiring efforts to make our base a success. I am pleased to be working alongside each of you." *That should please the crew and Beijing* he thought.

"Thank you, commander," from both men. The others in the command module had clearly taken note.

Xi followed up, "Commander, allow me to relay to you the very good news!" A small smile was evident on Xi's face. Xi was three years Li's senior in age but the respect that he had for Li was unquestioned... except when they talked politics.

Pulling over his intelliboard, Xi said, "Our iron ore exploration and refining operation has exceeded our early estimates. Let me pull up our draft report." His fingers flew over the surface without actually making contact, an impossible act since the intelliboard was a virtual representation of an old-fashioned keyboard. Most of the crew tended to talk to the intelliboard, giving necessary commands to the onboard computer or Skylake. However, older generations everywhere in the world, regardless of nationality and who had grown up with physical keyboards, still tended to use the keyboard approach. Old habits die hard, even for an accomplished taikonaut such as Xi.

All eyes were on the monitor as Xi brought up the most recent report prepared for CNSA covering the station's progress in ore extraction and refining.

"As you can see, commander, we were able to find several veins containing ore that were unexpectedly rich in iron and other metals we have been seeking. Consequently, excavation has been easier and faster than we had anticipated. The bottleneck is transporting it back here to the refining foundry. As a practical matter, this is a good thing as we do not expect the current find to last more than a few weeks, perhaps two months. So, we are not suggesting increasing the transport effort at this time."

"I was under the impression that the refining process was the slowing point," said Li.

"In truth, yes," said Xi. "But we will be able to increase that production effort given our current resources on hand and with what is expected to arrive in our upcoming resupply shipments. The utilization of the transport rovers, however, have been maximized for at least the next six to nine months."

"I see. Please continue."

"Despite these limitations, it is clear that we will exceed Beijing's expectations, I think. We will be expanding our iron ore processing ahead of schedule."

"Again, my congratulations to you and your team," said Li with an evident air of satisfaction in his voice. "What about extraction of Titanium?"

"Titanium, on the other hand, still seems to elude our search efforts, said Xi. "At least in form we can extract practically. There is plenty of titanium out there, but we continue our search for a viable vein that we can work with."

"Xi, I know you are doing your best. We can't extract what just isn't there for our equipment to work with."

"It simply has eluded us for so many years now."

Li needed to get things back on the upbeat. "Our time will come, Xi. Stay with it."

Li wanted to keep the positive momentum going based on the sound successes the Tiangong-3 crew had achieved to date, but it was necessary to broach the subject of which there was an unspoken level of division and discontent among the crew.

"Well, to my knowledge, the Gweilo astronauts have not succeeded in their pursuit of titanium either," said the commander. Although Gweilo was a Cantonese slang for light-skinned or Westerners, the use of the word among the Mandarin-speaking business, technology and political communities was very common.

"That is true," responded Xi. He quickly called up another report on his monitor. "And, our assessment is that we do exceed their efforts in iron refining."

"That is quite true, commander," added the other crewman, clearly pleased with being able to say that. "The Gweilo are operating about a fifth of our production."

"Gentlemen, I wish to remind you, we are not in a competition with the Gweilo. We have a defined mission here on the Moon and that is our goal. We are to achieve it and, if we can, exceed it. Do not lose focus on that."

Li knew full well that many of the crew of the Tiangong-3 did view the crew of the Venturous to be competitors to be beaten soundly. Li also ascribed to the belief that a competitive drive was often a very healthy state of mind. It challenged complacency for one. Competition stimulated creative thought. But competition could also sidetrack legitimate goals and efforts if left untethered.

The crew on the Tiangong-3 were highly educated, highly motivated men and women who stood far above the other billion-plus Chinese citizens. They were the county's finest in so many ways. They were trained to be the best and to seek out the best, to have an open mind about any issue that confronted them. This meant to have an open mind about what the Europeans, the Americans, the Japanese or the Russians were doing in their respective space programs to advance the science and technology of living off planet.

And for the most part, that is exactly how the crew thought and reacted. Many on board were eager to know and communicate with the Venturous crew, for example, to learn what they have learned and to share new technology and ideas that would help the extra-lunar survival effort.

Still, they all grew up in a somewhat contrary environment. If it were not the government and the party drumming the cause and the path forward of the Chinese communist philosophy into its people from the time they were born, then there was simply the consequences of growing up in that environment. It was a mindset where, generally, Europeans and Americans were considered greedy and could not be trusted; but let's conduct business with them anyway. It was an instilled mentality that many of his fellow modern city-raised intellectual colleagues had been subjected to. Few, like himself, who were exposed to a foreign education and lifestyle, were able to overcome that instilled mentality. But that was the point. It was something that you had to choose to overcome. For the rest, well… Xi Jian, his second in command, was of that negative mindset.

He returned his focus back to Xi and the crewman who were in discussion, some of which he realized he had missed. He added, "I don't wish to diminish any of your efforts. Keep up the hard work." And with a slight mellowing of his voice, "And, yes, a competitive quest with the Gweilo does have its benefits."

Chapter 4
When MET Meets

25 March 2039, 7:26 am PDT,
SpaceX Offices, Hawthorne, California, Earth

*M*y God, could we not have come up with a more boring name? Jeff Fund, the newest appointed director of *Moon Exploration Team* on behalf of the SpaceX consortium, still railed at the name given to the joint organization created by three world-renowned top-class entities. He had heard the stories from his SpaceX colleagues. Upon coming to an agreement in principal to form this public-private partnership venture back in early 2027, one of the first tasks was to settle on a name for the group. This seemed to be an overwhelming burden. Other than coming to terms on the extent of physical and financial participation among the three participants – a year-long process in itself – naming the organization was viewed by observers to nearly stymie senior management and nearly resulted in its dissolution of the venture before it even got started.

SpaceX, being the more creative of the three, or so thought Jeff, had come up with some stimulating and modern, if not *stellar*, names, not unlike its own. Names like *LunarX* (perhaps too blatantly biased) or *Amaris*, from the old Spanish stories meaning child of the Moon, a popular favorite, were offered and rejected. Only as the participation agreement terms were being finalized and a name had to be agreed to, did the organizations' senior management settle upon *Moon Exploration Team*. How mundane!

Clearly brilliant minds did not implicitly mean creative nor cooperative minds.

These were the thoughts going through his mind as Director Fund prepared to join in the monthly MET directors conference call. Unfortunately, these thoughts were also distracting him from what he really needed to focus on, the subject matter of the call. Most of the discussion would be routine and repetitive, taking no real effort on his part. But there were a few matters to discuss that did require not only his input but his political savvy to maneuver the other directors toward his position. Recently, for example, convincing the board to move up the production and transport of the metallurgy lab had been a calculated effort in swaying the opinion of the other directors; a sweet victory, one that SpaceX did not often receive.

Jeff Fund occupied an incredible corner office on the 26th floor of the SpaceX building in Hawthorne, California. It's two all-glass walls allowed him a bird's eye view overlooking the southeast corner of LAX, one of the world's busiest airports. In its day, Hawthorne and neighboring El Segundo were the hub of the aerospace industry. That industry floated to other cities in the US and other parts of Europe, but it was still a brain trust for space travel.

Fund's secretary came to his office to inform him that the video conference call had been initiated, that the other local SpaceX participants, of which there were three, were in the conference room completing the preliminaries of the meeting and that he should join them. Managers from each of the respective agencies and companies would be participating in the video call, but only the faces of the three voting directors would be seen continually on the four-way divided monitor screen, while a fourth image would show a current speaker or relevant documents that would be the subject of discussion at the time.

Entering the rather lavish conference room that was seldom used for anything other than these video conference calls, Jeff took his seat of honor at the head of the large oval marble table and in front of one of the Skylake video camera/monitors. As he did, his facial image took its place in the lower left corner of the monitor. The upper two corners occupied by his two counterparts: fellow director Dr. Cheryl Feskine, NASA's Director of Moon Exploration Team at the Johnson Space Center, in Houston, Texas, to the left and by Loukas Anagnostopoulos, ESA's Director of M-E-T out of European Space Operations Centre – or ESOC – in Darmstadt, Germany, to the right. The bottom right corner was still blank for the moment. To be sure, the order of the placement of the directors' facial images did not imply rank, as there was, supposedly, no superiority among the directors. Rather, the first to come online got the top left spot. The second got the top right...

"Good morning Jeff," said Loukas.

"Yes, good morning," said Cheryl.

"Well, good day, and good evening, to you both, and to all of you joining in today. Shall we begin?" Jeff did not feel it was necessary to apologize for his tardiness, which in truth was a matter of less than two minutes.

Accordingly, MET Mission Director, Kurt Vaughn, who was also a nonvoting member of the MET board of directors, took the remaining video spot in the lower right of the monitor. Although German and having been with the ESA for seventeen years, Kurt was technically employed by MET. As most of the MET operations were managed and conducted out of the Johnson Space Center Mission Control in Houston, that was where he resided and worked for the past five years.

The people he worked with were also from all over the globe, but his neighbors were mostly native Texans; all very friendly but they talked with an accent and used expressions that still through him off now and then. He had gotten the hang, as they would say, of backyard barbeques as the standard for social gatherings, but he did miss the Bavarian lifestyle he grew up with.

"Good day, everyone," Kurt said, with a slight southern German accent still present. This is our one hundred seventeenth Moon Exploratory Team Managing Directors' Meeting conducted today by video conference call."

Kurt's image was replaced by a MET document. "As set forth by M-E-T rules of order, we will adhere to the agenda, shown before you. Any new issues may be brought up by any one of our M-E-T directors or by myself."

And so, the board meeting continued. Consensus was that all life supporting systems were running optimally, but after ten years in use, the potential for problems was an ever-increasing concern. Planned maintenance and replacement programs were in effect and backup systems were online, but there was still that tinge of concern. The board concluded that every effort was being taken and will be taken to assure the safety and wellbeing of the crew.

And on the subject of the crew, Kurt Vaughn addressed the agenda item concerning its morale and condition. Physically, as had been reported by Dr. Reisberg in her recent monthly update to MET, all crew members were doing well. This was reflected by the fact that they were eating well, getting in programmed physical exercise and that there were no reported physical ailments. Kurt noted that the physical health of the crew as compared to a comparable population located at a US or EU military base was above that standard norm. It was a health standard that was already very high as compared against the average population.

As concerned the morale of the crew, Dr. Reisberg's reports for the last several months did allude to some decline. She could not attribute this observed decline to any specific element of living on the Moon. Most of the station's planned experiments and work schedules seemed to keep the crew upbeat – they loved doing what they do best – and this was despite some minor setbacks and delays to planned experiments such as with the astronomical and astrophysics team where its research equipment had been sidetracked in lieu of other now-higher priority projects such as the search for titanium. She did, however, assert that there was a noted animosity between some SpaceX and agency astronauts, particularly at a senior level, based on observed aggressiveness heard in both casual and operational dialogues.

Personally, Jeff Fund thought that such an allegation was unfounded. The consortium's astronauts were highly trained and highly motivated to excel. While the crew on Venturous were all classic Type A personalities, that did not mean they were not able to work well in the team environment in space. To the board, Fund said that the doctor's observations should be noted, but without substantive and documented indications to the contrary, or a supportive report from the station's commander, which there had not been to date, no action should be taken other than to allow the doctor to continue to monitor the situation.

NASA's Dr. Feskine countered.

"Life, relationships and interactions in a confined world such as on the Venturous was new territory and nothing should be overlooked. The doctor's remarks should be weighed accordingly."

Loukas Anagnostopoulos concurred with Dr. Feskine. Still, that there were no reports from the station commander that alluded to such a problem, led to the board agreeing to continue monitoring. But the issue was not yet concluded.

It was off agenda, but several of the call participants felt strongly that there was a factor to be considered and discussed as a possible explanation for any impact to morale – and that was the concurrent actions taken by the only neighbors to the Venturous, the Chinese.

"I fail to see how the presence of the Tiangong-3, over 400 kilometers to the northwest, can have a negative effect on morale," interceded Dr. Feskine. "Their activities rarely cross paths with ours. They have kept to themselves, both on the Moon and on Earth. And they were there first."

"That's hardly significant," someone piped in. "We have both been there now for over a decade and…"

"And it's been uneventful, if not amicable," said Dr. Feskine, cutting off the speaker.

After a pause, she added, "Look, we have spent nearly fifteen years, developing a working relationship with the country after the devastation caused by the trade war of some twenty years ago. Our efforts to make the country a friend – even one we must keep an eye on – as opposed to an enemy continue to pay dividends. Look how they supported the West in the joint response to North Korea's foolish attempt to attack South Korea back in 2034. That would never have happened but for our advancing good relationship."

"Agreed, doctor," said Director Anagnostopoulos. "Any animosity at this stage reflects old and truly unwarranted biases."

"I agree as well," chimed in Fund. "SpaceX has enjoyed a very successful relationship with China Aerospace over the last decade. Some of our work products are, legally, part of their program. I do not think we have cause to be concerned about the Chinese presence."

Loukas, in a softer approached said, "Dr. Feskine, Mr. Fund, as much as I think the Chinese presence is not an issue, it is conceivable that it might be to some of the crew. I propose that we undertake an evaluation, a subtle one, to determine just how emotions and thoughts are trending by our astronauts."

"I can see that. Perhaps, doctor, your team can come up with a plan?"

"We'll look into it. I will provide a proposal early next week. Is that acceptable?" she asked.

"Done," said Fund.

The discussion turned to the station's endeavors to locate new viable iron ore deposits and the extraction and refining of the currently minable veins. Across the board, literally, this was viewed as a positive outcome for MET. SpaceX was particularly excited as this meant a financially rewarding endeavor for the companies involved. It was more than just SpaceX who had a capital investment on the Moon. There were a few subcontractors to SpaceX, such as Lockheed Martin and Blue Origin, an aerospace manufacturer and space technology firm out of Kent, Washington, that had a stake in the success of the minerals extraction effort. For this board meeting, Blue Origin's project manager was invited to provide an update since it was the principal firm that manufactured the lunar rover as well as several of the components for the metallurgy lab unit that would soon be heading to the Moon... ahead of schedule.

In line with the discussion of the refining effort, Jeff Fund introduced the project manager, "Fellow directors and MET team representatives, I would like to turn the call over to Chuck Fowler of Blue Origin."

Fowler's face appeared in the lower right corner, replacing the document that had summarized the latest ore extraction statistics.

"Thank you, ladies and gentlemen. On behalf of Blue Origin,

I am pleased to bring you up to date on our equipment and components that contribute to the successful operations on Venturous and in the Sea of Serenity," began Chuck.

Chuck had been a mechanical engineer in the Seattle area after college and had no thought to becoming an aerospace type. Most of his friends were Microsoft or other brand name IT techs, but that didn't interest him. Still, he hung out with them at their favorite haunt near Pike Place Market in downtown Seattle. Apparently, so did Jeff Bezos, owner of, among many entities, Blue Origin. Their paths did cross one evening. The rest was history. Chuck joined Blue Origin, and in the years to follow, he became one of the senior executives of the firm.

Chuck gave his prepared presentation. It was upbeat, effective and promising. It seemed that there was full support of the iron ore extraction and refining effort. Chuck pointed out that the success of this effort benefited all mankind in many ways – a sales pitch but an unnecessary one. He reiterated one of Jeff Bezos' goals when he formed Blue Origin in 2000: to see one million people working in Low Earth Orbit (LEO) and on the Moon; to remove heavy industry from Earth into space; and to improve life here on Earth.

"Mr. Fowler, can you address the state of the Moon Automated Rover/Transport," asked someone. "I understand you have had a problem with the gear box."

"Certainly. The rover, or Martin, as the crew calls it, has been in successful operation for eight years now. It has been well maintained over that time, but we are operating it on the Moon and the Moon has sharp objects! Upon encountering one of those objects, the gearbox become cracked. Unfortunately, this condition had gone undetected for some time. That lead to the infiltration of dust and dirt. In turn, that condition lead to the unexpected wear of a gear referred to as a screw drive. The good news is that the box panel is easily repaired. And I understand that the crew has devised a plan to temporarily replace the screw drive. Replacement parts, including the addition of supplemental gearbox shielding, will be on the next supply run."

"Thank you, sir, for that update."

"Mr. Fowler, your success is unquestioned. However, some of us here do not want to lose sight of the fact that we have a plethora of priorities that each must be addressed and receive the same degree of attention that the iron ore exploitation effort has received," said one of the agency reps with obvious sarcasm. "I would not like to see these other projects be diminished. Yet that has occurred with the advancing of the delivery of the metallurgy lab, an action that required the setback of other planned equipment."

"Whoever is speaking, you are out of line at this board meeting," asserted Fund. "This matter has been discussed and settled by the board."

"Well, Jeff, if I may," said Chuck. "Blue Origin's goal is very much in alignment with NASA and ESA. We want to save the Earth and we want to do it through advancing efforts off-planet. That does mean we support all scientific research in space and on the Moon." Showing a small smile, Chuck continued, "I do not see the Moon Exploratory Team doing anything else. The mere shifting of one element further along does not defeat any other project and we would not want it that way."

His statement seemed to settle the group. Silence prevailed for a long thoughtful second.

"If I may reiterate Blue Origin's motto: Gradatim Ferociter or 'step by step, ferociously.' We want to succeed; we want you all to succeed. And we want to do it one step at a time, but there will be no stepping back."

Well that was impressive, thought Fund.

Chapter 5
Making Other Plans

That could not have gone better if I had said it myself!
The board meeting continued after Chuck's presentation, but the issues brought up and discussed by the others were inconsequential to Jeff Fund. He was still gloating to himself over the phenomenal presentation of, well, someone who was actually his competitor, but in this instance a comrade in arms. He needed to call him though. It was the same time zone up in Washington, so it was still morning for him.

Jeff placed the video call from his jPhone. "Vid call Chuck Fowler," he said to it.

Within a second, Chuck answered, smiling on the screen, "Well, that didn't take you long."

"Hey, great presentation to the board and that gang of bureaucrats. Their view of the program is just too constrained. It seems like they just don't see the bigger picture."

"Ah, they're just doing their jobs," said Chuck. "You know as well as I do, their bigger picture just happens to be in another room!"

Jeff chuckled at that. "Yes, you're right. And we do need every one of them to keep this project moving in a common direction, generally forward." Settling down, Jeff's face turned more formal.

"So, our iron extraction and refining effort is definitely going well. We are way behind the Chinese, but then, there is plenty of ore to go around. And they don't seem to be any more interested in our operation than we are in theirs."

"True enough." Chuck also took a sterner persona. "But I don't think you called me to talk about iron. What's on your mind?"

"Right to the point. OK, I am concerned that we're not succeeding in our other pursuits. Titanium is there in plenty. Damn near 30% of the surface elements within the Sea of Serenity comprise titanium. But we have not found a viable source that can make extraction practical for us. Your firm operates the rover and works with the crew on this matter. Is there anything new you can tell me? Are we pursuing this properly?"

Chuck hesitated as he thought about it. "As you know, we have just the one rover and it's use must be rationed out to the various projects that require it as well. You also know another rover is in the works and will be sent to the Venturous in about a year from now. The rover itself will be completed later this summer, but it will need to be commissioned, tested and prepped for shipping. Perhaps you could do your thing and get that expedited."

"I already pressed the board to move up the delivery of the metallurgy lab. And it was at the cost of deferring some of their other experiment packages. But getting a second rover there is not only essential, I think it's critical. Look what happened when it was out of commission for just a few days. I think it's a good argument to expedite delivering a second one."

"If anyone can do it…" said Fowler.

"I will need to talk to my CEO, but I doubt it will be an issue. The company truly wants to expand its presence in space and achieve its goal of saving the Earth and helping mankind." Then he added, "Of course it won't hurt that we benefit as a company, especially when I tell them it could result in accelerated payments to us," added Fund.

"No doubt Blue Origin won't object."

⳾

At the same time, but two time zones later, Dr. Cheryl Feskine and MET Mission Director Kurt Vaughn stayed in their Houston Space Center conference room to continue discussion of MET issues that had been brought up during the board meeting and also those that were not brought up.

Cheryl Feskine at age 52 was perhaps one of the most accomplished overachievers in her field. Make that fields. After graduating from UCLA Medical School and serving her residency in the Los Angeles area, she went back a few years later to USC, UCLA's very big and very local rival, to earn a doctorate in astrophysics. Afterall, it was her hobby.

Married, still, and with two children, both overachievers like their mother, she had also been an amazing wife and mother. Her husband had risen to become a senior vice president of a global engineering firm, an achiever in his own right. There were times when the two of them were separated for months at a time, due to a work assignment that took one to a far-off state or country, while the other stayed at home. And home was often a loose definition for where one adult and the kids happened to reside.

However, with their son finishing college in Stanford and their daughter starting out at JPL, there was no keeping Cheryl on the ground, at least not figuratively. Five years before, NASA, seeking such multitalented doctors for its future manned space, Moon and Mars programs, approached her to join its Moon Exploratory Team. She had become a natural choice as a director, despite less than five years of experience with NASA and MET.

Add to all that, Cheryl was still lean, quite physically fit – having maintained a workout regimen that included full-contact martial arts – and she kept very attractive.

Cheryl Feskine had it all. Oddly enough, she did not flaunt it. She took everything in stride.

"You sidelined the action item concerning Japan's request to be a formal partner in MET." Kurt was reviewing the hard copy of the agenda – he was old school about that – bringing up Dr. Feskine's decision during the board meeting.

"Yes, but as I said, the action required more investigation into the elements and the merits of JAXA's request. That part is true enough," responded Dr. Feskine.

The Japan Aerospace Exploration Agency had placed a 500-page proposal, offer and request before the three prime entities of MET. Bottom line, the Japanese were seeking entry into MET and a participating role. It was a worthy proposal. Since the turn of the century, JAXA had developed an incredible base of knowledge and experience in the area of satellite development, deployment and utilization emphasizing a high degree of efficiency and effectiveness. And it was an accomplished space agency in other areas of endeavor such as its asteroid exploration program with the Hayabusa series of spacecraft. These were areas that MET could take advantage of if it could bring JAXA into its fold.

JAXA might well have had its own space program years ago, but it seemed, quite surprisingly, that its conservative base had no interest in expending funds on a program that other countries were already vigorously advancing. The cost to the Russian economy was a prime example, albeit not a fair one. Russia's economic demise had little to do with space exploration and more to do with its attempts at space dominance... via missiles and expensive cyber-attacking satellites.

"The other reason I tabled it is that NASA wants more time to flush it out through the Washington, D.C., political machine and ESA equally wants to do the same in Brussels. I'm under the impression that our commercial counterparts are all for it simply because Japan would be another government entity to share the financial burden."

"Yes, of course," responded Kurt. "I have to admit, though, I am not up on JAXA's current activities. MET keeps my fully occupied. But I was under the impression Japan was going to team with Israel to form their own Moon mission."

"Yes, at one time that was discussed at length between Israel and Japan. As I heard it though, Israel's budget wasn't ready to take on such a load and still keep up its defensive posture. Also, I think it was going to be a challenge for such distinct bodies with little common ground, separated by so many kilometers, to be able to pull it off effectively. And Japan definitely shies away from inefficiency."

Kurt paused in thought, acknowledging Dr. Feskine's remarks, "Agreed. I'm just glad Russia can't come up with the cash to expand its goals in space. Otherwise, they would want a piece of this action too!"

"Well, outside of their participation with the ISS program, I don't think too many of our government colleagues want to see Russia anywhere near the Moon."

Moving to other matters, Dr. Feskine reviewed with Vaughn the issue of morale on Venturous. The concept of even having low morale among the most elite of humankind's best representatives was not unheard of, but it was considered very low on the rather long list of human priorities. Perhaps that was a mistake now that there were so many more people in space for periods exceeding what past decades of space missions had asked for of its astronauts.

Dr. Feskine thought to herself: *Did the experience of being in space even compare with that of sailors that lived in the very confined spaces found in our fleets of submarines.* Moon living certainly was a newer concept and there were, she thought, considerably different physical and mental pressures involved. It was worthy of further study, but for now...

"Kurt, can you get with our medical team and come up with a program to evaluate this concern about morale and possible animosity? I promised to offer one to the board in two weeks. I would like it to be done right, so if you need more time, let me know."

"I will get right on it. And I will ensure that it stays lowkey."

"Thanks. This is new territory and we don't need to let it get out just yet."

"And you will have it in two weeks. I will be taking my family on vacation in three weeks."

With a smile, Dr. Feskine said, "Oh I know. And good for you. You deserve a break from here. But I understand you decided not to go back to Germany. You are going to England instead?"

"Correct. My wife and I would like to go back, but in truth, our ties to Germany have faded over the years and we are mostly American now, or at least international. Our children are only German by name. They don't remember growing up in Würzburg near the old cathedral nor do they remember the beautiful mountains of Bavaria. They only know cities and places where spacecraft are launched and controlled. We want to expose them to what the countryside offers – beautiful scenery, sparse but elegant architectural structures, and more animals than people."

"I see."

"So, after thinking about a few options, we have opted to stay in an old English castle."

"I'm impressed," said Cheryl. "But isn't that a bit pricy?"

"Not at all," said Kurt elatedly. Ever since that Brexit debacle, the economy there has been so distressed, the Brits – not the isolationist British government, but the people – are practically begging for EU and foreign businesses to come, invest and spend their money. What it cost us to stay there shows it. The five of us will be able to stay in a castle near Cornish for ten nights for a price less than a three-night stay at a Hilton here in Houston."

"Excellent! I might have to consider doing that with my family one day… if I could round them all up that is."

"I will let you know how our stay goes, but I can only imagine it will be worth the effort."

Their meeting wrapped up. Kurt moved on but reiterated that he would have an evaluation program proposal before her by Friday, April 1st, no joke.

Chapter 6
It's an Old Story

I tell ya, when it rains, it pours… even on the Moon!
So many things were just not going right, for one reason or another, thought Jon Miles. He stopped short of thinking everything was going wrong because he knew better. Jon, an ESA astronaut, hailed from Ireland. He was not the only astronaut from that corner of the world, but there were extremely few, especially from Ireland. Though the Republic of Ireland was not in any way a part of the United Kingdom, Brexit still took its toll on all the islands in its circle of reach.

Jon Miles had been on the station for twenty-two months and it was his first actual space mission. Even though he was a junior-level member of the crew by ranking and listed as a mission specialist with no actual specialty to speak of – more of a Jack-of-all-trades guy – he was a bit older at 42. He was lucky perhaps.

Jon's best friend was 36 – Hal Lindstrum – with whom he had trained on Earth, spent 10 weeks together in the isolated low-grav environmental simulator in Houston and had traversed space with to get to the Venturous 22 months ago. Of course they were buddies.

To no one's surprise, Jon and Hal were together in the equipment and experimentation module, affectionately known as the 'Science Lab.' The Science Lab was jam packed with various pieces of scientific equipment of every kind allowing for research and experiments in just about any field from astronomy to zoology. Hal, the team's official astronomer, was there organizing his astronomical equipment with the help of Jon for an upcoming planned observation.

In another part of the Science Lab worked Penelope Brightling, the computer tech on station, and perhaps one of the busiest among the crew. She was continually updating the software of some motherboard, Skylake panel or equipment processor throughout the base station. And if she wasn't doing that, she was repairing or replacing the hardware of an older component that had failed at some point on this mission.

Penelope was technically a UK citizen. In fact, she was the only astronaut from the UK throughout the various space programs such as ISS and the Mars Expedition. Because of her notable work with SpaceX in the US on space-based systems and her very upbeat personality, she was a natural to be selected by SpaceX to be part of the Venturous crew. On board, Penelope was well liked by her counterpart NASA and ESA crew members. SpaceX was thrilled to have her.

"I don't know," said Jon. "It just seems that everything we want to pursue around here gets pushed back for one reason or another. Either the equipment fails, it's not adequate for the task or we simply can't get it delivered as scheduled. I can't believe MET is delaying your new space telescope just to accelerate the delivery of the metallurgy module. Our work has a priority, too!" Jon seemed quite animated yet kept his concentration on the task at hand at the same time.

"It is ridiculous," agreed Hal. "I have not been able to accomplish half the experiments and observations that MET itself laid out for me. My research is far behind and I don't see how

I can catch up without some intervention." Hal looked up from his work noting that Penelope Brightling was in earshot of their conversation. No big deal, she was practically one of them. He thought however: *She does seem to get whatever she wants from her SpaceX consortium.*

Lowering his voice, Hal continued, "Personally, I think MET has created a program that is too ambitious and asks for too much. The base is going to be here for a while and more will come, but we're only here for such a short period."

I agree, Hal. But what can we do?" asked Jon rhetorically.

"I would prefer not to leave here without achieving a majority of the tasks I set out to do. This is a once-in-a-lifetime opportunity to be on the Moon. It's killing me to see it go to waste. I need to do something about it." After a pause, "As if I could," he said softly.

"We have fourteen months left in our mission, but it seems like we will be leaving tomorrow. It just goes by too fast."

"Speaking of which, what is today, Jon?"

"March 27th. What, are you counting the days now?"

"No, it's just that my girlfriend's birthday is coming up soon. I don't want to forget to SpaceTime her or she will kill me."

"That's news to me. All this time we've served together I did not know you had a girlfriend!" Jon had to think back if he had missed that tidbit of information. "Well, good for you. Don't miss that call!"

"I won't."

Hal and Jon wrapped up their work on the radio telemetry equipment and packed it to take out to the research platform, a level base created years ago for just such experiments. Equipment like this, though quite bulky and required careful maneuvering, was not heavy. Over the years, crew members often took on similar or bigger equipment relocation challenges instead of using the specially designed Moon dollies simply because these items did not seem heavy. So far, no calamities had been reported.

Once the equipment was set to go, Hal and Jon headed to the dressing and staging rooms. These were the compartments in which the crew would suit up to head outside the protection of the base station environment.

"Later, Penelope," said Jon as they exited the Space Lab.

"Good day, guys." Penelope looked up and smiled to her fellow crewmen, pleased that they said something to her. She decided to add, "Hey, just for the record, Hal, I think you have been getting the short end of the stick."

"Hmmm." That was all Hal could say.

"Thanks, Penelope," said Jon, not wanting to let Penelope feel disregarded. Well, after all, Jon did like her. Unlike Hal, Jon did not have either a wife or a girlfriend back on Earth. He had a number of female acquaintances, and more than his share of romantic experiences – some pleasant but short affairs, some very unpleasant entanglements. And this seemed to be particularly notable whenever the women in his life found out that he was an astronaut. Oddly enough they would be more interested in him when they learned he was going to the Moon for three years. What's wrong with that picture?

It just seemed that none of his relationships had meaning. He occasionally thought that perhaps a woman that was distraught that he was going to the Moon, would be someone he could have a solid relationship with. But then, how would that ever work out!

Well, maybe, he could get to know Penelope a bit better. He knew her background since everyone on the station knew the history of everyone else there. She was a UK citizen, but had lived in the US for much of her adult life, given the limited opportunities at home. And she was single too.

Oh, what would his family say if they knew that he might be thinking of a relationship with a Brit. That didn't matter really. Jon was a forward thinker, probably why he was selected for the mission, and did not let family politics or life choices affect his. He did not follow the family footsteps into the retail trade. It had been a good and profitable way of life for nearly all his siblings, aunts, uncles, nieces and nephews, but it was not for him. He saw the stars and aimed for that. He would not have changed a thing... except, perhaps, to have a bit more mission support here.

Entering the corridor to the dressing rooms, Hal said to Jon, "I think things are going to change for the better."

"What makes you say that?"

"I don't know. I have no real basis for saying that." Then Hal added, "Actually, that's not true. I have been talking to Commander Wedmond about these setbacks. He seems to understand and recognizes the impact. I think he's taking it up with MET back on Earth."

"You think so? It seems to me, he is just sitting back and letting Dr. Kormendy have whatever she wants," countered Jon, clearly not pleased with Dr. Kormendy's influence over project priorities that seemed to disregard the scientific pursuits.

"I just think things will change for the better."

"Maybe you're right," said Jon, somewhat reluctantly agreeing with Hal. "I suppose if we're very successful with the iron refining and, hopefully, achieve steel production, and if we recover Titanium efficiently and in a usable quantity, M-E-T will be pleased and will get us more funding for our other projects," said Jon, trying to be upbeat.

"Right,"

The conversation dropped off as each man entered his designated dressing room.

Suiting up was still a three-step process but not as demanding as it was ten years ago when the Venturous was just a collage of modules and corridors under construction and the original Moon crew of six were living in the Lockheed Martin lunar landers and shuttling back to the then 3-year-old Lunar Orbital Platform-Gateway.

Even today, if there were a 'least desired' assignment, it would probably be an assignment on Gateway. Gateway had been built as an independent station in lunar orbit created to support not only the future base station Venturous but any other lunar operation. It was not, however, a program of MET, but of NASA in conjunction with the Canada Space Agency and, later, with ESA. Gateway comprised tighter quarters than the ISS.

Hal and Jon commenced the suiting up process. Crew would wear their station attire as the first layer of clothing before adding any of the lunar space suit paraphernalia. It was designed for that purpose, ideal for both internal and extra lunar functionality and comfort.

Over clothing, a basic pressurized accoutrement was necessary to maintain an internal suit pressure equivalent to no more than 2,500 meters Earth altitude. This was what a typical passenger airliner was pressurized at when in flight.

Over that came the modern lunar-based space suit, constructed of an incredibly strong and lightweight polyethylene material known as Dyneema, a manmade fiber fifteen times stronger than steel. This layer contained just about everything else an astronaut would need to live, work and survive on the surface of the Moon, day or night. It comprised a complex system of monitors, regulators, electrical and hydraulic controllers, and environmental components tied together to keep the extra-lunar astronaut comfortable while performing his or her tasks.

Despite the plethora of essential accessories, the suit was

able to minimize the effort required to bend limbs and still over-come the traditional suit's natural tendency to stiffen against the vacuum of space. And then, of course, there was the fully self-contained air supply and temperature control system that per-mitted complete independence of the base station.

Some of the crew were heard to call their lunar space suits 'suitcases' given the number of items they carried or were packed inside them.

Once Hal and Jon were suited up, they met up again in the corridor that led to a controlled pressurized exit to the Moon's surface, nicknamed 'the *Door*.' No other entry system used that name – they were either hatches, or lids or ports. This was where the astronomical equipment waited for them.

Per procedure, they checked each other's suit for proper seal and function. There were a small set of test switches that only another astronaut could access, thereby guarantying no one went out alone without some assurance of survival.

Via his communications radio, Hal Lindstrum, as senior as-tronaut, contacted Command Center.

"Command, this is Lindstrum and Miles. Suit checkout is complete and operating within norms. Equipment on stand-by and ready to exit. Request exit authorization."

"Stand by, Hal," he heard in his right ear. Procedure had re-quired a prior filing of a 'request for extra-lunar activity' stating the purpose of the activity and, for safety purposes, the filing provided assurance that those outside were being monitored accordingly.

After a short pause, "Two authorized to exit. Two-hour ex-cursion. We have you in sight. Enjoy your day, gentlemen."

As they approached the airlock corridor, Jon happened to look back and see one of the new crew members approaching them with a video camera in hand. They were being filmed, though he did not know the occasion. Rarely was anyone filmed anymore unless it was for a specific purpose or for sending back home to family and friends. Just the same, he tapped Hal. They both turned and waived to the camera. There was no use speaking, they would not have been heard.

Chapter 7

For the Record

27 March 2039, midday UTC,

MET Moon Base Station Venturous, Sea of Serenity, Moon

I can't believe this is real! I am really on the Moon!
Eleni Dimopolous had been at the base station for a little more than three weeks but was still thrilled at being here. Coming from Greece, a country still in a recovery mode after years of economic stagnation, being here was a true accomplishment for her as both a woman and a Greek. Growing up near Athens, she was taught to work hard for everything she needed and even harder for whatever it is she wanted. It was instilled in her by her family to want only the best, to reach for the highest goals. Joining the European Space Agency's European Astronaut Corps and becoming an astronaut was what she wanted most.

ESA initially did not accept her for the astronaut program but did give her the opportunity to be a part of the space agency's development program in recognition of her education and accomplishments in botany and her award-winning studies in space-based plant reproduction and growth – at only 27 years of age. Assigned to ESA's research division in Darmstadt, Germany, she worked for Loukas Anagnostopoulos, a fellow Greek and, in those days, Director of Research and Development.

She had worked hard and well for the research group, just as she always had in her life. So, when Loukas became a director of the ISS missions overseeing astronaut training and qualifications, he helped her make the move to the astronaut corps that resided and trained in Cologne, Germany. She trained with her heroes and mentors; an assembly of pioneering leaders – people like Alexander Gerst of Germany, who had spent more than a year on the Russian Soyuz TMA-13M and MS-09 in its early days.

That was back in 2032. Seven more years of hard work and here she was. Anagnostopoulos, now a director of the M-E-T program, was pleased with her success and selection to go to the Moon. He might even have had something to do with it.

Also, back in those years, when M-E-T first implemented a program of growing plants on the Moon, its efforts were small and tightly controlled. Frankly, the controlling factor was the very limited space available for such a program within the confines of the early Venturous station; nor were the personnel specifically trained or tasked for that activity. There was simply too much else to be done. But after some early successes, M-E-T managers decided it was time to advance that science of plant growth if they wanted to truly inhabit the Moon. Three years ago, a module was sent to Venturous for the sole purpose of being a greenhouse to support botanical research and mission specialists were selected to carry out that task.

Eleni was M-E-T's currently assigned botanist for Venturous. Although she was taking over a botanical project started by her predecessors, the science behind it had been her development back on Earth. Eleni had been tracking the progress and achievements, so it was almost as if she had been here for three years, not three weeks.

At least from the science side that is. From the years of anticipation, months of training, weeks of low-grav living, and actually physically being Moon side, it was as if she just arrived yesterday.

Today, she was performing her other dedicated role on

board, that of Venturous historian. Like her crewmate Luca Barolo, and everyone else before her for that matter, she was very unsteady moving about the corridors and spaces. To document life and accomplishments at the station, NASA, with the help of a Hollywood production company, developed a small, lightweight efficient (like everything in space) video camera designed to resist excessive movement and remain stable in the low-gravity environment. The camera itself, using dual operating lenses, took functional 3-D video. This was technology advanced by Avalanche 3D Entertainment, a company that was ahead of its time back in 2010. It could be instantly replayed on any 3DTV.

There was already an extensive library – a virtual library – of videos that documented the birth and growth of the base station known as Venturous. It contained videos of all the pertinent milestones that were achieved in building Venturous to what it had now become. Videos also included the milestones reached by the crew over the last ten years. There were memorable videos of when the station was pressurized with breathable air (some of the modules were shipped with argon to preserve certain interiors sensitive to low- or no pressure) and when the first crew members moved into the berthing areas. Videos documented the celebrations that took place immediately after.

Videos were taken of the discovery of ice in the northernmost regions and of the iron ore finds a few years later. Videos were also taken of crew doing their mundane tasks, but some were taken of their very successful research and experimentation, some of which were held in either secret by governments or in copyright by SpaceX.

There were, of course, videos of the day Mission Specialist Friedrick Kooler bounced off a Moon rock back in 2032 and, trapping his leg on the way down, broke it in two locations. Thankfully, his suit stayed intact – no rips or seals broken so no loss of air pressure – but with a broken leg, he was damaged goods. Though Friedrick practically begged to stay with the mission, MET did not want to run that kind of experiment on human regrowth and restoration of bones and torn muscles. At least not yet. And they did not want to contend with someone who was not up to full capability.

Many of the legally obtainable videos were garnered by both the public services, such as PBS, and private entertainment firms. They were then repackaged with added storylines and packaged into the glut of documentaries and made-for-3D films that have educated the Earthbound public about the life on the Moon – documentaries and films that kept the public interested, in touch and willing to keep funding the program.

And then there were videos of the greenhouse…

Despite her excitement, Eleni controlled her voice, to keep it professional sounding while she continued with her documentary video.

"And this is the botanical module or greenhouse," Eleni stated for the benefit of the camera as she entered the space. Despite her intended level demeanor, she could not help but express pride when she added, "As the new on-station botanist, *this* is now in my charge. In this module, the past and present crew members of the Venturous have, perhaps, realized our greatest accomplishments on the Moon."

She panned the camera around the 12-meter-square room, capturing footage of the greenhouse that seemed to be quite confined, due mostly to the various hydroponic and potting benches jam packed with plants in every square centimeter. And there was the variety of special lighting systems, watering and liquid fertilizing systems, and heating systems along with hand tools, measuring cups and devices, and an array of other testing and working equipment.

But the plants that grew in the greenhouse were, quite literally, phenomenal.

Hues of green was, by far, the overwhelming color characteristic. Every plant radiated green. But green was not the only color. Flowers of red, yellow, white, pink and colors in between could be seen – and they were massive compared to the same plants on Earth.

Continuing with her video, Eleni said, "While extensive narrative and video documentation already exists of the twenty-two plant varieties currently occupying the greenhouse, this panoramic view provides a grand view of all twenty-two growing together in harmony. Everything from the high-oxygen output of the Philodendron to the very nutritious but compact hybrid microcorn efficiently grown on very small stalks have proven to grow beyond our initial expectations. My American counterpart and mentor, Mary Musgrave, would have been ecstatic to be here personally."

Back on Earth, plant physiologists such as Eleni and Mary Musgrave, and the many others like them, spent much of their careers experimenting with plants under conditions of space travel and under low gravity habits like that to be found on the Moon. Experiments were also conducted not only on plants but on seeds, studying the effects of intense 4g acceleration on their ability to grow and produce. Such accelerations might be encountered in long-haul space flights to other planets.

Eleni recalled some of Mary's early work that became the basis for her own research. Mary had experimented with plants that were near relatives of crops like canola, broccoli, and cabbage. To address low- or no gravity environments, her team had designed tubes that ran through the plants' roots, releasing water directly into the soil substitute when necessary. To assure drainage of excess water or fluids, they replaced conventional soil with a special porous clay, a compensation for the lack of one of the Earth's environmental factors not found on the Moon.

On Earth, its environment provides various stimuli, such as sunlight, soil for nutrients and support, and gravity, that are a direct inducement to a growth response from the plant life that inhabit it; what botanists call tropisms. For decades, they had found viable substitutions for sunlight and soil. Gravitropism, pertaining to a plant's response to gravity, was still new science.

Gravity primarily affects the development of a plant by determining the direction of the growth of its roots in relation to the gravity's pull by growing earthward. Plant roots sense the pull of gravity through specialized cells known as statocytes, which are contained in plant structures called statoliths. Working together, they send chemical messages to the tips of the plant's roots, which in turn, grow in the direction of the gravitational source. The opposite effect occurs in the stems of most plants, which grow, typically, in the direction of the source of light.

In Eleni's mind, this was the science that she knew, understood and lived with daily. However, what was happening in the greenhouse was pure magic! What the botanists before her had discovered was that the Moon's gravity, at one-sixth of the Earth's, had a two-prong effect on plant growth of a number of plant varieties. What they discovered was that, all else being equal – as equal as can be reproduced in the greenhouse – plant growth was essentially uninhibited. Plants just grew faster and sometimes bigger!

Among the plants that tended to grow more vertically than horizontally, such as stalks or vines, they tended to grow taller, as if they were stretched upward. To Eleni, this unexpected effect was exhilarating. And that was when she could only see photos and 3D videos of Moon-grown plants, during the years that she was Earthbound. But now she was here, among these miracles of nature. She could not be happier.

Still recording, Eleni continued narrating, "On the subject of high oxygen-producing plants, the greenhouse nurtures several varieties of Philodendron and Dracaenas. As a result of their rapid growth, their ability to generate and excrete oxygen is coincidingly enhanced. For the purposes of expanding both current and future inhabitation of the Moon, this discovery has profound consequences yet to be fully realized."

To Eleni, the ability to generate oxygen was of prime importance, considering where she was. What she did not mention in her documentary was that the heartleaf philodendron and the elephant ear philodendron have proven to be excellent plants for helping to counter indoor air pollution. Eleni had worked with NASA during its early studies of 19 different basic houseplants, including four species of the Dracaena, also found at the station. NASA wanted to determine which were most effective in removing pollutants such as benzene and formaldehyde from indoor air. These two philodendron species were at the top of their list. Now they were part of nearly every space platform, including the Venturous. And they had one more benefit, they were attractive. Crew members would grow them in their berthing areas giving them, well, a touch of home while benefiting their physical environment as well.

Panning by the racks of Philodendron and Dracaenas, she brought into view the Areca Palms that had clearly overgrown their containers. Continuing the narration, she added, "The Areca Palm, also known as the Butterfly Palm, the Yellow Palm, Golden Cane Palm and Madagascar Palm, were brought to the base station because of their penchant for removing airborne toxins and introducing more oxygen into the environment, more than most other plants. Known also to be grown indoors in large containers because they retained a compact size, that 'fact' turned out to be a false assumption on the Moon. Its untethered growth exceeded expectations, as did their toxic cleaning and oxygen production characteristics."

While MET took precautions to avert toxic, carcinogenic and other unhealthful air pollutants by avoiding or minimizing their use on the base station and, for that matter, on all its space-craft, some of these air pollutants simply could not be avoided. Consequently, Venturous incorporated an extensive and complex air filtration system throughout its modules and corridors. But the system was a high-energy consumer and degraded over time, requiring continual maintenance and replacement of filters. Several of these greenhouse plants lightened that load immensely.

Eleni continued, "As our research and experimentation demonstrated, cost of inhabiting space, the Moon and someday Mars can be significantly reduced when you've got Mother Nature to assist in the process. We now know that there are plenty of plants that consume harmful particles in the air and release fresh oxygen – all while adding a decorative touch."

NASA, ESA and now MET, had spent years in research and experimentation, and it had paid off immensely. And when other problems came to light, the agencies took them on. In other labs on Earth and on the ISS, Eleni was familiar with the efforts of some physiologists that had devised a system that circulated exhausted air dense with CO_2 from the space craft's main personnel spaces found on the ISS, through the chambers and facilities where the plants were grown. This development enhanced the plant's exposure to the carbon dioxide that they needed to survive and process. The air now richer in oxygen produced by the plants and cleaned of toxins was pumped back to the living spaces. It was after adopting systems such as these that it was discovered that plants could thrive in space and on the Venturous.

Eleni loved the greenhouse. She could stay here for hours. But she knew she had other responsibilities as historian, such as documenting the other work, research and experimentation taking place. Hesitantly, she completed her video of the greenhouse and moved on to other modules.

She moved through the Science Lab, the toolshed, the common area, the mechanical module that was the heart and lungs of Venturous. She avoided the berthing areas this time, wanting to give a heads up to the crew first – these areas were, after all, personal space.

Passing through one of the many corridors of Venturous, Eleni happened upon two crewmen near the Door, in their suitcases, clearly preparing to go extra-lunar. "Here we have a pair of astronauts who will be exiting Venturous for the Moon's surface. Looks like they will be taking out some sizable equipment. Probably to conduct one of the many research projects that go on here daily."

One of the two turned. It was Jon Miles. He reached for the other. Both now facing Eleni, they give a slight wave to her. "It appears to be Hal Lindstrum and Jon Miles. They must be preparing to conduct one of the astronomical experiments or observations." She waived back and a bit loudly said," Moon luck, guys!" She knew they could not hear her, but she liked using the expression that had evolved on the Venturous in lieu of the old 'good luck.' Moon luck was a pleasant greeting but had a subtle implication that whatever was going to happen to you on the Moon, luck, whether good or bad, was going to be a factor.

Chapter 8
What the...

Why are we always just one step behind?

Bruce Holmann was in the maintenance and repair module, better known as the toolshed. He was bent over the damaged gearbox that had been pulled out of Martin after its unfortunate run-in with a protruding Moon rock. It was taking longer to repair than he thought. He just didn't have the right tools and materials – a common plight of components that occasionally failed. He had promised to complete it before now, but here he was on a Sunday, in the evening hours, UTC evening hours, working to get it done.

He wasn't alone. Jim Sheppard was also in the toolshed, working late, repairing a section of the automated watering system for the greenhouse garden.

The toolshed was a bit cluttered lately with various pieces of equipment lying about on tables. It was all equipment in some state of maintenance, such as one of the berthing area dehumidifiers that had been changed out for maintenance. And there was one of Sylvia Levander's laser devices that she used in her comms and materials identification research. But why was one of the tool carts left out and left so disorderly? A housekeeping lecture to the crew was going on the list of things he needed to do.

"So, you heard that the crew of the Tiangong has now found

lead," said Bruce, keeping his concentration on the tools in his hand.

"Just heard it at dinner," responded Jim. "Everyone is talking about it. The Chinese are a step ahead of us again,"

"Exactly what I was thinking!"

Both men kept at their work. Jim, however, had been successful, or at least a bit faster in his repair task. Bruce was clearly struggling with the gearbox.

"Done." Jim examined his repair. Satisfied that the leaky piece has been adequately patched, he began cleaning the area and restoring the tools he used. He wasn't ready to leave though. This was a heavy subject matter – the achievements attained by their Chinese neighbors – and he was very interested in getting Bruce's take on it.

"The report I heard says they found an outcropping of anglesite ore, in which lead is frequently a component back on Earth. This find happened to contain a sizable concentration of lead in it."

Bruce said, "That's what I hear."

After a pause, Jim asked, "I am curious, though. Were they seeking the anglesite, or did they just encounter it?"

"Good question. We will probably never know," stated Bruce.

"Still, finding lead is one thing. Do you think they will be able to do anything with it?" asked Jim, hoping that Bruce would open up a bit more to appease his curiosity.

Bruce could think of a few things. "Considering that there is no need to worry about inhaling or ingesting lead particles when applied in our current controlled environments, particularly outside Venturous, there are a variety of uses for processed lead. It could be used in our exterior shells to greatly enhance our radiation shielding. That alone would make it invaluable.

It could be used in insulation of external piping. With time and more resource recovery, lead batteries could be constructed which would also greatly improve our living capacity and offer a reliable backup energy source, if not a primary source."

"Good points." Jim thought about that. Just finding resources, regardless of who found them, would show the world – the Earth-bound world – that living on the Moon can not only be realized, it could be self-sufficient. Maybe even profitable to Earth. He stated, "I guess it's fair to say that the Chinese are making progress. We will be able to build off of that. So, then, really, it's good for all."

"Exactly. Now that we know it's out there and can be found, we will be able to do the same in time," said Bruce.

"It's not my field, so I have not really kept up with it as I should. I tend to want to make things from what we have. But I know we have a plan in play to seek out usable resources. Otherwise, let's face it. SpaceX would have dropped us and focused its efforts toward the pursuit of Mars.

"SpaceX is a pain in the ass about our lack of progress in 'resource acquisition,' using their terminology." Bruce Holman did not think highly of SpaceX as part of the team. In truth though, it was Dr. Kormendy he had his reservations about. The other SpaceX crewmen naturally tended to side with their senior representative. His ability to get along with them was merely a reflection of his ability to get along with her. Early on, he had every intention of working alongside her as past XO's of Venturous had worked alongside their SpaceX counterparts. But Dr. Kormendy was not like her predecessors, or so he came to believe.

Upon reflection, Bruce felt compelled to add, "Still, our American as well as the European governments need to demonstrate some benefit and return to their respective constituents.

The people whose tax dollars and euros fund our efforts. They do need to justify and continue to support our mission here," asserted Bruce. He was not unmindful of this concept.

Jim seemed content with Bruce's assessment. Like many of the space agencies' crew members, Jim thought Bruce was an outstanding leader in his own right. He was an unrelenting force bucking up against an inexorable wall. "Well then, I better let you get Martin fixed so we can get on with it. See you in the morning."

Jim headed out, the repaired watering system in hand, leaving Bruce alone with his repair work.

Bruce Holmann had spent his life either finding a way to get into space or actually being there. At 17, he entered the United States Air Force Academy, Class of 2003, with the driving goal of entering NASA's astronaut program. He graduated near the top of his class as a mechanical engineer, to become an accomplished fighter pilot while serving in the Iraq war. In recognition of his service, he got his wish to be considered for the astronaut corps in 2010. He was a shoe-in. The downside was that the space program in those years was nearly nonexistent, at least as far as going into space. Then in 2020, he got his first chance – he was selected to be on the crew of the ISS.

He excelled at that experience and was an exceptional crew member and leader.

Then, an incident occurred on ISS. A very small meteorite shower crossed paths with the station. Normally, ground-based radar systems tracked such showers and are able to direct ISS to maneuver out of the way. This one was too small and too fast and, proportionally, destructive. A strike to the berthing unit made a pinprick hole that proved to be disastrous. Normal procedure would have been to suit up, but the suits were right there where the penetration was. Bruce quickly reacted to the escaping air and pressure, trying to fit a loose food container over the hole. But due to the tight space to work in, Bruce's arm became close to the hole and was sucked against it. It was several minutes before other crew were able to free Bruce to repair the hole, but by then, the damage to his arm was done.

Skin tissue and, of course, blood vessels were sucked into the micro-hole by the vacuum of space and what got up against the hole froze. Post assessment was that the damage was not serious – Bruce would recover quickly – but it hurt like hell at the time.

Despite the recognition he received for his bravery in the face of such a peril, the injury put him out of future missions for a while. But not indefinitely. In 2026, Bruce was one of the first of a four-member crew to take up occupation of the newly constructed, Lunar Orbital Platform-Gateway, when Gateway was led by NASA, and three years before the establishment of Venturous on the surface.

Back on Earth, Bruce worked with NASA on a variety of projects that included both the Venturous on the Moon and the Mars Exploratory program. He did not get selected for a mission for the remainder of the 2020's, and by the early 30's, NASA was looking for younger astronauts for the three-year-plus missions on the Venturous and the even longer Mars missions. Bruce had married late in life. Not having to prepare for and go on a space mission had given him time to socialize and find a nonorbiting love in his life. But there were no children.

MET, however, viewed Bruce differently. The managers and leaders of MET saw Bruce as an ideal candidate for a mission where his space-based experience impressed them and where age was not the factor it once had been. Had it not been that a mission commander was already instilled on the Venturous, he might have been that person. And MET board politics, not performance, kept him in that position when Dan Wedmond took command. That was Moon luck.

Bruce chose not to dwell on the negatives and was thankful for the positives – a true sign of his character. He and Commander Wedmond, his junior in age, got along very well and worked well as a team. He was on the Moon for Heaven's sake! He did have friends here, Jim Sheppard was among them, and when he was working, he was doing what he loved. Aside from his wife, the crew of the Venturous was his family, his only family really. So, if he didn't get along with some… well… he'd seen worse behavior among the closest of siblings. It would work out between Dr. Kormendy and himself. She was an incredibly smart and capable professional after all. Bruce really had no complaints.

"Ok. I think I've got this," he said aloud to himself as he started restoring the parts and pieces of the gearbox back together. He needed one special driver to attach the extender rod to the gear face.

"Where did that go… oh, yeah." Rifling through some of the haphazardly placed tools and equipment in an adjacent cart, he found the driver. In the process, he uncovered an odd box he didn't recall being kept in the toolshed. Not that it mattered since crew often shifted equipment around from module to module.

Odd though, it looked like an old handheld calculator. The red LED digits were counting down. And it was wired to something else. "What the…?"

As he realized what it was, there is an explosion. Not a big one, but enough that it ripped a series of holes in the toolshed's nearest wall to the exterior shell. The outer shell also ruptured letting the air vacate to the void of space, instantly freezing to ice particles, and continuing unhindered on their trek to nowhere. Bits of tools and metal hit Bruce in the face and chest, knocking him back into other equipment, before collapsing to the floor.

Sirens began to blare in the station, but Bruce could barely hear them – the air in the toolshed had become too thin.

Despite the immediate high-pressure infusion of oxygen-nitrogen from the emergency system, it could not keep up with the breach in the exterior wall. There was nothing he could do to stop the escaping air. He couldn't get up.

His face and body pop as body fluids began to boil due to the loss of air pressure. The pain is intense. His whole body reeled in agony as he succumbs to unconsciousness there on the floor.

Chapter 9
When Your World Changes Quickly

27 March 2039, 11:02 pm UTC,
MET Moon Base Station Venturous, Sea of Serenity, Moon

*W*e *have what it takes. Let's get it done, dammit!*
Laying in her rack in one of the berthing compartments, Dr. Kormendy listened to Hungarian folk music, as adapted by Béla Bartók in the 1930's and 40's. Anna had grown up with this music; it always soothed her and allowed her to think at a slower pace.

Her roommates were not disturbed by the music as she always played her music using the Bose Personal Space Speakers. Bose had developed a speaker system that allowed the user to listen while positioned within the sphere of space created by four speakers. Outside that sphere, sound waves were unable to carry the music waves due to a sound cancellation process similar to active noise reduction technology developed around the turn of the century. Thus, the speakers created a personal space for the listener, while only a bare murmur could be heard outside the sphere. And the really cool thing – the listener was not insulated from other sound nor silenced. If you wanted to have a conversation with someone outside the Personal Space Speakers, you could… provided you had the music volume low enough.

The speakers had only been developed four years ago and though they became popular among the 30 and older crowd, only Anna had them on Venturous. She reveled in that knowledge.

"ALERT. ALERT. EXTERIOR SHELL PENETRATION. LOW PRESSURE WARNING IN THE MAINTENANCE AND REPAIR MODULE. ALERT. ALERT." The computer-generated warning sounded loudly in conjunction with a low-level whoop that far exceeded the sound from the speakers. Because it was computer generated, the location of the penetration was known and stated.

As the lights automatically increased in intensity from soft to full, Dr. Kormendy sprang out of her bed. Her roommates did the same. As had been drilled into them, they each grabbed their face masks and mini-tank from within reach of their beds. But Anna did not put hers on just yet. It occurred to her that the tool-shed was several corridors and spaces away. She slipped on her shoes and threw on her crew jacket and ran toward the toolshed. Reaching the central area of the berthing spaces, crew members were quickly gathering in various degrees of dress.

Glancing at the pressure gage, found near every corridor hatch, she saw the indicator was well in the green. Moving as rapidly as she could, encumbered by corridor hatches and the Moon's low gravity, she made her way to the hatch of the corridor that led to the toolshed. By now, about fifteen of the crew were in the module that would lead to the toolshed. This was a workspace that held very sensitive equipment and could hold ten astronauts comfortably. It was getting packed. Commander Wedmond had arrived and taken command.

"Is there anyone in the toolshed?" he yelled, speaking over the alarm and the din of the crew. There was no response at first.

Working his way into the module, Jim Sheppard was able to get Wedmond's attention, "Commander, I was in there about fifteen minutes ago. I was there with Bruce Holmann. He could still be there!"

"Holmann! Bruce Holmann!" yelled out Wedmond, hoping

he might be in the crowd. No response. "Has anyone seen Bruce Holmann?" No response.

The alarms finally stopped.

Per procedure, three assigned crew were required to fully suit up as if to exit the Venturous. This, of course, was a considered precaution in the event of a significant pressure loss in one of Venturous' corridors or modules in anticipation of an even worse situation arising. When they finally arrived, their pathway was blocked.

Commander Wedmond ordered, "Make a hole! If you are not essential here, clear back to the other spaces." Accordingly, several of the crew exited out of the module through another corridor to make room for the arriving response team. Many still stayed regardless.

Someone handed Wedmond a headset so that he could communicate with the response team. He recognized that Luca Barolo was the lead responder of the three. This was good as Wedmond knew that Luca had extensive experience in an external "no air" environment. "Luca, we only know that there is loss of pressure and air from the toolshed. Cause and the extent of any damage is unknown. It is possible that the XO is inside. Be careful but move fast."

"Understood," said Luca, heard over Wedmond's headset.

Seeing acknowledgement from the other two responders, they entered the corridor leading to the toolshed and sealed the hatch behind them. As they approached the corridor hatch that accessed the toolshed, the pressure gage was clearly in the red, confirming a total loss of pressure. Not hesitating, Luca pressed the keypad combination to open the hatch. It was an override code as the hatch would not open normally under a pressure differential scenario.

As the hatch opened, Luca stepped forward. "Merda"

On the ground was Bruce Holmann's body. It did not look good. The skin of the face and arms had been obliterated. Pieces of metal fragments had punctured and penetrated his body. Blood was exiting and boiling away instantly. There was a red haze that seemed to hover above his body. There was what appeared to be a series of various size holes in the toolshed wall, apparent only because there were various tools and pieces of equipment that were wedged into these holes.

"Let's get him out of here now," said Luca to the other two. "Commander, Mr. Holmann is… here. He is dead I am sure. We will bring him out."

Luca heard from Wedmond over his helmet speaker, "Understood."

Luca directed one of the team to stay behind and assess the damage. He and the remaining response team member picked up Holmann's body and headed back through the corridor to where everyone was waiting.

It was after 11 pm, UTC, but all twenty-nine members of the Venturous were awake, anxiously standing by at or near the maintenance module. Commander Wedmond contemplated asking everyone to return to their berthing areas but he knew that they were all desperate to know what had happened in the toolshed. Dr. Reisberg had arrived bringing a makeshift medical bag. As the response team exited the toolshed corridor, she saw immediately that she would not need it. Bruce Holmann was dead.

The two put his body down, while those that could see, gasped and turned away. Despite the obvious, Dr. Reisberg made a quick check of the body to confirm its status. Spotting Marc Laboe and Jon Miles in front of the group, she said, "Marc, will you and Jon please take the body to the clinic." They nodded and proceeded accordingly.

"Well?" asked Wedmond.

"I'm sorry Commander. There is nothing I can do."

Wedmond nodded then turned back to Luca. "What is the situation in the toolshed?"

"Very hard to say, Commander, but it appears that there are many ruptures in the toolshed wall. It appears that is was a rapid depressurization sucking up metal debris and lodging it into smaller holes." Pausing, and knowing that only Wedmond can hear him over the headset, he added, Commander, it looked like there was an explosion of some kind that might have caused the damage. The tool cart near the wall is destroyed and was dark… blackened."

"Understood. I am going to turn off the airflow to the shed. No need to waste it. Get back in there and see what you can do to patch the wall."

"Certo… certainly, Commander," replied Luca.

Luca and the response team removed the debris from the wall and applied quick-sealing patching compound, designed to harden rapidly and seal any hole the size of a half-dollar coin instantly, to the holes they could actually fill. Some of the ruptures were just too big and in some instances the debris could not be removed. Larger patching methods would have to be employed, but it was evident that the toolshed could not be sealed anytime soon. This was reported to Commander Wedmond.

Per procedure, Wedmond had taken his position in the command module. With him were Dr. Reisberg and Dr. Kormendy, as ordered. Wedmond spoke into his headset, "Thank you, Luca. For now, do not attempt to repressurize the toolshed. Leave everything as is, but double check for any other potential damage. We'll send in a team tomorrow morning to assess the damage."

Turning to his two remaining senior officers, Wedmond told them, "Almost immediately after the accident, MET registered the abrupt loss of pressure on their monitors. They attempted to contact us and when we did not respond, they contacted Gateway. Of course, Commander Fascar was unaware of what happened and tried to contract us as well. Neither were pleased it took nearly seven minutes before I could respond. When I did, I informed them that we did, indeed, have an unexpected rapid pressure loss in the toolshed, that it appeared to be attributed to a detonation of some kind within the shed, and that Holmann had been in the shed at the time and was a casualty."

Both women could not do much else but look down at the table.

Dan continued, "They asked questions. Other than reassure MET that the extent of the damage was limited to the maintenance and repair module and that Bruce was the only fatality, I could not answer their questions as to cause. I told them that I needed to address the most urgent matter at hand and that I would get back to them. That was now fifteen minutes ago."

Dr. Kormendy looked up at the commander, "Do you think it was something that Bruce was working on that caused the explosion?"

"I don't wish to speculate on anything at this point; however, I was aware that he was working on the gearbox of the rover. I doubt that any part of it was explosive."

"Perhaps something caused a spark that ignited... something," she persisted.

"Unlikely. As you know, with the lower air pressure that we maintain, even with a rich percentage of oxygen in the air mix, it is still lower than what exists at, say six thousand feet above sea level. But as I said, I don't wish to speculate." To Dr. Reisberg, he asked, "Were you able to examine Bruce's body?" He could not yet think of the body as an inanimate object – he was still Bruce.

"Not really, sir," she responded. "I could only scan the body and verify the lack of vital functions before you called me here. I had it placed in the clinic on one of the examination tables for now. But I can tell you, preliminarily, he received numerous abrasions and, basically, was riddled with metal debris – I believe the term used in the military is shrapnel – before his blood boiled from the depressurization."

"So, *preliminarily*," said Wedmond, "he was likely killed or incapacitated by the explosion before depressurization took its toll." That was a statement, not a question.

Dr. Reisberg nodded, "Yes, most likely."

"Ok, so I am told by Luca Barolo that the explosion of whatever it was, was relatively small but that its proximity to the toolshed exterior wall resulted in a significant rupture in the wall. For now, the ruptures cannot be fully repaired preventing us from repressurizing the space anytime soon."

Dr. Kormendy was clearly affected by this news as she sat back in her chair to contemplate the consequences.

"In a small way, that's a good thing for the moment. It will allow us to conduct a very careful and methodical investigation of the space without risk of unintended corruption by the crew." Wedmond then asked, "Is there anything else we need to consider before I give my updated report to MET?"

"Just one thing, Commander," said Dr. Kormendy in an uncommon show of respect. "I think we also need to assess what other damage was done in the toolshed. I am guessing, for example that the gearbox for Martin was further damaged, putting it out of commission for the time being. What other tools or equipment did we lose?"

"Good point, doctor," said Wedmond. "We will need to take

inventory of all equipment in the space and assess its status, once we have repaired the wall and returned it to a habitable state."

Dr. Reisberg interjected her concerns to the commander. "Sir, I think we must also take a moment to examine the impact the explosion and the death of Bruce Holmann will have on the crew. This could have some unexpected ramifications on their mental state."

Jumping in on Reisberg's assertion, Anna stated, "I don't think so. These are highly trained, top notch professionals selected for their mental strength and resilience, as much as anything else. You should give them more credit."

"I... think... Dr. Reisberg makes a valid point, Anna," Calling her by her first name was now an attempt to minimize her vocal assault on the medical doctor. "I suggest, Dr. Reisberg that you monitor the crew accordingly. You might want to be mindful of Jim Sheppard. He was a close friend of Bruce's and he was in the toolshed moments before the accident and he has been here on Venturous for much longer than most of us."

"You are right about that, sir. I keep an eye on the crew all the time as part of my overall responsibilities, but I will elevate that effort in light of our discussion." She could not resist a smirky smile at Anna.

"Ok," said Weddell. "It's late for all of us. I need to prepare my update to MET, and because of our current alignment with the sun, I will have to give it to Commander Fascar on Gateway for further relay."

"Yes sir," came from both of them.

"Go get some rest. We will start developing our repair plan and investigation plan in the morning following breakfast."

Again, from both, "Yes, sir."

✑

Moments later, having composed his notes and thoughts, Wedmond initiated his call to Gateway via a video link to Commander Fascar. Marianna Fascar was an experienced ESA astronaut and a good friend as well. Though she was German-born, you would not know it from her unaccented English.

"Commander Wedmond," said Fascar as she came on the screen. "We are still in shock up here. I hope there is no more terrible news to report."

"Negative. I can only give you an update on what has happened. The damage is confined to our maintenance and repair module, but the ruptures to the exterior wall might take some time to repair. There are no other injuries and, sadly, the one fatality – Bruce Holmann."

"Understood. How can we help, Dan?" Fascar said expressing a sincere wish to ease the difficult situation Wedmond was facing.

"For now, I must ask you to relay this message to MET. We are in a blackout area at the moment."

"Of course. And if we can do anything else, you will let me know?"

"I will. If we are to continue on Venturous, it will be necessary to return to some semblance of normality, and the sooner the better."

Commander Wedmond relayed the details of the accident and the status of the toolshed and its contents to Commander Fascar, whom he considered a true friend in a place so far from home. He completed his report stating the he would be initiating an investigation of the cause while a separate team would be assessing the full scope of damage and how to effect repairs.

"I will relay your message immediately, Dan," she said to him. "It appears that you do have a plan going forward. I won't say Moon luck to you. I think you need straight up good luck right now."

"Thank you, Marianna. You will hear from me again very soon."

Commander Fascar took a moment to soak in the events that had happened below on Venturous before initiating a video call to her Mission Control in Houston. She needed to think.

Marianna Fascar was a person of two worlds in so many different ways and she succeeded in both. Born in Offenbach, Germany, just outside of Frankfurt, Marianna grew up in a diplomats' world, both parents being career diplomats, learning English from a very early age and speaking as if she were a native. As a consequence of her parents' career moves, she spent her youth shuffling between the sphere of UN families in New York and the influence of the kids growing up in Frankfurt that were focused on the arts and sciences. This was her first exposure to two distinct worlds.

She was inclined to favor engineering but at the same time, Marianna turned out to be a world-class athlete, having come up just shy of being selected for Germany's Olympic track and field team. Consequently, she gave her all to engineering. Again, two different worlds.

Out of college, she landed a job with Lockheed Martin in its Lunar Lander development program due to her exceptional communications skills and ability to relate human needs to physical processes. In 2017, she decided to jump ship and be a part of the agency that was utilizing the Lunar Lander; she joined the European Space Agency. When ESA was seeking women to join its astronaut corps, she was right there – the right age, the right education, the right physical adeptness and the right social aptitude – she had the right stuff for a woman of that era. Two different worlds.

Nineteen years later, on her third space mission, Marianna Fascar became ESA's preferred choice as a command astronaut on the NASA-led Gateway program. And that was because NASA saw her as a natural for the program as well. Two more different worlds. Today, she was the first ESA astronaut to command Gateway.

Speaking to the Mission Control Comms Manager on watch, Fascar had relayed the report from Venturous and reiterated that Gateway stood ready to support MET and Venturous if called upon. Wrapping up the call, she said, "I will inform Commander Wedmond that I have forwarded his report and that it is, officially, received by MET."

"Very good, Commander," said the Comms Manager. "And let them know, we here in Mission Control are with them in spirit."

"Will do. Fascar out." She terminated the call. It had gone as expected.

ℐℓ

Because the message was sent via Gateway and not direct from Venturous, there turned out to be an unexpected listener to Fascar's message – the Tiangong-3.

"Commander Li," said one of the Tiangong-3 crewman in Mandarin Chinese, waking him from his sound sleep. "We have important news about the Gweilo base. You must hear this."

Sitting up quickly, he looked at the crewman, "You refer to the Venturous?" He knew what the crewman was referring to.

"Yes sir. We intercepted a message from its orbiting station to NASA on Earth."

"Well, what is it?" asked Li.

"The orbiting station…"

"Gateway," interrupted Li.

"Gateway relayed a report that there had been an explosion on the Ventor…"

"Venturous," corrected Li.

"… Venturous. There was a rupture to one of its modules resulting in an isolated loss of pressure. Their second-in-command was in the module and was killed."

"This is very distressing," said Li, more to himself than the crewman. "Inform Xi Jian. I will discuss this with him in the operations center right away."

Chapter 10

The Aftermath

28 March 2039, morning UTC,
MET Moon Base Station Venturous, Sea of Serenity, Moon

I must keep going. I must keep the crew going. There is no going back. We are on the Moon.
Activity on the Venturous the next morning was minimal and quiet, but not at a standstill. Functions, necessary to sustain life on the base station, continued, as did the crew's monitoring, recording and adjusting to the somewhat changed physical environment. But it just wasn't the same.

Wedmond had stayed awake last night contemplating what he must now do. The safety of the rest of the crew was paramount. And he knew that their safety rested on what he did in the coming days, particularly on what he did to keep them staying focused on where they were.

He had already talked to everyone on board who were not asleep – some were up late dealing with the accident, a few had come off necessary night shifts.

Finding Dr. Kormendy, he pulled her aside. "Doctor, after our discussion last night, I have given it some thought. In consideration of your knowledge and capabilities, I would like you to head up the investigation of the cause of the accident."

"I can do that, Dan," said Anna, setting aside some of the formality she had shown last night.

"And I would like Luca Barolo to assist you since he will

have to be in the toolshed anyway to effect repairs, and he has extensive experience with equipment failures and malfunctions through his past missions on ISS. You can pick anyone else you need to back you up; however, I think that you should take advantage of Eleni, as the historian, for purposes of documentation. No doubt, whatever we do, will be scrutinized and I think a proper documented effort by the base historian will relieve any credibility issues."

Dr. Kormendy was going to say something but hesitated. She thought it best to proceed as directed. "Yes, of course. I will have them suited and outside the toolshed corridor in half an hour. Anything else?"

"I don't think I need to tell you," although Wedmond actually did think he needed to tell her, "Jim Sheppard would have been a natural choice for the team, under the circumstances, he needs to be sidelined for the time being."

"You are right," Anna said. To herself, *you didn't need to tell me that!*

"Very good. I will see you at the corridor in thirty minutes.

He arrived there at the appointed time with Hal Lindstrum alongside. The investigation team had yet to arrive. Frankly, he thought, thirty minutes was not enough time to select a team, explain the task at hand, get suited and get to the corridor. Yet, three minutes later, Dr. Kormendy, Luca Barolo, Eleni Dimopolous and Stan Rivers, the sole representative of Blue Origin on Venturous, entered the module, suited but carrying their helmets. Stan was in his early thirties but an expert in the operating equipment and, generally speaking, making things work. Her was the Venturous handyman. Although Anna had not picked a NASA crewman for the team, Stan's expertise made him a wise choice.

The Commander greeted them, each nodding in acknowledgement. It was pep talk time.

"What you are about to do is, potentially, both dangerous and important. MET and I are counting on your skills and expertise to do what on Earth would be carried out by a team of trained experts. But I don't think we need such experts when we have you four."

The spirits of the team were elevated noticeably. "It is your task to determine what went wrong so that we can correct it and not let it happen again. So that nothing harms another of our fellow astronauts."

"Be safe in there. You must be aware that we cannot say with any certainty that the ruptures will not reopen nor that whatever caused the explosion won't do it again. Keep your suits on and fully functioning, your eyes open and do not hesitate to exit the space if you are unsure of anything. Stay in contact with Command Center. We are expecting to hear your voices every few minutes."

"Understood" they said.

"Hal will be outside the corridor here to also monitor you and assist in exiting." Again, each acknowledged.

"Are there any questions?" asked the commander. They all shuck their heads no.

"Ok, you know what to do. Let's do it." Dan had thought about saying Moon luck to them but thought better of it. Now was not the time for luck of any kind.

Wedmond left them to it as Lindstrum helped them place the helmets and go through the final suit-up protocols. Hal had been quiet during this exchange, but then, so was everyone after the accident.

Wedmond entered the medical module referred to by the

crew as *the clinic*. The clinic looked not unlike a doctor's examination room, except this one was crammed full of storage cabinets, examination equipment and medical scanners. In the center were two adjustable exam tables. On one of the tables was the body of Bruce Holmann. Dr. Omoné Reisberg was examining the extremities. It was not a pleasant sight.

"Dr. Reisberg, good morning. Is there anything you can tell me?" Wedmond asked, distracting her from the examination.

"Good morning Commander." she responded. "There is nothing I can say at this point beyond the obvious. He was impacted by the force of the explosion and the bits of tools and metal parts that were projected by it. That was followed by a rapid decompression and loss of oxygen."

Wedmond nodded and the doctor continued with her report. "It's hard to say what killed him – the trauma to his body or the boiling of the body fluids due to the decompression."

"Did he suffer, doctor?"

"Unfortunately, I would have to say yes, but most likely not for long. Perhaps, if the impact of the blast and debris was sufficient, it could have left him unconscious before the loss of pressure. Worse case, the blast might have disabled him, preventing him from exiting the toolshed. Frankly, if he had been further away from the blast, perhaps… and had been subject to less of an impact, the emergency air compression system would have allowed him to escape. But that is just speculation."

"Understood. And how are you holding up?" asked Wedmond.

"I'm OK. We train for the worse and, of course, in my profession, I have dealt with significant loss. But this is the first time I have had to address it in this environment… on the Moon."

"It's the first time for all of us." He thought about it, then added. "Hang in there, Omoné. I can't think of anyone else I would want with me here on Venturous."

"Thank you, sir."

"Is there anything else?"

"Well, I can tell you that the crew has taken the loss of Bruce Holmann very hard. While he had his run-ins with some of the crew, particularly from the SpaceX contingent, he was very well liked and recognized as a hard-working leader."

Commander Wedmond was aware of the people issues. Among such a large diverse group of one-percenters from so many backgrounds and with different agendas, there were bound to be some personality clashes. He just didn't think it would manifest into anything detrimental on, of all places, the Moon. He would have to give this some more thought.

"Also," added Dr. Reisberg, "I need to point out to you that for some of the crew, they must now be thinking of the vulnerability we are all subject to on a world that is very much anti-life sustaining!"

That was a consideration he had not thought of. "Duly noted. Let me know if you see or hear of any negative trends in attitude."

"That goes without saying," she responded.

"In the meantime, I will need to find a way to reassure them that their safety is not any more at risk than before the accident; to restore their faith in our technological world." *Which will require that we find out what really happened and correct the situation accordingly,* said Dan to himself.

"I will be glad to help you there, too, where I can."

"Thank you." Pausing, "Let's get to it then."

Commander Dan Wedmond had a lot on his mind, but the safety and security of his crew was uppermost in his thoughts. He needed to know what happened in the toolshed and why.

Chapter 11

The Business of Government...
and Business

29 March 2039, 6pm CET, ESOC, Darmstadt, Germany, Earth

I knew this day would come. I just prayed it's never today.
Nearly forty-five hours had passed since the accident. Loukas Anagnostopoulos was still devastated by the loss of one of M-E-T's senior astronauts. At 63 and in the space business most of his life, he had experienced tragedy before and far too frequently. You just go on after each experience with the false hope that it will be the last time.

The M-E-T board of directors called an emergency meeting with senior staff following news of the accident. Since the condition of the Venturous and its crew appeared to be stable and under control, and thus, there was no exigent need to take action, the board deferred having an emergency conference call. Rather, it was decided that a face-to-face meeting would be held as soon as possible. For a number of reasons, the decision was that it would be held at ESA's European Space Operations Centre in Darmstadt, Germany. That decision was made very early Monday morning (for most). It took all day Monday and most of Tuesday to get the directors and about forty staff into Darmstadt.

One of the reasons for holding the meeting at ESOC was that offices and conference rooms were already in preparation for the next scheduled board meeting that had been planned to convene in one of the buildings' four stories. Another very significant reason was that ESOC would most likely be managing the next space launch to Gateway. If an urgent launch was called for, the M-E-T directors wanted to be close by.

It took no time for the world to learn of the accident and that a member of the Venturous crew had been killed. MET's public affairs offices had no choice but to issue a very brief statement to the press in Europe and in North America. Prominent government officials from countries everywhere were offering condolences while affected countries were demanding more information that MET simply did not yet have.

Tracking down and informing Holmann's wife, Jennifer, quickly, quietly and with due remorse had been no easy task either. She had been travelling out of the country with her sister in New Zealand. It had taken nearly twelve hours to reach her. Thankful for small mercies, there were no children.

One of Loukas' senior staff approached him as he sat at the circular conference table, waiting to get the meeting started. Many others were still coming in. "Herr Direktor, I can confirm that the maintenance and repair module is the only known damaged area. It has been temporarily sealed but the state of repair is not permanent. There is no other known damage and no other reported injuries. The damage was caused by a low-level explosion inside the module."

"Danke, Henri."

At least there was some small bit of good news. Loukas had already been apprised of the situation many times over the last two days, but it was reassuring that the conditions were stable and satisfactory. Now they would have to move on from this.

It was evident that the other two board members and the majority of the senior staff were present, evident because where there was a name plate at fifteen seats around the table that identified a significant senior member of M-E-T and someone was sitting behind each one. Sitting on either side of him were MET directors Dr. Cheryl Feskine and Jeff Fund.

As the host representative, it fell upon Loukas to start the meeting. He had been handed a gavel but banging it to get attention was not his style. Speaking loudly, also not his style, he said in English, "Ladies and gentlemen..." People finished taking their seats or positions near the walls. Conversations were brought to a halt and everyone turned to Director Anagnostopoulos.

"Ladies and gentlemen, fellow directors, thank you." Loukas had given his opening remarks some thought. "It is a terrible tragedy that has brought us together here today. Under any other circumstances, such a gathering would have been a wonderful event. Even if we were, on occasion, arguing with each other over policies, implementation or funding, we all knew it was for the greater good and advancement of the prevailing goals of M-E-T and of mankind.

"Regrettably, today we come together to deal with the loss of one of our beloved colleagues – Bruce Holmann – an experienced astronaut who loved his work and was an inspiration to his fellow astronauts.

"We have all known this was a lofty but risky business, this going to the Moon, and we took on the challenge gladly and with fervor. But today, we cannot dwell on his loss, for we owe it him and the astronauts still inhabiting the Moon to do what we can to prevent any further damage or loss, now and in the future. So I ask you now to take a moment of reflection in silence, and then that you set aside your feelings and return to the tasks that you have all performed so well for the benefit of those who must continue on."

"A moment, please."

Thereafter, the meeting proceeded. A copy of a dossier

containing only a few photographs of the damage and a two-page report of the assessment of the damage was distributed and reviewed. To the credit of participants present, whether it was attributed to Loukas's words or simply because they knew within themselves that the right thing must be done, each contributed to the Moon Exploratory Team in a true team-like and congenial manner.

"Can I have your attention, please," said Kurt Vaughn, Mission Director.

"You have the dossier and I am sure, at this time, you all have been fully briefed as to what has taken place on the Venturous. We can add very little more, since it occurred nearly forty-eight hours ago. The team on board, at the direction of Commander Wedmond, has carried out an initial investigation of the matter to the best of their abilities given the circumstances of where they are."

"The good news is that we believe there is no further likelihood of another similar incident. Additional precautions have been implemented to secure any further potential explosive or hazardous events. While we are still assessing what lethal combination of materials would lead to such an explosion, we do know very well every material that is on the Venturous and we will narrow it down in due course. In the meantime, we have asked Commander Wedmond to continue his investigation as best he can. We are providing some guidance where we can."

"Mr. Vaughn," asked one of the attendees, "can you tell us about the rest of the crew? How are they handling the situation?"

Expecting that question, Vaughn responded immediately, "There can be no doubt that the twenty-nine members of the crew of the Venturous are shaken. But as you all know, these are not just any people. They are not just very talented people in their field. These are astronauts. They are the cream of the cream to begin with and they have been trained to manage catastrophic failure, including the possibility of death."

"But, Mr. Vaughn, might these be considered extraordinary circumstances?" came another question from someone at the table. "Might this be an instance where one of our crew could be substantively impacted and possibly falter in light of what happened?"

"Yes, of course, that is possible. Perhaps even probable," replied Vaughn with evident sincerity in his voice. "We have discussed this with both Commander Wedmond and Dr. Reisberg. In fact, before we brought it up, the commander had discussed such a possibility with Dr. Reisberg. While observing the crew is normally her responsibility there, she will be more diligently watching for signs of depression that might be considered debilitating or detrimental. Be assured, the crew has been hit hard."

At this point, Dr. Feskine stepped in. "I would like you all to know that this concern – a very valid concern – has been at the top of our priority list, along with trying to determine the cause of the explosion and preventing a reoccurrence. Our best medicine, if you will, is to keep the crew active and moving ahead with their normal workload. Work, for many, can be therapeutic. We feel this is what our crew needs right now."

Adding to the sentiment, Loukas added, "If I may doctor, in support of that concept, let me point out that what they are doing is dangerous and, as we have just seen, it can be fatal. Our 'star sailors' need our support at this time." Loukas often used the endearing Greek term that was the origin of word astronaut, especially when he wanted to invoke the emotions of the audience around him. In this instance, he was seeking their heartfelt concern for the astronauts. "Still we also cannot let the crew be any less diligent or complacent in their duties now or at any time, or we could experience more disaster."

Loukas Anagnostopoulos was only a year younger than the European Space Agency for which he had worked nearly his entire adult life. He was a tall and forceful man growing up, but not that athletic, as he had been held back by asthma. Not one who could travel to the stars, he had no qualms being there to support that effort.

Out of college, he went to work for ESA and by his midforties, his obvious leadership skills placed him as the head of ESA's research and development division. Some of advances in physical exercise equipment, body massaging beds (later replaced with the massaging body suit) and air circulation devices, used on ISS and other space missions, were attributed to Loukas and his team of scientists. In the late 20's he became a managing director of some of the ISS programs, such as astronaut training, at the European Astronaut Centre in Cologne, Germany. In this role, Loukas met, trained and worked with nearly every ESA astronaut who was currently or had recently been assigned to M-E-T and several of the NASA astronauts as well.

In 2031, Loukas was asked to take over for ESA's then-retiring former Director General of ESA and its original director on the M-E-T board, Jean-Jacques Dordain. To date, Loukas Anagnostopoulos has been the longest-serving board director of M-E-T with nearly eight years under his belt.

Following Loukas' remarks, there were a series of questions asked and concerns aired; however, in the end, there was a strong consensus among those around the table. All work on the Venturous would continue in accordance with in-place plans. Further discussion was followed by a concurrence – no choice really – to allow Commander Wedmond to complete the investigation, supported to maximum extent possible by MET researchers here on Earth.

Vaughn closed the subject, "With the board's approval then,

we'll direct Commander Wedmond to continue to investigate this tragedy," then added, "but for now the results will be kept confidential, at least until we can identify and overcome whatever malfunction or failed procedure he uncovers. Needless to say, we don't need bad press right now."

"Agreed," said Jeff Fund. "And on that note, I would like to turn the discussion to our counterparts in China. It has come to our attention that the Chinese are fully aware of our situation. Do we know yet how that happened?" asked Fund with a clear level of antagonism in his voice.

"We have an answer for that, sir," said M-E-T Communications Manager Manuela Lusk. "When the Venturous had its status report relayed through Gateway to Houston Mission Control as an audio-only transmission, we believe that the Tiangong base station was able to intercept it. Video transmissions are encrypted, but audio is not primarily because it is used for mass data transmission of standard operations that are seldom of a confidential nature. Gateway, for example, can often pick up their transmissions as well."

"Interesting," said Jeff as others discussed that among themselves. "But perhaps more interesting is that the China National Space Administration has contacted us to offer their condolences as well as its support and assistance. I admit, I did not expect that, but I should have. There are any number of reasons why they would offer assistance, none of which would be altruistic."

Responding, someone said, "Agreed, outside of trade between China and the EU or North America, which has nearly doubled since the trade wars of 2018, they have shown little interest in establishing a relationship with any of our countries."

"That is not entirely true," said Dr. Feskine, "nor is that a fair assessment. We have made numerous attempts at establishing working relationships with the Chinese. And though they have not made outward efforts to cultivate such relationships, they have clearly acknowledged them. The Chinese support in the United Nations, and of course their full support during the one-day war with North Korea, is evidence of their alignment with the West."

Jeff Fund reacted with some agitation, "Cheryl, that's very speculative to presume that they might truly want to help us! They have been ambivalent for decades. I am not sure this response of theirs is due to a change of heart."

"Then that is something we need to find out," Feskine responded.

Dissention among some of the MET leaders over the intentions of the Chinese continued leading to a discussion of the political climate among the US, EU and China. Loukas Anagnostopoulos saw that the group was getting off subject. It was agreed that for now, without more information, the CNSA would be thanked for their offer of help but not accepted.

Refocusing, they did turn the discussion to the consequences of the accident, what it meant for MET ethically, financially, and publicly.

For now, MET would have to wait and see.

↬

On Venturous, it was about 1600 UTC. Concurrent with the board meeting in Darmstadt, another meeting of consequence was taking place in the Command Center.

Commander Wedmond was taking in the update from Dr. Kormendy and Dr. Reisberg. Dr. Reisberg had informed them that Holmann had died of rapid decompression compounded by blunt force trauma. That was what the death certificate would say. The body had been sealed in plastic and had been placed in a designated storage space in the clinic. It was a little known and seldom discussed point of the design of the base station that storage space in the medical module was intended not just to cold store medical supplies and biological experiments, it was also designed to hold bodies for whatever reason that would become necessary… like now.

The conversation turned to the status of the toolshed.

"We can deal with meteorite strikes on the base. An explosion like this we did not plan for," said Dr. Kormendy, giving her update.

"We just don't have the right materials to adequately patch the ruptured exterior wall frame at that particular location where the support beams and braces meet. Just about anywhere else and it would not have been an issue," she said. "For now, we have some permanent and some temporary makeshift patching in place. The provisional patches are holding for now, but they are not safe under pressure. I cannot guarantee they will stay in place. I recommend that we have replacement panels brought down in the next Earth-Moon supply run.

"I doubt that will be a problem. Although, if we're stable now, MET might not expedite a launch to us right away. They will want a full assessment of our condition and all our replacement needs."

Thinking about it, Wedmond looked to Dr. Kormendy, "let's not give them a reason to delay. Anna, I would like you to develop a detailed shopping list of what we need to fully restore the toolshed. Confer with the other senior crewmen. And be sure to prioritize the list just in case. I would prefer not to have MET second-guess us on this."

"I will do that," said Kormendy. "As for the cause of the explosion, that is still being looked at. Luca Barolo is leading that team, as you know, and he is the best we've got for the task that none of us are trained for."

Anna Kormendy was bold, assertive, frequently outspoken and occasionally abrasive for a reason. As a young adult she was very ambitious, striving to become both a lawyer and a scientist in a Hungarian social environment that disdained women with ambition. It didn't help that she was a very attractive blonde with a slight build. Men in her sphere simply had other expectations for her. Even in marriage, her husband could not accept that she was of a far superior intellect. They wound up separating – he basically could not keep up with her – leaving her with two children to raise on her own while still butting against her Eastern European social and political systems.

Anna did rise above it, but at a cost. She had become callous and aggressively competitive with anyone she saw as being in her way, while still wanting to selflessly achieve great things for mankind. She was a bit of a paradox.

She had the talent. She had the skills and she spoke several languages including German and English. But when she tried to pursue a research opening at ESA back in 2018, they passed her up. ESA did not say why, though she suspected that it was due to her own aggressive personality. But it didn't matter. She was bitter and had never really forgiven them.

Somehow, SpaceX had found her. Elon Musk, himself, had interviewed her and hired her on the spot, with almost no experience. She and SpaceX never looked back.

Dr. Kormendy had proven herself many times on such projects as the very successful Falcon 9 and Falcon Heavy reusable launch vehicle programs and the Dragon V2 capsule. At the time when Dr. Kormendy was an instrumental member of the SpaceX science team, the Falcon Heavy could lift more than twice the payload of the next closest operational vehicle, the Delta IV Heavy, and it could do it at one-third the cost spent on their rockets by NASA or ESA.

Now, twenty-one years later, her children on their own and following in her footsteps, SpaceX granted her what ESA had not, a place of honor on Base Station Venturous and as the lead representative of SpaceX on this mission.

She was still her antagonistic self and managed to alienate those she considered 'the opposition' – Bruce Holmann had been one of them – but she was still brilliant, hard-working and full of great ideas. Those who were on her side, loved her.

Wanting to close this meeting, Commander Wedmond said, "Alright, I'll be following up with Barolo and his team. Hopefully, they will be able to give me something tangible in the next 48 hours. MET is anxious to know what caused this and frankly, so is the world right now."

But Dr. Reisberg had one more concern she wanted to bring up. "Commander, I do have one question."

"Certainly, Omoné, what is it?"

"Well, what will happen to Bruce's body now? Do we send him back to Earth?"

"Well, we will have to take that up with MET," he answered.

With that, he adjourned the meeting and they headed off to the dining area for dinner.

Chapter 12
Blue Moon

30 March 2039, 8:33 am UTC,

MET Moon Base Station Venturous, Sea of Serenity, Moon

I can't believe this is real. I thought I would be so happy to be on the Moon.

Four weeks on the Moon and Eleni Dimopolous could not be much more depressed than as she was now. The crew could not be more depressed. She felt terrible about what had happened to Bruce Holmann. Under the vail of uncertainty of what went wrong and the specter of a recurrence, Eleni had lost that upbeat, can't lose, outlook that drove her to get her to the Moon. Now, she just wanted to go home… back on Earth.

Since the accident, like many of the crew, when she didn't have a task to perform or chore to carry out, she sat quietly in the common dining area while eating some processed food for breakfast. Sitting with her at the table was Luca Barolo.

"It was a very difficult thing," said Luca to Eleni in his charming Northern Italian accent. "I had not seen anything like that. When you train, they tell you what can happen to the body when it decompresses. But to see it for the first time… not so good."

"I guess I can say I was fortunate. I did not have to see that part. But I did have to go in right after you completed your repairs to document the conditions. There was a reddish mist still in the air. I can only believe it was vaporized blood."

"My team were working on repairing the rupture, but I looked around," said Luca. "The explosion was not very big. Had it not been near the toolshed wall, it might not have damaged it. Of course, had Mr. Holmann not been there…"

"Have you learned anything more about the accident?" asked Eleni. "I overheard some say that the XO might have caused the explosion himself. Although, no one can say what it was yet."

"We are still investigating, but it does not look as if that were the situation. Mr. Sheppard says that the XO was only working on the Martin gearbox and that there was nothing on the bench he was working at that was dangerous. Whatever it was, it was on the tool cart. We will know more this afternoon."

After a pause to think, Luca adds, "In fact, are you not coming back there to examine some of the greenhouse supplies that are kept there? Dr. Kormendy told me your expertise will be needed."

"Yes, she asked me about that. I am coming there just after breakfast. I will need to suit up since the toolshed cannot be assured to maintain pressurization. I suppose you will be there, too."

Luca nodded, "Yes, I will be there. I hear that she has a theory, but hasn't really shared it with anyone yet."

"I tell you, I don't know what to think of her. You and I are newcomers on Venturous, but if you talk to the other ESA crew who have worked with her for a while, they say she is very critical of our work and makes no effort to be friendly. And she was particularly belligerent to Bruce for some reason."

"Belligerent?" asked Luca.

"Like argumentative with him, even though he was the XO," Eleni clarified.

At an adjacent table, Hal Lindstrum, overhearing the conversation, commented that, "The hole left by Holmann's loss is going to give Kormendy the opportunity to press her influence and power over the operation of the Venturous. If she gets her way, our research agenda will change and not for the better. We will be doing what SpaceX wants to do, not what is good for the mission."

A crewman from NASA sitting with Lindstrum added, "I think you're right about that, Hal. Commander Wedmond cannot see through what SpaceX is doing; he is too… accommodating, trying to get everyone to work together despite the personality conflicts that have burdened our team and impacted our research efforts. And now we lost the one person who was standing up to her."

Luca frowned at what he was hearing. "I think that is a bit strong," he said. I have been here only four weeks, but I thought that we were all one big happy family. Everyone was getting along."

Hal looked at Luca. "You have only been here a short time. You haven't really experienced the negativity yet. You will."

The crewman jumped in to add, "You're Italian. From a big Italian family perhaps? Tell me, does everyone in a big family get along all the time?"

"I see your point," said Luca nodding.

"It's sort a like that."

Although he was an only child, he did understand the crewman's allusion to big family issues. But before he could respond further, Jim Sheppard entered the room.

And the room went quiet.

Until now, he had been keeping to himself and away from the common areas, perhaps understandably so. With little thought, Jim grabbed up a container of 'instant breakfast' and some juice. Noting that the few tables in the area were taken by crew, he saw a place by Luca and asked if he could join them.

"My God, yes, Jim, please do" said Eleni. As he set his plate down, it was evident on Jim's face that he was very distraught, to say the least. From many of the other crew came quick words of condolence and comfort; that they were glad he had not been caught in the explosion.

"*Incredibile!*" said Luca in his native Italian. "Are you OK?"

"You've got to be shaking, given how close you were to being in the toolshed at the time..." said Eleni, not finishing the sentence.

Nodding, with a forced but notable smile, Jim said, "Yes, it was devastating. It's all I've been doing for the last two days; thinking about Bruce... and how close I came to dying with him." He paused.

"I happened to finish my repair on the waterline and left just minutes before the explosion. I had even hung around to chat with Bruce for a few minutes. It could have been me in there, too." Others were listening intently.

"Dr. Reisberg talked to me Monday about it. She told me to take it easy. And I was kinda avoiding everyone. My mind was racing, going over the accident, wondering if there was something I could have done that might have prevented it. Maybe there was. I don't know.

"But last night I realized I can no longer dwell on it. Bruce is dead, I am not, and we still have a mission to do here. The Moon can be harsh, but we must keep going if we are to overcome its challenges. I remembered that this is what it's all about and that I need to be actively doing my part. I need to get back to work."

"Good for you," came from one of the crew. "We are here to support you, Jim." As one person walked by to leave, she patted Jim on the shoulder and said, "Jim, I think it's fair to say we admire your strength and attitude. You are an inspiration."

Suddenly, Jim Sheppard truly felt better. He was going to

recover from the doldrums he let himself fall into. He was going to be stronger for it. He knew it inside.

♪♪

On the Gateway, orbiting in near stationary orbit south of, but not too far from, the Venturous, the crew of six on board were also quite solemn. But as on the Venturous, they, too, knew that the work goes on when you are in space.

Their lives were more pent up, more confined, than the thirty who inhabited the Venturous. They would occasionally do space walks. But those below got to do more extensive Moon walks and they did it under some degree of gravity. The Gateway crew did conduct research and experiments, many of which were co-ordinated with the Venturous. Bottomline, it was considered a harder life on Gateway. Thus, rotation in and out was typically about two years.

Occasionally, there was an exchange of personnel between Gateway and Venturous. The justification of this was, again, to carry out more research on the human condition; similar in concept as the research conducted with astronauts Mark and Scott Kelly twenty-five years ago when one astronaut twin stayed on Earth while the other spent a year on board ISS. The research revealed unexpected changes to the telomeres molecules, found at the ends of DNA strands, of the space-bound twin – they tended to expand in space. The significance of that fact, however, had yet to be determined. A theory prevailed among researchers that the extension would lead to a prolonged life. Unfortunately, empirical data had yet to bear that out. Now, similar studies were being conducted with crew exchanged between the base station and the platform. There were no twins this time, but crew with compatible DNA structures were part of this program.

Knowing that Commander Fascar was anxiously awaiting

an update, Commander Wedmond had contacted her via video link. "I'm expecting a conclusive report from the team investigating the accident later today. I hope to have more for you then."

"That would be great, Dan. Regardless of the pressure you must be getting from your M-E-T folks, it would be a relief for you and the station to know what happened. Hopefully, it will be something that can be avoided in the future," Fascar told him.

"That's pretty much what we want down here, an answer to why it happened, and could it happen again or was it just a one-time occurrence. Was it a faulty device, a mix of things that should not get together or is it a systemic problem in the design of the station? We need to know."

"I'm with you there," she said.

Changing it up, Fascar asked, "What about the repairs to the exterior? The last report said your team was having difficulty with a durable fix."

"True. We have implemented a temporary fix that has held so far, but it's not a permanent solution. MET is aware of this. They have reviewed the structural plans. I'm told a fix is feasible, but we cannot get the materials we need – and the tools we need – for about two months plus. They will come on the next supply launch from ESA."

"Nothing sooner?"

"For now, no. Needless to say, to send up an unscheduled flight that would go to ISS, then to Gateway and then from you to the Venturous, is costly. They would rather we make do for now," said Wedmond with a touch of frustration in his face and voice.

"Nature of the game, I suppose," said Fascar.

"It just means that we cannot use the toolshed without being suited up. An inconvenience for the time being."

"I suppose that means you will have to keep Bruce's body for a while, as well?" she asked.

"Yes. For now."

Commander Wedmond did not want to stay on this subject, and he had some other business to discuss with the Gateway commander. "Are we still good to go with the Lunar Lander?" asked Wedmond, already knowing that the lander would be making its scheduled supply and exchange run shortly after lunch today.

"Yes, it is loaded with your supplies and will be departing in about two hours."

"Very good. We could use a diversion with the arrival of the lander. Keep everyone focused on a critical task."

"As you know, we will also be exchanging one of your crewmen for one of mine," Fascar said, referring to the exchange of one Gateway crewman for one Venturous crewman. "I think you will be doing quite well. William Sosa has been exemplary up here on Gateway. A true asset."

In response, Commander Wedmond did not hesitate to say, "Good to hear that, because that goes both ways! You will be getting one our best astronauts in exchange. I'm pretty sure Ms. Miramontes would prefer to stay Moon-side. But she works well under all conditions."

"We look forward to having her join us on Gateway," said Fascar. Then, with a more serious note, "We do have one matter that is out of norm, but we think will benefit your crew."

"What is that?" asked Wedmond.

"We have had a discussion with Dr. Reisberg about conditions there. While all appears within expected norms, it was brought up and agreed that our Dr. Laurent Benet, would come down for the six days the Lander is there. Being independent of the Venturous crew, it was felt that he will be able to assist Dr.

Reisberg in assessing crew condition. I hope you don't mind." Commander Fascar added a quick smile to her last statement, hoping to not have tread on Wedmond's toes.

In response, Wedmond said, "Commander, you are not sneaking anything by me." Smiling himself, he said, "Omoné already informed me. We thank you for your support."

"Well good. Everyone here is always looking for an excuse to go Moon-side. This purpose seemed more valid than most."

"Does that mean you might be coming down yourself one day, Marianna?"

"I suspect that might not be in the cards for me, Dan." Then she added, "But you never know!"

"You will be most welcome, if you do."

Chapter 13
Silver Linings

*I*f *anything is a silver lining in this mess, it has to be that Jim escaped being a casualty.*

His conversation with the commander of Gateway was, as always, a good experience, and lately they left him feeling less alone, despite the intense proximity of his very sizable crew. Commander Wedmond's thoughts were now fully focused on the positives. That was, after all, his job, his responsibility.

And part of that role was to assure himself that Jim Sheppard was getting through this... as well as could be expected.

No surprise to Dan, he found Jim working in the greenhouse. If anyplace was therapeutic after an event that Jim experienced, this was it. And Jim did need to complete the replacement of the watering system parts that he had repaired that evening of the accident, nearly three days ago.

Spotting the commander entering the greenhouse, Jim looked up, smiled tentatively, and said, "Commander, welcome to the greenhouse."

"Thanks, Jim. I really need to spend more time here. This place is just amazing. You and your predecessors have done some miraculous work, here," said Wedmond very sincerely.

"Hey, it's not me. Nor any of the botanists per se. This is a truly unique environment under which these plants are growing."

"Don't understate your contributions. If it wasn't for the dedicated scientists, engineers and plant physiologists, of which you are one in that group, none of this would exist at all. I am proud to be just standing in the shadows. Well, if there were any shadows." The both laughed at that concept.

"I am just glad to see you are not overcome by the accident. You seem to be in exceptionally good spirits," said Dan, getting on to why he was there in the first place.

"Well, to be sure, it was not just a devastating incident. Just knowing I could have been there when it happened had me down for a day or two. Not to mention wondering if there was something I could have done to prevent it."

Wedmond just listened, nodding his head in acknowledgement.

"But then I realized that that way of thinking was not healthy and not going to help. I had to get back into the routine and do whatever I could to keep us alive and well here."

"I'm impressed. I don't think everyone here could have made that comeback, and certainly not so fast."

"Now who is understating?" said Sheppard. "We do have some exceptional people on Venturous, all operating at peak performance under extraordinary conditions. I just told myself that I was not going to be one to let everybody down."

"Rest assured, you haven't. I am glad you are one of the team."

"Speaking of which, I should be part of the repair team. It is my area of expertise," said Jim.

"Don't worry. You will be. I do need a clean bill of health from Dr. Reisberg before you can do that, but I doubt that will be an issue. For now, however, we have plenty of expertise here and back at MET as well. But I'm counting on you for the final repair effort," said Wedmond.

"I'm looking forward to it," Sheppard said. "What about the cause of the explosion? How's that investigation going?"

"I would like to tell you that I know something, but I can't. I'm getting an update later today, but so far, there has been no clear indication of what could have caused it."

"Not good. Well, I can tell you, I did not see anything out of place when I was in there with Bruce. And as I've already told Anna Kormendy, Bruce was working on purely mechanical elements. Nothing electronic, nothing... nothing chemical. Just the gear box."

"So I understand. I am under the impression it had nothing to do with either one of you. We'll know more shortly."

"That'll be good," said Jim. "Let me know what I can do."

"I certainly will, Jim. The sooner we figure out what happened, the sooner we can correct any problems or conditions – if there are any to correct – and the sooner we can get the tool-shed repaired and up and running again. It's holding us back on some of our work."

Before departing, Commander Wedmond took a moment to take in the greenhouse. He talked with Jim about some of the plants, the amount of oxygen generation from them and the impressive levels of air filtration and cleansing that were being achieved. Dan, like the rest of the crew, truly appreciated the vitality of the plant growth and how it made one feel just to see it, to take in the aromas. It was invigorating. This would be what would transform the Moon someday, if people were going to live here.

⚛

The Venturous did not have the only greenhouse on the Moon. The Tiangong-3 had, perhaps, an equally impressive greenhouse that was built in a classic Chinese style. It was designed to experiment with solar radiation. It had a thick heat-absorbing wall and a partial roof that were positioned away from the sun's rays and it had very thick, slightly concave acrylic panels that did face the sun. Though there might not be an atmosphere on the outside, there was one on the inside. Thus, the Tiangong crew were able to experiment with heat sinking walls and materials to absorb solar energy and then radiate it back into the greenhouse during the 'night' side, away from the sun. The results that the Tiangong-3 botanists were achieving received critical acclaim in the plant physiology world.

The Tiangong-3 station had some other impressive features as well, including a lab module dedicated to solar power experimentation and the transmission of power back to earth via microwaves. The technology to do just that had been developed by a Japanese firm, Shimizu, as early as 2013. Shimizu wanted to build Lunar Solar Power arrays on the Moon by 2035 out of very lightweight materials. Unfortunately, it had no way of getting it there. CNSA offered them a ride.

Ideally, Shimizu wanted to build its arrays within a narrow band around the equator of the Moon. CNSA had other plans and wanted to be much closer to the pole. Shimizu decided to work out an agreement with CNSA such that at least they could get on the Moon, build a facility within Tiangong-3 and, eventually, venture southward to the equator to build its array.

So far, their research and experimentation were proving successful. Power from the sun was being used to power the Tiangong-3. And early attempts to transmit it back to Earth in the form of microwaves were showing promise.

Within the coming six months, CNSA and Shimizu had plans to take a crew and some rovers with solar arrays down to the equator to set up an experimental station there. The logistics of getting there were still in the planning stages, but CNSA thought it was doable. Ultimately, the plan is to construct a solar array called the 'Luna Ring' around the lunar circumference that would be up to one hundred or more miles wide. It is planned as a major undertaking that would be years in the making. Two of the 40-person crew on the Tiangong were Shimizu employees responsible for this project. Pedro Yoshitake was the current head of Shimizu's Lunar Solar Panel project.

Pedro Yoshitake was, like so many of the taikonauts, an exceptionally brilliant engineer who could not keep still. Born in São Paulo, Brazil, home of the largest Japanese emigrant communities outside of Japan, he rose quickly in an environment that fostered few success stories. He spoke Portuguese (his native language), Japanese and Modern Standard Mandarin Chinese fluently by the time he was 16.

Probably due to his location in the warm sunny climate of São Paulo, he gravitated to the solar energy field. After college, Pedro worked for a few solar panel companies in Brazil, but that was not good enough for him. He pursued an opportunity in Tokyo to work for a solar research lab. There he encountered Shimizu and learned of its plans to build a solar array on the Moon. He was all in for that.

He went to work for Shimizu in 2028. Nine years later he was heading to the Tiangong-3 lunar base station representing Shimizu's interests in the Lunar Solar Panel project. On board, he was well liked by the other Chinese taikonauts where he not only conducted his solar energy experiments but pulled his share of the workload. He loved what he was doing on the Moon.

"It is confirmed, Yoshitake-san," said Guan Nuan, in Mandarin, but stating his name in the respectful Japanese fashion. "Several additional solar panel arrays will be transported here within four months' time." Guan was the senior female taikonaut on Tiangong and chief of sciences and research. It was her responsibility to oversee all research and experimentation. That included overseeing the Shimizu solar energy project.

"That is excellent news," Yoshitake responded. "That will help accelerate our program immensely."

As the two continued their conversation about the project in the solar energy lab, they were approached by Commander Li, followed by second-in-command, Xi Jian, and the chief engineer, Yang Junlong.

"Sorry to interrupt," said Commander Li. "Guan, can we have a moment of your time?"

"Certainly, Commander," Guan responded. Looking to Yoshitake, "Excuse me Yoshitake-san. We will continue our discussion later?"

"Of course, excuse me." Yoshitake moved on to continue his work.

Commander Li continued, "Guan, we would like to discuss with you the situation on the Venturous."

"The Gweilo base station?" she asked.

"Yes, the Westerners' base station," Li said, choosing not to use the slang term. "We know that there was an explosion of some kind inside one of their modules that caused a breach in the exterior wall. That breach resulted in depressurization of that isolated module and that their executive officer, equivalent to our second-in-command, was killed."

Everyone nodded having heard this much about it already.

"Also, from what we have heard, it is being treated as an accident," Li continued. "But they do not yet know for certain what caused the explosion." Again, nods of understanding. "What we are uncertain about is the status of their attempts to implement repairs. Messages that we have intercepted have been unclear on this point."

Yang, thinking like the engineer that he was, asked the first question, "Sir, those exterior walls are irregularly shaped in a manner that reinforces the strength of the wall material and there are numerous tubes or ribs closely spaced as part of the structural frame. The tradeoff is that a sizable breach or rupture becomes very difficult to repair. Is this the nature of their breach?"

"I cannot answer that," said Commander Li. "But I believe that is the issue that is affecting their repair efforts."

Xi Jian interjected, "So Commander, why are you telling us this? We are not concerned about the problems of the Gweilo." Xi was assertive in his question to his commander, and by Chinese standards, less than respectful. But Xi was a nephew of Xi Jinping, the beloved president of the Chinese Communist Party and leader of China back during the trade wars. It was known, or at least suspected, that Xi Jian was a taikonaut because he simply wanted to be. He got what he wanted. But he also happened to be good at it, so he was accepted by the crew. They just had to accept his attitude. Back on Earth, it was rumored that CNSA was very glad that he was on the Moon... and not on Earth.

In response, Li said firmly, "Xi, we are all Yuháng yuan, especially here on the Moon. I am compelled to be concerned about our fellow inhabitants, regardless of what country they come from."

"Yes sir, you are right," conceded Xi. "Forgive me. May I ask what you are proposing?"

"Our leadership at CNSA, the Ministry of Industry and Information Technology, and in the Party have reached out to the entity called Moon Exploratory Team that operates Venturous. They have offered our assistance. The Western entity did not accept our Earth-based offer.

However, I wish to take it a step further. I want to talk to the Venturous commander directly and reiterate our willingness to provide support and assistance and our offer to help however we can. I want to do this out of basic human compassion."

The three looked at each other, nodded and smiled. Guan Nuan spoke first, "I think that is the right thing to do, commander."

"What can we do, sir?' asked Yang. He was suddenly very proud of his space-venturing family legacy.

"Thank you for your support. That is all I can ask for right now. I will contact the Venturous commander tomorrow morning."

He paused for a moment and added, "I will, however, need one of you to translate for me."

They laughed. They knew his English was perfect.

Chapter 14

Revelation

30 March 2039, 1:16 pm UTC,
MET Moon Base Station Venturous, Sea of Serenity, Moon

*W*e are only pale under Earth's bright light…
I should be a poet, thought Eleni. *Ahh, but I have got enough on my plate already!*

It had only been three days since the worst few days of her life and she was slowly returning to her normal upbeat self. She did have a few guilt pangs about it. And it reflected in her elegiac thoughts of the significance of what had happened. Life continued – on Venturous and on Earth. And she realized she needed to get back to being a constructive part of that life… at least here on the Moon.

Earlier, the investigative team had taken a break for lunch, discussed their findings with Dr. Kormendy, and then convened in the science lab awaiting Commander Wedmond to brief him on their findings. Dr. Kormendy had to see to the arrival of the Lunar Lander from Gateway, due around 1300 UTC, and could not be there for the briefing.

"So, what have you got?" asked Wedmond as he entered the science lab. There, working around some of the debris from the toolshed, were Luca Barolo, Eleni Dimopolous and Linda Miramontes, the NASA electrical engineer who had come on board Venturous with Wedmond but would soon be heading for Gateway for her last eight months.

"Commander, with the help of Eleni and Linda, here, and Dr. Kormendy, we have determined what exploded and perhaps what had caused it." Luca looked to Linda before continuing. "Based on residue found, we know it was ammonia nitrate that exploded."

Wedmond displayed only a modicum of surprise in his expression, but he was surprised just the same.

Luca then picked up a white plastic container labeled as fertilizer. "This is one of the fertilizers that are used in the greenhouse. Several of these containers are kept in the toolshed. This fertilizer was selected because it was relatively low in nitrogen, a necessary ingredient for plant growth, but considered safe for our purposes on the Moon."

"Apparently not," interrupted Wedmond.

"Yes and no," Eleni added. "By itself, and even under most circumstances around the base station, this product is safe."

"However," continued Luca, "there were some containers of ammonia-based products on board used for a variety of onboard purposes such as cleaning, refrigeration and water purification. These two products were very close to each other. Somehow they were i-nited... ah." Luca did not know the English word he was looking for.

Linda jumped in, "They ignited. The problem is that the ignition process is not simple. It takes either a great deal of heat or a shock force, maybe by a smaller explosion. Right now, we don't know yet what that was that could have caused the ignition."

Linda's face was very somber and almost bleach white as she explained it. It was almost disconcerting. Though Linda was of 'Hispanic' origins, she was pale-skinned and blonde, naturally. It was a misconception that people of Hispanic backgrounds were dark-skinned. Much of South America and parts of Central America and Mexico where inhabited by a variety of pale European settlers, their traits carrying through in subsequent generations.

"How do you know this, Linda?" asked Wedmond.

"I might be an electrical engineer, but I was going to be a chemical engineer first. Explosive materials was one of those lab classes I took back in the day."

"Something else, commander," said Luca. The ammonia products are not kept in the toolshed. They are not used here and there is no reason for them to be here." Pausing, Luca said, "Linda, explain the explosion step, please."

"Sure. We looked through the debris. It was all very badly demolished and misshapen, but we did find what appears to be an electronic device that we cannot account for. I think what happened is that some of the fertilizer came in contact with the ammonia and the device might have been heating it up. Perhaps the device heated up enough to first melt the plastic containers and then, secondarily, initiate the explosion. We just don't know with certainty."

"Will you be able to make that determination?" asked Wedmond.

"It's possible but not likely," responded Luca. "We are just not equipped to handle these things."

Linda added, "We do think it's unlikely that it was caused by anything Bruce or Jim were working on. We base that on what Jim reported."

"There is one more thing you should be aware of, commander," chimed in Eleni. "As you know, many of the modules have video camera coverage available for purposes of documenting experiments and research events." Eleni was now in her area of expertise. "There was no reason for Bruce and Jim to be recording what they were doing at that time. But just in case, I checked to see if there was a recording."

"What did you find?"

"As I suspected, there was nothing," Eleni said. "But it wasn't really nothing, it was blank for that time frame. It was as if there had been a recording, but it was erased."

"What's your take on that?"

"I'm not sure, but I think the camera was recording at the time. The explosion did not damage the camera, but perhaps it caused a corruption of the video."

"Alright, good work everyone," said Wedmond. Turning to Eleni, he said, "Why don't you discuss your findings with Penelope Brightling. See what she can come up with. If anyone on board knows these systems, she does."

Turning then to Linda Miramontes, Dan said, "So you will be leaving us here in a few days. I hope you enjoy your next eight months on Gateway."

In response, Linda said, "I am sure I will, but I will miss it here on the Moon and being part of the Venturous crew. What happened to Bruce Holmann and the toolshed was terrible, but the experience of the past twenty-eight months has been more than just rewarding. It goes without saying, my life will never be the same."

"Fantastic, Linda. I want to thank you for your help in the investigation and with all you have done to make this mission a success. It has been a pleasure working with you! I guess the next time we see each other, it will be Earth-side."

"Yessir. Thank you."

Wedmond left the team as he had found them in the science lab. But their report had not been what he had expected and, if anything, very disturbing leaving him with even more unanswered questions. For now, however, his responsibilities, took him to 'the Door' to greet the new arrivals after they had settled in.

⚜

The arrival of the Lunar Lander from Gateway was always a spectacle to observe. The entire crew would stop what they were doing, when they could, to watch the process. A flat and level clearing about fifty meters from the Venturous was laid out and marked for the purpose of receiving the lander. It was just bare surface, but there were both visual and electronic 'targets' in place to assure a consistent and safe landing.

Preparation for an arrival took some effort. A checklist of tasks had to be completed long beforehand. Once completed, however, from the Venturous' point of view, the landing was automatic. And for the pilot of the lander, it was pretty much automatic as well. He or she was, almost, along for the ride.

Per procedure, two crewmen were suited up and standing by outside the Door during the touchdown. This was more out of respect and courtesy to the arriving astronauts as opposed to providing any safety function. If something did go awry, what could they do?

But nothing ever did go wrong.

Dr. Kormendy, as the current senior representative after Dan Wedmond, was out there for this arrival along with Jon Miles.

"1305 UTC. Right on time," Anna said to Jon.

Lockheed Martin's Lunar Lander was not that dissimilar to the original lander used during the Apollo missions seventy years ago. It was a bit bigger for hauling components, supplies and a lot more personnel. It also had cleaner lines and all elements of it were reusable. The top was a flat docking port that was used solely when docking with Gateway. Once on the Moon, however, with its gravity in effect, crew could exit out of a side portal to a ladder on one of the braced landing legs;

supplies were handled out of a second port on the opposite side, closer to the ground.

It would take about five minutes for the pilot to shut down and secure the lander. While he was doing that, two of the Gateway crew on board, in their suitcases and, thus, indistinguishable, exited the lander and approached the welcoming committee. Clearly they both had not experienced gravity for a while. They were unsteady and moving cautiously, slowly across the fifty meters of open moonscape as if heavily burdened. Their muscles were not used to working this much, even under the Moon's much lesser gravitational pull. It would be days before any level of normality would be felt in their legs.

Procedure would not permit the welcoming astronauts to go out to meet the new arrivals until the lander was fully secured. They had to wait near the Door. After several minutes, the two Gateway astronauts arrived at the Door.

Seeing their name patches on their suits, Dr. Kormendy was able to recognize and greet the new arrivals via the comms radio, "Welcome to the Moon, Doctor Benet, Susan Ly. I am Doctor Anna Kormendy, and this is Jon Miles. Glad you could make it."

"Thank you, doctor," said Laurent Benet. "We are very excited to be here."

"Yes, thank you," said Susan Ly, the Canadarm operator out of Montreal, her French accent just slightly noticeable. Susan's parents had immigrated to Canada from Vietnam, but she was born and raised around Quebec. "It's good to feel the weight of my body again," she added.

"I am sure you would love to wander and take a look about. Perhaps in a few days when your muscles are more acclimated. Let's get you inside the Venturous. Dr. Reisberg is anxious to meet with you both. Jon, will you wait for the pilot?" Jon nodded.

"Command, three returning, Jon Miles to await the lander pilot."

"Understood, Dr. Kormendy. The retrieval team is standing by to unload the lander. Welcome to the Venturous."

The three entered the Venturous. Jon Miles stood by while the pilot, William Sosa, of NASA, shut down and exited the lander. Jon could see the difficulty William was experiencing as he worked his way down the ladder and across the half-football field distance toward the Venturous. With the lander secured, Jon went out to meet him halfway.

"William, welcome to the Moon and to the Venturous. I'm Jon Miles, ESA. Let's get you inside quickly." They both continued to the Venturous, William taking it slowly.

"Thank you, Jon. I knew this was going to be a challenge despite a regular workout on Gateway, but I did not know it would be like this."

"No worries. It happens to everyone who spends time on Gateway before coming here. You will adapt quickly, especially at your age."

"So those who come directly here from Earth do not experience this wobbliness?" asked Sosa.

"Actually, they, like myself, have a totally different experience. Despite having spent about five days in space getting here, that is not a very long time for muscle adaptation. Consequently, we typically have a sense of feeling too strong. Inside the Venturous, newcomers from Earth tend to bounce off the walls."

"OK, then."

"You are actually lucky that your first gravitational experience is the Moon. Those returning from Gateway, ISS or other long-duration missions under zero gravity are significantly affected when they reach Earth. Some astronauts report taking up to eight months to get back to Earth normal."

"Great!" exclaimed William.

"Don't worry. As I said, you will adapt very quickly to the Moon's gravity. Still, you will not be expected to do any heavy lifting for a while." Both men were smiling, though neither could see the other through the heavily tinted visors.

"Speaking of heavy lifting, here comes the retrieval team now. They will unload your lander." Three crewmen were coming toward them from the Venturous. All waved as they approached each other.

"Oh, good news, guys and gals. We have your lunar rover replacement gearbox onboard, special order from Blue Origin. Your guy, Stan Rivers, will be looking for that," said William.

"That's me," came the voice of one of the retrieval team. "That is great news. I knew they wouldn't let us down. I will have Martin back up and running in no time."

Stan Rivers had picked up the task of repair of the Martin that Bruce had taken on before his death. With the new parts in hand, he went right at it. And with gusto. He was going to get it done in memory of Bruce.

After getting settled in, Dr. Benet conferred with Dr. Reisberg on the condition of the crew, but they quickly recognized that the mere presence of the Gateway crew had a positive benefit, as did the supplies and new equipment that came with them. While both Laurent Benet and Susan Ly would only be here for six days before returning to the Gateway, the change was welcomed, and smiles were seen again. That afternoon, with the mingling of the two crews, it seemed that everyone on the Venturous was clearly more upbeat than they had been in days.

Luca Barolo, having completed his investigation and being the social Italian that he was, wanted to be part of the evening welcome dinner. The event would also include saying good-bye to Linda Miramontes as well, with whom he had worked closely during the investigation, and would now miss.

For now, Moon luck was looking good.

Chapter 15
The New Kid in Town

31 March 2039, 7:10 am UTC,

MET Moon Base Station Venturous, Sea of Serenity, Moon

It's great to feel gravity again, even the Moon's!

At thirty-two, William Sosa was now, officially, the youngest person to inhabit the Moon. He had gone to his assigned berthing area rack early, missing part of the evening's festivities. Frankly, he was feeling the soreness in his muscles and the tiredness in his body due to the new feeling of exertion that came on since arriving on the Moon.

Naturally, having gone to bed early, he woke up early, found the Venturous gym – one of the modules set aside for exercise as well as the conduct of various human physiology tests. No module could have only one function. There in the gym he met more members of the crew he had not met the evening before. Breakfast in the dining area followed. Even that was a new experience for him, eating at a table where the food didn't float in front of your face.

Unlike most of his astronaut colleagues, it had never been his goal or secret ambition to be an astronaut. Growing up in San Diego, he just wanted to be around cars, not even necessarily fast ones. He just liked cars – driving them, fixing them, admiring them at car shows.

That love for the automobile waned as he got older, but never left him. In college, he studied to be an electrical engineer. In the back of his mind, he thought he might actually apply that skill in the automotive industry, but it was only a thought.

Out of college, a friend steered him, figuratively, to check out opportunities at JPL. He did. He found a new love. It might not be an engine running on four tires, but the engines and the equipment that he got to play with far exceeded his love for cars. Now he was working with the best and the brightest in the field of space vehicle research. As it turned out, so was he.

He was part of a team carrying out some very forward-thinking research focused on travel to Mars and other off-world destinations that he could not talk about. Additionally, he was interacting with some of the world's best engineers and research scientists working for Lockheed Martin, Blue Origin and, of course, SpaceX. He was in heaven... almost.

Well, he was in heaven, he thought, when some dozen years later, he married his high school sweetheart. They were a match made in... heaven, of course. All was going very well. He was rising in responsibility with significant management roles at an early age. He was in great health and loving life. At thirty years old, he thought it couldn't get any better.

Then one day out of the blue, he was approached by a NASA senior administrator, or so he thought. NASA was in the market for a bright young electrical engineer who had hands-on experience with rocket engines and spacecraft systems, someone who was a standout among others of comparable skills and yet a team player; someone in good physical condition who wouldn't mind going to the Moon if called to do so. He was asked if he would consider applying to its astronaut corps. William had not given any thought about getting off the Earth's surface, but having been approached by NASA, he gave it consideration. He did not think he would actually make the cut – there were several other very qualified candidates who most likely really wanted the job – but he was very curious to see how far he could go. His wife, on the other hand, told him flat out he had better go for it.

That was two years ago. His engineering experience, mechanical prowess and good-natured approach to life's challenges got him selected for the corps. He was a rising star among rising stars. He was also in the right place at the right time. That got him fast-tracked for the Gateway mission after only a year of training.

Still not thinking that he would be stepping on the Moon any time soon, when they wanted someone for the NASA-MET exchange program, he was their ideal candidate as he was a good match for the Venturous-based electrical engineer, Linda Miramontes. He was going to the Moon and he loved it.

And here he was, on the Moon, eating breakfast, feeling a bit drained.

"Good morning, William," said one of the crewmen whom he had met in the dining area last evening, "Did you sleep well?"

Marc Laboe – that's his name. "Good morning, Marc. "Yes, but I wound up getting up early. Gave me a chance to check out your exercise facilities."

"Ah, you found our gym! Good. As you know, spending quality time there is a must if you want to maintain your muscle mass."

"Exactly. It felt a bit odd, though, having spent ten months on Gateway with close to no gravity to speak of."

"Well, again, welcome aboard. But don't relax yet. Commander Wedmond would like for you to join him and some of the others in the Command Module right away. Do you know where that is?"

"Out this corridor and two modules to the left?"

"You got it," said Laboe.

William washed and put away his utensils quickly and

lumbered through the maze of corridors to the Command Module. Already there were Commander Wedmond; Stan Rivers, whom he had passed on his trek from the lander to the Venturous; Jim Sheppard, who had greeted him last evening; and a lean, blonde-haired woman he had not yet met.

"Good morning, William," said Commander Wedmond. "And good to see you are up early."

"Good morning, sir, ma'am," Sosa responded, acknowledging the others as well.

Kormendy jumped in, "We haven't met yet, William. I am Doctor Anna Kormendy. I am with the SpaceX contingent on the Venturous. Welcome."

Sosa shook her hand and did the same with Jim and Stan, greeting them.

"We need for you to get right to work, William," started the commander. "We have a problem and we would like your participation in the resolution of it."

"Of course. I will do what I can."

"Good." Then, turning toward Rivers, Wedmond said, "Stan, you were about to tell us some good news. Please continue."

"Well, with the delivery of the gearbox and parts for Martin… William, that is our pet name for our Moon Automated Rover/ Transport… I was able to get them installed yesterday and complete operational testing this morning. So, the good news is Martin is good to go!"

"That is great news," said Dr. Kormendy, "We are desperate to get back on schedule with our geological explorations."

Jim Sheppard subtly shook his head at her comment, but no one took notice. "I am sure Bruce would have appreciated it's return to service." His cutting comment took away Anna's smile.

Wedmond ignored the comment but took note of it. "Good work Stan."

"I was also able to make some modifications that should minimize further infiltration of dust and dirt. That will keep the gearboxes in good working condition longer. We will also implement a procedural maintenance task that will inspect these parts regularly."

"Alright. I think you should share the news with the rest of the crew and start figuring out who will be taking it out first."

"Will do," Rivers said and left the meeting.

"Blue Origin came through,' said Wedmond as a kudo to the company. "Dr. Kormendy, what has SpaceX got for us to get our toolshed usable again?"

"I would like to say that we can fix the wall panel now, but the damage was too significant to the structure and the ribbed exterior panels as well as the interior wall panel. We will need to have some very significant replacement panels brought up from Earth, plus some special equipment to properly attach and seal the panels. We cannot do it with what we have here on Venturous."

Jim added, "Commander, we have extracted most of the mobile tools and some of the equipment that is not locked down. Of course, finding places for these items is also burdensome since free space is an indulgence we can't spare."

"Understood," acknowledged Wedmond, grudgingly, then turning to Sosa, "William, I have asked you here for two reasons. First, since Linda Miramontes was part of this repair effort but is leaving us, I would like for you to pick that up from her. And second, I have been made aware of your skill and experience gained when working at JPL. I think that will come in most useful in this situation."

"I'll be glad to, sir. We worked with componentizing equipment and such at JPL."

Anna added, "All components of the station are designed to

be quickly removed and either repaired or replaced in the event of a minor failure, even a minor meteorite strike. An internal explosion was not anticipated."

"What about a large meteor strike?" asked Sosa.

"Well… let's just hope it never comes to that," Jim Sheppard answered. "Commander, if we need to expedite the repair of the toolshed and suitable parts and panels must come from Earth-side, it will be necessary to delay the transport of the metallurgy module in order to fast-track delivery of those items."

"You're jumping to conclusions, Sheppard," asserted Kormendy, irritated by his comment and fearing the delay of the lab. "We don't know that yet."

"I am concerned about not only the use of the toolshed, but the impact the rupture might have on the integrity of the entire station. To be able to build this facility with materials that could be brought to the Moon meant that safety factors were minimal-ized. MET shares my concern and are planning to act accordingly.

"William, sorry to say your starting off here under a very stressful situation. But don't let it get you down. We still have plenty of good tasks, experiments and research in front of us to accomplish of which you will be a significant part."

"Jim, work with William to come up with a parts list and what, if any, equipment we will need to assure a proper repair. Anna, since Martin is back in service, I would like for you to revise and update its operation schedule." After a round of "Yes sirs," Wedmond said, "Ok, let's get to it."

And so the day started.

Wedmond had remained in the Command Center, taking care of his other administrative tasks that came with the job. About 0900 UTC, Dr. Reisberg and Dr. Benet entered the module wanting to confer with him.

"Commander, a moment?" asked Dr. Reisberg.

"Certainly, Omoné. What's up?"

"As you know, I have been tasked by M-E-T to assess the crew's adaptation to the conditions including the impact of the nearby Chinese station. The original task was modified after the explosion. I have only begun to carry out the task as there are past assessments to review and a baseline that I must establish before I talk specifically to our crew. In the meantime, Doctor Benet and I have reviewed my contemporaneous notes on the matter of the mental health and stability of the crew. And he has had a few hours to meet and talk to several of the crew since arriving."

Dr. Benet added, "My general impression is that by design, if you will, your crew is highly resilient to distressful events, events that for many typical individuals would likely succumb to various levels of depression. I think you will not see much of a setback and that the crew will bounce back to their normal state, if they haven't already."

"Well that is good news."

"Having said that, I have suggested to Dr. Reisberg some indicators to be mindful of as she observes the crew in the coming days. Just to be certain that all is well."

"Makes sense. I appreciate your coming down to assist us. I think, under the circumstances, we should consider ourselves fortunate that we have not one but two very competent doctors available during our tragedy."

"A pleasure, sir," said Dr. Benet, smiling. "Since I am here for a few more days before my ride returns to Gateway, I plan to further assist Dr. Reisberg. And, since we were collaborating on a mutual research endeavor, we will be working out those details as well."

But before Wedmond could continue, Penelope Brightling,

who was the on-duty Command Center officer, approached him. "Excuse me sir, I have a very urgent communication for you."

"Really? From Darmstadt? They would be the only ones awake right now."

"No sir," she said softly, "It's from the commander of the Chinese station, Commander Li I believe."

"Ok. I guess I better take that," Wedmond responded. Turning back to the others, "Doctors. We'll have to continue later. I need to take this call."

As the two doctors left, Commander Wedmond walked over to the comms desk and sat down in front of the video screen. There on the screen was a very serious-looking senior Chinese man. He looked as if he could be in charge of more than a base station. "I am Commander Wedmond. Do you understand me, sir?"

From the video speaker came Commander Li's voice, "Yes sir. I am fluent in English. I hope you do not mind if we converse in this manner. I am Commander Li Yuen of the China National Space Administration and in command of the Tiangong-3, not far from you."

"I do not speak Mandarin nor Cantonese; however, as commander of the Moon Exploratory Team's base station Venturous, I am honored to receive your call."

"In truth, I wish to apologize, Commander Wedmond. I should have reached out to you quite some time ago. Perhaps our own workload got in the way."

"I could say the same thing, sir," said Wedmond. "If I may say, not only is your use of English excellent, but you seem to know our expressions as well."

"Very true. You might be surprised to know, sir, that I was taught English from a very young age. In China, it is very much a desired course of learning. Additionally, I received a post-graduate education at Stanford University in California. I do miss California."

"Commander, I am impressed. And I am embarrassed that I cannot say that I have much experience with your country, although I have traveled the Yangtze River from Shanghai to Chongqing and I have visited the site of the famous Terra Cotta Warriors."

"Ah, something even I have not done," said Li.

"We should compare notes. But I am sure that is not why you have called. Is there something that we can do for you, commander?"

"To the contrary, commander. I want to know if there is something that we can do for you?" After a brief pause, allowing it to sink in with Wedmond, Li continued, "The CNSA is aware of your accident and the death of your... Executive Officer. We do not know much about what happened, but we can only surmise that the damage to your facility is... detrimental to the safety and condition of you crew. If I have overstepped my position, please excuse me. However, my crew and I are genuinely concerned. We want to offer you our full support."

Dan Wedmond did not see this coming. Nor was he prepared for it. He did not know how to respond to this very surprising offer. Was it serious or just a gesture? He needed to dig into this more.

"I am grateful for your offer, commander. I can tell you that, while it was a tragic accident in which we did lose one of our crew, the damage was confined to one location. There was a rupture to our exterior wall. It is most likely the sudden decompression that resulted in the death." So far, Wedmond had not told Commander Li anything other than what the world, at this point, already knew.

"I am sorry to hear that. Were you able to repair your facility's wall?"

"Yes. Well, temporarily. We have parts and equipment on the way with which we can implement a permanent repair. For now, we are airtight and secure."

"I am glad for you. Please know though, if conditions change, we will be at your disposal. We do have here at Tiangong a portable high-arc welding machine and personnel with the necessary experience."

"That is good to know. We just might call upon your assistance if conditions do change."

"Very good, commander. You can reach me anytime here. I won't be going anywhere soon!"

"Again, thank you for your offer, Commander Li. And… we should talk again soon."

"I agree. Until then."

"Xié xié," said Wedmond, saying thank you in the only Chinese he knew. Li smiled at that.

"Until then."

Chapter 16
Eureka

Oh my God, we did it. We hit the mother lode!

One hour after the confirmation, and with a thousand other thoughts racing through his mind, Marc Laboe was still ecstatic. It was a geologist's dream come true. He and the two crewmen with him had not been out twenty-four hours since Martin's return to service, that they found what they had suspected they would find all along. Of course, credit rightfully goes to the researchers and scientists before them. The find was based on sound science and a lot of planned, detailed exploration. They had found titanium in large extractable and refinable quantities. Lots of it!

He knew that Dr. Kormendy and the rest of SpaceX would be thrilled with the find. In fact, everyone on the Venturous and most back at MET will be thrilled as well. This kind of find could help the mission pay for itself and then some!

It had been on the schedule for weeks. The team had planned to explore a few cave-like indentations found at the northeastern ridge of Mare Serenitatis, around the Posidonius Crater. This was near the location where small but significant traces of titanium had been identified in the surface layer. But that was just before the untimely breakdown of the rover, at which point all such activity that far from the Venturous was put on hold.

In retrospect, the only consolation from the delay was that by deferring this run by two weeks, it allowed for more direct sunlight on the area in question.

It's conceivable that had the run been made as scheduled, they might not have taken the exploration into the caves as deep and, most likely, would not have conducted the excavation and drilling where they did today. They very likely would not have found the rich titanium ore two weeks ago!

The Sea of Serenity would not be so serene for long.

Two hours after confirmation, the Venturous was abuzz with excitement. Everybody, except a few still asleep after a night watch, knew about the find. Those who were not asleep or on watch were invited to the dining area for the formal announcement. Twenty personnel were packed into a space that could seat fifteen; a few latecomers were standing in the back.

Up front, where the video walls were located for the intermittent entertainment of the crew, was a clear area were training sessions, presentations and the occasional formal announcements were made. Standing there now were Commander Wedmond, Dr. Kormendy and Marc Laboe. The buzz of excitement from the rest of the crew in attendance was notable.

"Ok, people, can I have your attention please," started Wedmond. "I know you are all excited about the news, but let us give you the formal report of our findings and then we can discuss what that means for all of us." It very quickly quieted down. "Thank you. Although this is a joint find by all parties to the MET agreement, our SpaceX partners were truly the discoverers. Therefore, 1 would like to turn the floor over to Dr. Kormendy. Doctor, if you will."

"Thank you very much Dan." Speaking louder to the group, "Very early this morning, our geotechnical team, led by Marc Laboe here, headed out to the Posidonius Crater north of here to resume their exploration activities that had been halted due to breakdown of the rover. Drilling in one of the suspected pit caves, it did not take long before they came across a vein of ore. Upon examination, the tests proved it to be high-grade titanium."

Cheers and excited adulation rose from the group of astronauts, scientists and researchers in the room.

"Needless to say, this is just the proverbial scratch of the surface, pun intended. But it goes toward proving what we have suspected – that refinable titanium is accessible and can be mined here on the Moon. It's impossible to say the commercial value of this find or the overall potential. That will have to be a question to be answered in the months and years to come. What I can tell you with confidence is that with this find, along with the work that we have achieved in mining the ice, the iron and the lead so far, these successes assure that we can continue to stay on the Moon."

Lindstrum interrupted Kormendy, "That's great for you and SpaceX and the other companies, but how does that help those of us who are here for the pure science and research? We seem to be the stepchildren in this deal. Our research programs are constantly being deprioritized or deferred in lieu of the interests of SpaceX."

"To the contrary, this find is a win for all of us. This discovery directly affects us all, whether you are a geologist who thrills at any discovery here on the Moon regardless of its commercial worth, whether you are a botanist who is advancing the science of plant life and the benefits they bring to the air we breathe, or if you are a physicist playing with the gravitational fields of the Moon and its applications toward meteorite deflection, because now, the companies and governments back on Earth can afford to let all of you continue with your research, your experiments and your advancements.

"With this discovery, we cannot only stay on the Moon, we will be able to afford the significant cost that it takes to expand our presence here and continue to do good things for all mankind!

"These are exciting times in our lives."

Commander Wedmond jumped in. "It is too soon to tell, but I think there is no doubt that this will go a long way toward continuing our presence here. And we can only be here if we show the rest of the world that our presence has its benefits."

Hal Lindstrum, Ken Herron – one of ESA's electronics experts – and some others were still skeptical of the benefits-for-all concept. For the most part, though, they all had to admit that the discovery of high-grade refinable titanium would definitely bring about change... most likely change for the better! Expansion of the mission here had to be a good thing. Otherwise, why were they here?

Luca Barolo spoke up somewhat hesitatingly, asking the question that weighed on his mind. "Commander, I am still new here on Venturous, but if you would not mind, could you please explain how this very interesting find will benefit so many, as you have stated?" The question was asked out of sincere curiosity as to how finding titanium on the Moon would benefit mankind.

Commander Wedmond recognized this sincerity. "You, sir, ask a very pertinent question, that many might be asking themselves, so let me put it this way." Wedmond paused to get his thoughts together on this very substantive issue.

"There are about thirty of us here on Venturous, a few more with the arrivals from Gateway. Then there are those who support us from Gateway. And every one of us each has our own reasons for being here, what we want to accomplish while we are here and what our own missions might be as directed by our respective agencies or companies. On Earth we have a huge support group, with thousands of people carrying out tasks whose sole purpose is to support us, but will never get to step on the Moon.

"Behind our agencies and companies are the millions of citizens in Europe and North America who support their governments who must pay for our dreams, along with the thousands of investors in the companies that also support us, and all these people also have goals and expectations.

"So when we're able to find and extract iron ore or lead and make practical use of it here on the Moon, or develop a thriving botanical garden that not just feeds us but regenerates our air and keeps it clean so we do not have to import these resources. or when we find a substantial mineral deposit such as titanium that has enormous market value, all these elements go toward lessening the financial burden of the millions who cannot be here. So, if in some way they can actually benefit from our resources, all the better.

"People want to support our efforts, but they want to see that there is benefit, if not to themselves directly, to mankind. In return, our reward is to continue to be funded into the future. And, if we are really fortunate, we will be given the additional materials and resources we need to grow and expand."

Mumbling and low conversations arose with Wedmond's pause. From the room, "We do kinda forget that…" along with someone who said, "Very good points, Commander."

Wedmond continued, "I didn't intend to give you a pep talk. But perhaps we just needed a reminder of the magnitude of the value of our presence on the Moon. Today, we can take a moment to reflect on this bigger picture and allow our geologist colleagues to truly savor the moment."

"Here, here!" could be heard

Dr. Kormendy, having heard the commander's words, said to the group, "Commander Wedmond, thank you. Thank you for putting it in perspective." Then smiling, "So, if I may, I would like to open it up for questions, and then I think we should take a moment to celebrate our successes!"

For the most part, that is what took place the rest of day. Other than essential activities, work on the Venturous was set aside this first day of April, 2039. The crew was much more upbeat than it had been since the accident. They celebrated the discovery, but there was a general festive sense for all the achievements that the crew, as a whole, had eked out of a singularly uninhabitable environment. It was a great day on the Venturous.

♪

April 1st, 2039, was not such a great day back on Earth, particularly in Northern California. In the week leading up to this day, California had been inundated with a heavy downpour of rain, off and on, all week. Rainfalls from south of San Francisco to well into southern Oregon had exceeded all prior records. There were allegations by some that this was a direct and predicted consequence of climate change induced by human impact on the environment. Others said, it was on the outer fringe of what could be expected of the extremes of a 'hundred-year storm." Still others said this was God's handiwork on the people of California. Regardless of what was believed to be the cause, it was extreme and devastating.

And on that day, in the early morning hours just after midnight, the worst rains ever recorded overran two of the dams in the region causing massive flooding throughout the state.

It wasn't instantaneous. The state and the feds had issued warnings days in advance, and those with any common sense and even some of the fearful-natured of the population left for other parts. But the majority felt they could stick it out. That had not been wise.

Several hundred lives were lost in the flash flooding, the toll yet to be determined, and billions of dollars in damage to property was incurred. The San Juaquin Valley, and several other agricultural regions were essentially wiped out early in the growing season. Entire coastal and inland towns were devastated. Lowland harbor cities like Eureka and Arcata, California, were inaccessible and half washed out. Small low-valley cities such as Willow Creek and Salyer were wholly under water. Redding was a disaster.

Other parts of the US had been impacted by such events, like the devastation to Louisiana by Hurricanes Katrina in 2005 and Tyler in 2024, or to Puerto Rico in 2018. And other countries such as Indonesia, India, Iran and countries in central Africa, witnessed death due to flood waters on a massive scale in just this century. But no one thought that this would happen to California. Their worries were of forest fires and earthquakes.

The news of this crushing disaster quickly reached the crew of the Venturous by late morning.

Except for Susan Ly, none of the others among the fourteen American and Canadian crew had family in the affected region of Northern California, but not surprisingly, many on board, even among the Europeans, knew someone who lived there or close to it. Jim Shepperd's family in Southern California were not entirely out of the way. Rains were impacting their lives both directly and indirectly. Even though it was four o'clock in the morning there, he called his wife.

The SpaceTime call caught her awake but still in her nightgown. "Jim?" she said sounding groggy.

"It's me, Lori. We are just learning of the terrible situation in Northern California. Are you and the kids alright?" Jim, very concerned, asked her.

"Yes, the rains here have been a lot, much more than we're used to. But up North… it's just been terrible. I have been listening to the news most of the night. There's been so much damage and so many people are missing."

"But you are ok?" Jim asked.

"Yes. Thank God we got the new roof on."

"What about your parents?" Jim knew they were in San Diego, and safe, but that would lead to his next concern – his parents.

"They're fine. And your parents are fine as well." Instant relief came over Jim's face. "They were evacuated to higher ground around Sacramento early yesterday. So far, it has only been precautionary, but the American River is overrun, and the Sacramento river exceeded its banks yesterday flooding most of the agricultural lands north of Sacramento."

"It's just terrible. Everyone here on Venturous knows someone there who might have been affected by the flooding. Everyone is worried."

Lori said, "You know my high school friend Katie? She and her husband live up in Paradise. They had survived the Camp Fire twenty years ago. Well, I cannot reach her now. I've been trying for the last hour."

"I'm so sorry, hun. I hope they're alright. You know, they are both very smart people, retired from the Sheriff's Department. They probably evacuated and just can't reach you. Just like when the fire went through Paradise. They're very likely on high ground somewhere."

"I suppose. But I can't stop worrying. They should have their jPhones though. They should be able to answer."

Jim wanted to ease his wife's worry. "They probably have

them, but there are all sorts of reasons you can't get through. Cell service is most likely down for one. They could have dead batteries. They could be required to stay off the line except for emergencies. They will call you when they can. It could be a few days."

"You're right. I've been up worrying. But I think I need to get some sleep. Thanks, Jim, for being there... so to speak." They both chuckled a bit. It relieved some of the tension.

They said their good-byes. He was so glad that his family and their parents were OK. Jim promised to check in regularly until conditions were better. The other Americans and Canadians with ties to California or Oregon made similar calls to family and close friends. Most were fortunate to get good news. Susan Ly did not.

Though most of her immediate family lived in the Quebec-Montreal area, she had an uncle that lived in Eureka, California. No one in her family had any word on him and his family. The family in Canada hoped and prayed that they had been evacuated. But they knew it would be some time before they would hear anything. On Venturous, everyone took a moment to console Susan.

Chapter 17

The Burden of Truth

1 April 2039, 1:37 pm UTC,
MET Moon Base Station Venturous, Sea of Serenity, Moon

*S*omething is very bloody wrong with this recording, but why?
For the last two days, since Eleni Dimopolous pointed out the discrepancy with the video recording, and time permitting, Penelope Brightling had been analyzing the video file at her station in the Command Center. Eleni had been correct. It appeared that there had been a recording taken from the toolshed video camera at the time of the explosion.

Like everything else, the recordings were taken and stored as digital files. Every bit of documentation on the Venturous was digitized. More importantly, the data storage system was designed so that nothing could be deleted. The concept behind this was that the data they contained was too important to risk inadvertent deletion or destruction. Better to have files that were unnecessary or superseded, then to lose an important file. If files were necessary for a specific research project, experiment or observation, copies could be downloaded to the workstations as needed.

The storage drives did not require an on-board backup system per se. There was a regularly scheduled data dump back to Earth every two weeks, a backup of sorts. Every three to four months, the physical drives were replaced with new drives that arrived with the supply run from Earth. The current set of drives were about to be replaced, had it not been for the analysis that Penelope was conducting on the video records.

Glancing at the wall clocks, she saw that it was Friday, 1337 UTC, 1st of April. Seemed like she just had lunch. For that matter, it seemed like it was just a few days ago that all hell did break loose. But it was five days ago. She wished it all was just a big April Fools' joke. Regrettably, she knew all too well that it wasn't

While working at her station, Eleni approached her, having been very curious and even concerned about the discrepancy. "Penelope, how is your analysis going?" Eleni asked.

"Your timing is great. I was about to report my findings to Commander Wedmond. But I would like to review my findings and thoughts with you first."

"Certainly. If I can help, that would be good."

"Great. As you know, I have been able to confirm that there had been a video recording going on at the time of the explosion. Based upon what I can get from the data logs, it had been started two days prior."

"Two days? What does it show?" asked Eleni.

"Nothing. In accordance with procedure, when a video file reaches a specified size limit, the file is closed out upon completion of that recording. A new file is started with the very next recording. That new file, which would have recorded the events leading to the explosion, has been corrupted."

"Do you think the explosion did it?"

"No. At least I don't see how it would. The video file is placed on a server drive here in the Command Center. There would be no physical action in the toolshed that could cause the corruption. I can only conclude that the file was corrupted after the fact and by someone here on board."

"Whoa, that's a very serious accusation." said Eleni, clearly not expecting that revelation.

"Well, how would you explain it?" asked Penelope.

Eleni, having experience with video recordings, but not with the digital file creation system on board, considered the concept. She, too, was coming to the same conclusion. "I think you might be right. One file corrupted. All others are good. They cannot be erased, but if someone wanted to corrupt the file, why would they do it?"

In response, Penelope pointed out, "Files cannot be deleted. If there was something in the video record that someone did not want seen, it is conceivable that a program could be introduced that would basically corrupt it." Eleni was letting that sink in.

"Having come to that conclusion, I have found something in the system log that indicates that a program, possibly the one that caused the corruption, was introduced into the computer system. I cannot prove that was the file, but there is no other reason for adding an operational system file."

"If you are right, and if someone tried to corrupt a record file, that implies that..."

"That someone has something to hide," interrupted Penelope. "That, possibly, someone rigged the explosion ahead of time and did not want to be seen doing it."

"So, out of curiosity, did the prior file show someone in the toolshed?" asked Eleni.

"Yeah, I checked it and it does. It shows Dr. Kormendy in the shed doing something with the parts on one of the tables."

Penelope Brightling was distraught by her findings, but the conclusion was undeniable. After wrapping up her discussion with Eleni and urging her to keep it to herself, she knew she now had to tell Dan Wedmond. It would then become his problem.

Penelope found the commander in one of the lesser used

equipment modules quietly talking to Susan Ly – she knew what that had to be about. The word got around that Susan's uncle lived in the area of Northern California inundated with flood waters and that he was unaccounted for. She waited patiently just out of sight until Susan, very distraught with her head low, left toward the berthing area.

Penelope approached Wedmond, "Sir, I take it there is no good news from California about Susan's uncle."

"It's still too soon to know anything, but no, there has been no new news. What can I do for you, Penelope?"

"I've completed my assessment of the video record. Unfortunately, I have very bad news to report."

"How could it be worse than what happened in California," Wedmond groaned. "Tell me what you got."

Penelope did just that. She went over her approach, how she came to certain conclusions and, then, what she believed had happened. She could not, however, say who had taken such an action.

"You should know that I might be wrong… but not likely. It's possible that with the right tools, experts back on Earth might be able to unravel the corruption. Here on Venturous, I don't have that kind of equipment and, frankly, it's very much out of my area of expertise."

"I understand," said Wedmond. "Anything else?"

"I also looked to see how far back the corrupted file goes. Looks like all of Sunday and most of Saturday were affected. The last recorded image of anyone in the toolshed was that Friday," said Penelope.

"Oh, and who was there?" asked Wedmond.

"It was Dr. Kormendy."

Dan Wedmond was not happy.

"I need you to keep this to yourself, until further notice,"

Dan said, ending the briefing. Penelope decided this was her que to leave.

If someone did cause the explosion that killed Bruce Holmann, he didn't want that person to know that there was evidence to that effect. More evidence could disappear or possibly others could become victims. And the crew had already experienced one hellacious emotional rollercoaster ride this day. They did not need to worry about a possible murderer amongst them.

He needed to talk to someone about this latest revelation, but Dan did not want to share this with anyone on Venturous just yet. Normally, he might turn to Anna Kormendy, but she could be the person responsible for the explosion. There was Jim Sheppard, but he was under stress from the flooding situation in California. Omoné Reisberg was a good candidate. But then it occurred to him that the perfect person to talk to was just above him, on Gateway, Marianna Fascar, a fellow group commander and someone not on board whom he could trust.

From his private quarters, formerly shared with Bruce Holmann, Wedmond placed his call to Commander Fascar.

"Dan, this is unexpected," Fascar said upon seeing his face on the monitor. "What can we do for you today? And please express our concern for Susan Ly's uncle. We hope to hear good news."

"I will let her know. She is taking it hard," Dan said, "But, that's not why I called you. I need to discuss an important matter with you. I need your advice and I need it to be confidential. Are you out of earshot up there?"

Putting in an earpiece to prevent others on Gateway from overhearing, Fascar said softly, "Well, with some of our crew down on the Venturous, we have a little bit of breathing room, but we are still not as spacious as being down there. I'll do my best."

"Thanks."

Wedmond proceeded to relay the new information concerning the investigation to Fascar. She listened silently as she took it all in.

"So, there you have it," Dan said to Marianna. "It appears that the explosion might have been intentionally set off. If so, we don't know if Bruce was an intended target or just someone in the wrong place at the wrong time. We don't know who might have done this, but the last person known to be in the toolshed was Anna Kormendy, two days beforehand, for what purpose we don't know as of yet."

"Don't you think you should inform M-E-T right away?"

"I would like a bit more information before I make such an accusation. I just don't like knowing so very little about what really happened."

"Dan, that is not your call. I understand you concern, but you need to let them know, if for no other reason than to help answer those questions."

"Yes, you are right, of course," Wedmond responded.

"Further, we are not prepared for this kind of… of problem. We are trained to deal with many different space- and Moon-caused problems, even disasters. We are not trained to be forensic investigators and we are certainly not policemen."

"Oh, I don't know. I think we did a pretty good job investigating this. But, you're right about the latter. We are not police."

"And you still have too many unanswered questions, Dan. I'm thinking you need to turn this over to M-E-T. We shouldn't even be having this discussion," stated Fascar forcefully. With a little softer tone, she said, "Look, I understand you don't want uncertain accusations made against one of your crew. But the possibility strongly exists that someone is a murderer. And you don't know what that person will do next."

"I get it," Dan acknowledged. "I'll contact MET once I've laid out the facts based on evidence and not assumptions."

"Good. I support you in this. After all, that is my job here."

Chapter 18
Now What Do We Do?

1 April 2039, afternoon UTC,
MET Moon Base Station Venturous, Sea of Serenity, Moon

*H*umans can't go ten years off-planet without committing murder among ourselves.

Commander Wedmond had been keeping it together quite well, but this got to him – coming to the realization that among a highly trained, highly motivated, very small select group of professionals was a man or woman who could resort to killing another and possibly killing the entire crew in the process. He had to take a moment, stand back and think through this situation.

He tried to come up with a viable motive. One thought that he could not get away from was that Bruce Holmann and Anna Kormendy were far from compatible workmates. Dan knew he had a role in that by insisting that Bruce deal with it. Maybe he should have acted sooner. But was that really a reason to kill someone. It didn't add up.

But what if it wasn't Kormendy? What other motive might exist for someone to do this? He was truly struggling with that thought. Could Jim Sheppard have been the target, not Bruce? That made no sense either. Everyone liked Jim and he was not in a leadership role. Was it suicide maybe? That seemed unlikely for two reasons. First, these were people who very much wanted to be on the Moon. And he saw that in all of them every day. Bruce was no exception. The second reason to rule out a suicide – there were far better and more certain ways to do it. This was messy and, unfortunately, painful for Bruce. No, it was not suicide.

There was just no rational explanation. Yet, someone had done this terrible thing.

Dan paused to reflect on other trying times and personal challenges in his career and in his life. He had had a few. He had grown up in a military family, his father a senior officer in the Navy and his mother an officer in the Coast Guard. That existence was fraught with difficulty since getting both mom and dad together in the same city, even the same country sometimes, was rare. But he and his two siblings, one older sister and one younger brother, were brought up well and with the understanding that nothing was fixed except family. His sister went to the Naval Academy like dad; his brother became a doctor serving humanity around the world. Dan aspired to be a pilot. He didn't want to get caught between mom's service and dad's. It was only natural that he chose the Air Force Academy, graduating with the Class of '09 with a mechanical engineering degree.

Shortly after graduation, he married his high school sweetheart, Deneen. Children followed thereafter.

While serving overseas, he and several of his fellow pilots were off duty at Bagram Air Base, in the Parvan Province, Afghanistan, when a Taliban rocket strike hit the canteen where they were hanging out. Dan and two of his colleagues survived with minor injuries, but three others, including his closest friend, died in the attack. It was a life changing experience to say the least.

Because of the injuries and impact, Dan was rotated stateside early. He served at Vandenberg Air Force Base near Lompoc, California, for nearly five years. Two of his three children were born there. The third was born in Okinawa, Japan. In Japan, two more friends were killed in a helicopter accident, one that he had been assigned to, but taken off the flight manifest at the last minute to address the commanding officer's concerns about relations with the local Okinawan residents.

He'd been in the midst of a clash between the base command and the locals who were not pleased with the base relocation project. There had been a series of helicopter and other aviation accidents, along with other 'incidents' among some of the local women and some of the enlisted. The death of his two friends made the task of dealing with the local residents that much more difficult to bear. But, as before, he would cope with it in his own way.

Dan needed a change. Thinking back on his exposure to the space program at Vandenberg, he decided to pursue an opportunity with the NASA astronaut program. In recognition of his accomplishments and experience, he was taken in.

He, his wife and family of three boys moved to Houston where his astronaut training took place. He was a natural and recognized as a leader among the best. He served two missions on ISS and one on Gateway in 2031-32.

Later, in 2034, his very loving and accepting wife, Deneen, who had been there for Dan, raising three great kids, and helping him get through the worst of his experiences, contracted brain cancer. She passed away six months later.

His three boys were devastated. The youngest was about to go to college and was still at home. Dan took some time off and the four men – and one daughter-in-law – spent some time together. He helped them to cope with the loss of their mother while doing the same for himself.

Three years later, he was asked if he would like one more mission – this time to go to the Moon as the base commander of Venturous. With the boys now on their own and no one else in his life, it seemed to be the obvious choice.

Now, once again, he was coping with the death of someone close.

Marianna had been right, of course. They were not policemen. He would now have to hand this off to MET. He was not used to passing his problems on to others.

Dan was postponing the inevitable call. But he had his reasons. By making the call around 1600 Venturous time, it would be too late to talk to someone in Darmstadt. The call would have to go through Houston. He wanted NASA to have first crack at this matter.

♂♪

"Mr. Vaughn, this is Manuela Lusk," came the voice across the intercom in Kurt Vaughn's office. He knew that she was the Comms Manager on duty at Mission Control, which could only mean that ISS, Gateway or perhaps the Venturous was making an unscheduled call. Most likely, it would be Venturous, given their situation. It would be very late in the afternoon for both Gateway and Venturous.

"Yes, Manuela, what's up?"

"Sir, you are needed in the command operations center. Commander Wedmond asks to speak to you."

"Ok, I'll be right there."

Kurt Vaughn headed down the short hallway from his office to the Mission Control command operations center. As he entered, he could see Dan Wedmond's face on about a dozen monitors including on the largest screen where everyone in the command operations center faced. Looking quickly at the clock displaying the time on board Venturous, Vaughn said loudly, "Good afternoon Commander. What brings you out this late in the day?"

"Good morning, Kurt," he responded, knowing it was just

after 11 am in Houston. "I am prepared to give you the update to our investigation of the cause of the explosion."

"Good news, I hope. Something we can rectify or avoid in the future?"

"I'm afraid not. In fact, I think we have a bigger problem than anyone could have contemplated." Dan proceeded to state the facts of the investigation up to that point, particularly the matter of the apparent corruption of the video file. He did, however, gloss over the point that Dr. Kormendy was the last person seen in the video taken in the toolshed. There were a dozen other NASA staff in the center who had just become aware of the problem. Dan knew that this was inevitable and unavoidable once he reported in. Keeping secrets was never part of the mission communications plan.

Dan said, "At this point, I cannot say with any certainty, who might be responsible. It only happens that Anna Kormendy was in the toolshed two full days beforehand, just before the video record file closed out."

"Did you ask her about that?"

"That, I did not," said Wedmond. "To be quite frank, except for Luca Barolo, Eleni Dimopolous, and Penelope Brightling, the three who conducted the investigation, I have not talked to anyone else about it on Venturous." Dan was accurate in that statement. He did not want to mention just yet that he had talked to Marianna Fascar.

"I understand completely," responded Vaughn. "Although I doubt you will be able to keep this quiet up there for long."

"Agreed. I advised Penelope to keep it to herself, but Venturous is a place where communication is expected. I'll need MET's direction on this quickly."

"I will get this to the MET board immediately. You will be hearing back from us very soon."

Turning to one of his aides, Kurt's face was dour, and his eyes narrowed. "John, please cancel my lunch meeting with the congressmen. Tell them I got called away. And see if you can get one of the deputy mission directors to fill in for me. I don't want them... concerned. Then get Dr. Feskine on the phone for me."

Then to those in the Mission Control command operations center, "And everyone, for now I want you to keep what you just heard to yourselves. We do not know all the facts yet and we do not need rumors and speculation to run rampant."

It took about thirty-five minutes to get the MET board of directors all on a video conference call. Just prior to that, Vaughn had talked to Dr. Feskine, who in turn had him call Loukas Anagnostopoulos and Jeff Fund. Vaughn summarized the reported facts of the investigation into the explosion and the apparent conclusion of Commander Wedmond – that it was not an accident, but an intentional act.

"So that's what we know, or, should I say, what Commander Wedmond knows, at this point in time. He has taken the investigation as far as he can with what he has at his disposal. He is very concerned, and rightfully so, that if this was an intentional act by one of the crew, that person could do something else, and maybe worse."

Jeff Fund chimed in first, "This is a God-awful thing, to learn that one of our brilliant, hardworking, cream-of-the-crop people, could resort to destruction and murder... on the Moon for God's sake."

Loukas, still maintaining his steady tone, asked, "If the commander alluded to the scenario that one person might have instigated this terrible deed, can he be sure that there is only one person involved?"

Vaughn responded, "That idea never came up, sir." After thinking about it, "I suppose there could be more than one person involved."

"Gentlemen," emphasized Feskine, "it is not our place to pursue this line of questioning right now. I think it best, so that we can contain the situation, to not let it get worse; that we turn it over to the proper authorities and let them handle it."

"I believe you are correct Dr. Feskine," said Loukas. "We should contact Interpol immediately…"

"Why Interpol," interrupted Fund. "If we're going to have a proper investigation, I think we need to have it done by an agency that can proceed with discretion. I believe that the FBI should do it."

Vaughn weighed in, "If I may, I would like for you to consider that MET's existence is based upon the formation of a public-private partnership and a contractual arrangement that came out of that partnership." The three board members were listening.

"That contract is very clear on the resolution of disputes… commercial disputes. Such disputes, if not resolved through the executive management of the affected parties, can be elevated to the United Nation's International Court of Justice. And if I recall correctly, the World Court does not have a policing agency. That is left to the member countries.

"The contract also says that for such matters, the laws, regulations and procedures of the country or state within which the dispute takes place, shall prevail. This was intended to address matters on Earth. With these two contract clauses, it was thought that all potential matters would be addressed. No one contemplated that a criminal act would occur, let alone how to address it."

Loukas said, "Incredible. Are you telling us that we do not have the mechanism to address this issue?"

"What I am telling you, sir, is that it is not immediately evident. I will have to look into it and discuss it with others. What others I am also not sure of at this time."

"Within NASA, we have our own Office of Inspector General. They are charged with investigating criminal and civil violations."

"I have thought of that," Vaughn said.

Fund said, "Sounds like we have a dilemma. How do you propose we proceed?"

Vaughn replied, "I have only had less than an hour to think about it. Regardless, we cannot do nothing. We might be unduly criticized if we did. But in the course of our discussion, it occurs to me that this was a NASA astronaut who was killed. Granted we do not know who did it, but with the victim being NASA, we should ask the NASA OIG for its opinion and to initiate the investigation."

"Dr. Feskine," said Loukas, "Kurt has a very good point. We cannot hesitate to act on the information we now have. Would your Office of Inspector General be able to attend to this matter?"

"I believe they could. At least we can get an appropriate authority involved quickly."

Jeff Fund said, "I don't like this whole thing, but I have to agree. We need to take action now and the OIG will be a good start."

"It's agreed then," said Vaughn. "I will contact the OIG immediately."

He then turned to the next critical matter. "Now, what do we tell the crew? They are going to find out very soon that this was not an accident."

A heated discussion followed by an agreement that it would be best to see what the OIG had to say. If one of the crew was... involved, it could be dangerous to let that person know that they were on to him... or her.

Chapter 19
Seeking the Truth from Afar

1 April 2039, 4:42 pm CDT,
NASA Mission Control, Houston, Texas, Earth

What in the world... wait it's not... of this world.
Special Agent in Charge, Aaron Ghiassi, had just been informed by his boss, the Deputy Assistant Inspector General for Investigations, back in Washington, D.C., that he had just been assigned to a very important case. *Please, not another cyber-crime*, he thought pensively. He hated those because, well, he wasn't a computer geek. He was told that it was a case involving the Moon Exploratory Team, also known as MET, and its Moon base station, Venturous. Well that could be interesting, perhaps it was a case of espionage or more likely a case of faulty manufacturing. He could deal with either. Then he was told what he never would have expected to hear.

"Aaron, you need to know, this case is to be handled as a murder investigation. You will need to proceed carefully, thoroughly and in accordance with procedure," said the Deputy Assistant IG, Robert Hamilton.

"Wait... what?" he said reflexively, not really asking. It had caught him off guard.

"You heard me correctly," Hamilton said. "The initial investigative effort of the astronaut in command of the base station Venturous, Dan Wedmond, has unearthed facts – curious choice of words, anyway – facts that plainly indicate that the explosion that killed Bruce Holmann six days ago was not an accident."

"That is beyond anything we have ever contemplated. I take it that such an investigation is within our authority," said Aaron.

"Yes, it is. Because NASA is a party to the MET partnership, and the fact that MET have formally asked for our assistance, that gives us the authority under current Federal regulations; however, what criminal laws that might been broken is an entirely different matter.

"OK. How do I proceed?"

"As with any case. The difference is, of course, you will not be going to the Moon. Interviews will have to be conducted via telecommunications and you will need to solicit the assistance of Commander Wedmond for the collection of any evidence."

"Understood. Anything else, sir?" asked Aaron.

"Yes. Three things. Since it was six days ago, we're losing the advantage of a quick response. You will need to get on this immediately. Sorry to do this to you on a Friday afternoon." said Hamilton.

"Well, that goes with the territory."

"Second, if one of the crew of the Venturous did carry out this act, that person is still on board and has nowhere to go. We could have a caged animal scenario, which means you have to be cautious, even if you determine who might have committed this act. We will need a strategy for assuring that no further acts of aggression occur. That scenario is potentially worse."

"Understood as well. Do you want me to outline my investigation with you before I proceed?"

"I don't think that will be necessary, Aaron. Follow protocol and proceed accordingly, as difficult as this will be."

"Got it." said Aaron, then asked, "So what is the third thing I need to be aware of?"

Hamilton hesitated. With a very firm and assertive voice indicative of a person in his position there in D.C., he said to Ghiassi, "This is a wholly unprecedented matter and it will be of great interest here in Washington. We are not just in the spotlight with the world, we're very much entangled with the interests of most of Europe and some of the most influential companies out there, none of which want an outcome that will jeopardize the Moon exploration program. I cannot emphasize enough the significance of these facts. You need to proceed knowing that much of the influential world will be looking over your shoulder."

"Oh, no pressure then," said Ghiassi clearly distraught about what he was just told.

"Look, Aaron, I know you. I know how you operate, and I know you get things done effectively. I was personally supportive of your assignment to this case. You can do it."

"Yes, sir. I understand."

"Good. One last thing. I want you to keep me informed daily of your progress and findings. Needless to say, this is a very sensitive matter, on the international political scale. If we believe it to be necessary, we can bring in additional help. We would prefer to keep this internal, but the resources of the FBI can be brought to our disposal. The last thing we want, though, is to let Interpol get involved. We will lose control if that happens. You got that?"

"Yes, sir. I will keep you informed."

"Good. You are authorized to take necessary action within the guidelines we just discussed. If you need help, ask me for it. Good luck, Aaron."

Did the weight of the world just land on his shoulders? Aaron Ghiassi was not unaccustomed to being under pressure on delicate criminal investigations, but he had tried very hard to get away from just such a life. It had taken its toll on him in the past.

For many years, he had worked for the FBI out of its New York District Office, the last five with its Critical Incident Response Group as part of the Hostage Rescue Team. It was hard work and there were more than a few occasions where the HRT could not accomplish its task. People died, good people, sometimes young people who were just in the wrong place when something went bad.

He wanted no more to do with death, even if he had been able to help many others survive. As a man of Syrian decent, second generation in the United States, he had grown up hearing of the death and destruction that was a constant part of his grandparents' lives. He thought that by going into law enforcement, he could make good on his promise to them that their sacrifices would be paid back by the subsequent enrichment of their lives once in the US. But when they passed on, the strain on his family took hold. He felt he had made good on his promise and he wanted to have a better life with his family.

It was just about that time, five years ago when his FBI boss, Robert Hamilton, decided to make the change as well and joined the Office of Inspector General for NASA. Six months later, Aaron Ghiassi was invited to come on board, provided he didn't mind moving to Houston.

It was a done deal for Aaron. The work had its own set of challenges, but nothing like his HRT days, and nothing he couldn't handle. And his family quickly adapted to an easier way of life as well in the Houston NASA community. Working for NASA for the rest of his career would be just fine.

Well, it wasn't a hostage situation on the Venturous. Or was it? He would have to work quickly and with focus to preclude just that possibility. And on the Moon of all places!

Ghiassi sought out and talked to Kurt Vaughn immediately, since they were in the same facility. He was given the facts as presented by Commander Wedmond including a copy of the video call he had made just a few hours ago. With this, he was able to get up to speed quickly.

Six days had passed since the incident; therefore, it was imperative that he talk to Wedmond as soon as possible. After learning that it was late in the evening for the Venturous, he decided to call him without further delay, even if it was just to hear the same facts passed on. But of course, first-hand was always more credible to a trained investigator.

Vaughn set up the call. Due to the nature of the call, it was channeled into a conference room. It was the best the command operations center could do. Private communications between spacecraft and stations and the center were never contemplated. It was just after 5pm in Houston, so it was after 10pm for the Venturous crew. It was a late evening for them.

Once set up in the conference room, Vaughn said to Ghiassi, "You will be speaking directly to Commander Dan Wedmond. He has been informed who you are and the nature of your call. He will try to maintain a private conversation, but, like here, the Venturous is not set up for that. He will be in their Command Center where operations must be monitored around the clock."

To Vaughn, Ghiassi said, "Thank you. I will keep that in mind."

"And one more thing, you must remember that it takes at least three seconds, perhaps four depending on conditions, for anything you say to get to the Venturous and a response to get back for the roundtrip, but you won't notice it as much after the flow of conversation starts. It's always tricky for first timers.

They sometimes lose patience. You need to understand and bear with it."

"Ok, that will be something new."

"Don't worry, the crew is used to it and have learned to adapt accordingly. Keep your questions succinct and don't hesitate or draw out your statements. And when you finish, do not attempt to talk again until the astronaut you are talking to responds; otherwise, you might start talking over that person and that just leads to confusion. You will catch on after a few minutes."

As Kurt left the conference room, Aaron turned to the monitor with the face of the Venturous commander front and center. Having been briefed on the comms system operation, he said, "Good evening, Commander Wedmond. I am Special Agent in Charge Aaron Ghiassi, NASA Office of Inspector General. I am sorry to be calling you so late your time."

After several seconds, which seemed to be a longer period of time to Aaron than it actually was, came Wedmond's response. "I fully understand. I have been expecting your call since my last report five hours ago," said Wedmond.

"Again, I am sorry about that. I am sure you can understand that it takes time to get word through all the proper channels before the call got to me. But I will be conducting the investigation from this point forward." Pause.

"Of course. And I am here to help you, sir, as much as you will be helping me," asserted Wedmond, with a trace of a smile. He did not want to alienate the agent who was very important to the task at hand. The stakes were too high.

"Please, call me Aaron. We will essentially be working together as a team for the next few days. I want you to feel comfortable working with me."

Dan liked the guy already. They were thinking along the

same wavelength. "Certainly. And please call me Dan. We try to be informal up here, though some are still set in their ways."

"I can understand you would tend to operate on a basis of familiarity, working in such a tight environment."

"It's more than that. If this were a military operation, in close quarters, military protocol would dictate relationship. But up here on the Moon, we are a bunch of researchers, scientists, explorers – we operate more like a family; a very diverse and sometimes eclectic family, but a family. Formality exists as occasioned by circumstance. In this family, I'm the current patriarch."

"I see. What can you tell me about… this family of astronauts, Dan? It might help me with what I need to do."

"Not much. Like any large family, we have some older and wiser aunts and uncles who have lots of experience with families of their own, if we're going to stay with this metaphor. And by that, I mean to say who some of the senior astronauts have been in space a few times before coming to the Venturous, such as on ISS, Gateway or other missions."

"I would take it those are the ones you can trust the most?" asked Ghiassi.

"For the most part, yes. But we also have our newcomers and first-timers, what you might think of as the teenagers of the family."

"Ahh, the rebellious types?"

"Yes and no. More like young eager minds with disparate ideas who want to learn, experiment with stuff, make themselves greater than they currently are, and do great things for humanity. I tell you this because I want you to understand the situation here. Someone in the family has gone astray. We need to find that person and, if possible, help him or her." He paused then added, "But we cannot let one dysfunctional member of the family tear apart the rest."

"Dan, I have to say, I am very impressed with your grasp of the situation. I do hope I can help you."

They got down to the facts at hand. Ghiassi asked very specific questions. Those that the commander could answer were definitive and without assumption. But it was getting late for Dan. It was time for him to dive into theory and speculation.

"Your portrayal of the facts has been excellent, but now I do need you to start to speculate. I ask you to do this so I can focus my efforts on plausible scenarios. You said that the last person in the toolshed was Dr. Kormendy. Did I say her name correctly?"

"Yes, that's correct, to both counts."

"And you do not know why she was there?"

"No. Nor have I asked her."

"Do you suspect that she might be the one to have caused the bombing?"

"In truth, I do not. But I am somewhat biased about it. I don't think anyone here on Venturous is of the mind to do such a terrible thing."

"But she did have run-ins with Bruce Holmann, correct?

"That is true."

"So, there is no point in me asking you if you suspect anyone else on board?"

"I have given you what I can. Yes, Dr. Kormendy can be difficult. But that is far from being capable of murder. I will tell you I suspect there must be someone else who could have done it. I just can't think whom that might be."

"Let me ask you this. Do you think it could have been a foreign agent, someone who could be committing sabotage?"

"I thought about that possibility. The fact is, the explosion was small-scale. But who's to say it couldn't have been worse. I am of the opinion that a foreign agent would not risk his or her own life like that. Also, why now? There is no significance to the timing of such an event."

"Unless he or she was about to be discovered and this was a way of terminating that possibility."

"I can't address that I'm afraid."

Ghiassi than asked, "What about the Chinese? We know they have a base very close to yours."

Dan quickly responded, "They're not that close, about 400 kilometers away. Also, until this happened, we never even heard from them."

"One more thought, commander," going back to a bit of formality, "What about the commercial aspects of your mission. Is there anything there that I should know about?"

Wedmond thought for a moment, but answered, "Our discovery of titanium is going to be a big financial opportunity for us, particularly the companies involved. But that discovery came after the accident and there was no way to predict the find. As for the other major finds, such as lead and iron ore, or even the ice, these are significant but have relatively low commercial value. At least not right now. Maybe decades from now."

"Ok, let's call it a night. We can pick this up in the morning, or afternoon for you. After I talk to your investigators tomorrow, I will make out a list of items I will ask you to collect as evidence and I will explain to you how to go about that. We will want to have physical evidence returned as soon as possible..."

"Unless you have more pull than I do, that won't be for a few months."

"Of course, and no I don't think I have that much pull. Well, I will need photographs and videos then, and digital copies of all communications that will not be available here at Mission Control. I will also want to conduct some interviews of the crew."

"The crew, for the most part, are not aware that we believe that it was not an accident. What do I tell them?"

"Simple enough. Tell them that the OIG is conducting a standard investigation as part of its support role to M-E-T. No more than that."

"Got it. We'll talk again tomorrow. Good day Aaron."

"Good night, commander."

It was a good call. Ghiassi had just gained an incredible amount of respect for Dan Wedmond. It was fortunate for NASA and for himself that such a person was there. It would be so much harder otherwise.

He sketched out his plan of attack for carrying out the investigation over the next few days. At the top of his list, he needed to obtain and review the background files on the entire crew. Not that he expected to find anything – astronauts were well vetted. But he would still have to look as part of the job. Since it was already late Friday, that would require some overtime from someone.

Chapter 20

A Quick Shower

2 April 2039, early morning UTC,

MET Moon Base Station Venturous, Sea of Serenity, Moon

*L*ooking at the Earth, being on the Moon. There is no better place to be.

Sylvia Levander lived for this moment – being 'outside' with a couple of the guys (or gals), in her suitcase, working on one of her projects, and not having a care in the world… or the Moon, for that matter.

Sylvia had been Moon-side six months now. Her specialty was the physics of lasers. And for the past half year, she had achieved some amazing things with lasers in this largely unrestricted environment of the Moon – almost no atmospheric elements to get in the way. And she had been instrumental in revitalizing the masers, the science of microwave lasers that evolved in the 1950's.

In 2013, Sylvia had been an intern on the LADEE program. While the 400-kilogram Lunar Atmosphere and Dust Environment Explorer spacecraft's primary mission was an assessment of the Moon's atmosphere, the craft utilized a laser system for transmitting data in lieu of a traditional radio wave transmission. The data download back to earth was completed at record-breaking speed.

Sylvia stayed with NASA and this field of research eventually developing the laser communications system that NASA,

ESA and other spacefaring entities utilized today for high-speed, high-volume data transmission.

A quarter-century later, NASA continued to carry out experiments and tests through its Lunar Laser Communications Demonstration program. Sylvia went from being a student to being one of the lead scientists in charge of that program. Then, her dream came true. She was selected to come to the Moon where she could continue her work with lasers and, happily, explore a few other lunar activities.

Today, Sylvia was doing her thing. She, along with Marc Laboe and Stan Rivers, were making some adjustments to one of the laser generators that the team had been experimenting with to communicate with one of the planetary explorer spacecraft in orbit around Mars. With the upcoming Mars missions looming less than a year out, Sylvia's laser experiments were considered vital for fast, accurate comms between the Moon and Mars.

Their work platform was about 70 meters from the Venturous. Why that far away? Supposedly protocol. Any potentially hazardous equipment – and a laser generator was considered hazardous – had to be a specified distance from the base parameter. To Sylvia, this seemed a bit too cautious.

Over their space suit comms, the three talked as they worked on the equipment. Marc said, "If this works, which it will, I think you'll make the history books… again!"

"Hey, you're just jealous!" said Sylvia over her comms link. "But I will be sure to give you guys an honorary mention at my awards ceremony for helping me." The guys laughed, which their auto-mics picked up and transmitted.

Stan said, "We're proud of you. You know that. We just have to tease you once in a while."

"Yeah, to keep you from getting too self-inflated and wind up floating off this rock!" said Marc.

"I knew there was a reason I keep you two around," laughed Sylvia. "And I don't know what you're complaining about, Marc. With that titanium find, I think you are going to be quite well off when you get back to Earth. And don't try to tell me otherwise."

"She's got you there," Stan followed up. "I think this tenth year of the mission is going to be historic for us all."

"Yes, but not all of it will be good," said Marc.

"What do you mean?" asked Stan. "Oh, you mean the accident. Well that was very unfortunate. And Bruce's death is terrible. Just Moon luck. But I think the world will rally around our achievements overall."

"I'm not so sure," said Marc. "The word is getting around that it was not just bad luck. That someone might have caused the explosion."

"Hey, you can't be joking about something like that," voiced Sylvia firmly.

"I'm not. I'm telling you I've heard that Luca and Penelope have come up with evidence that indicates the explosion was no accident."

"That's just a malicious rumor. If something like that had happened, we would have heard from Commander Wedmond."

Stan chimed in, "Well, I have heard something to that effect as well. But it was just others talking. Maybe it is rumor. Maybe there is some truth to it. Think about it, neither Dan nor any of the other senior astronauts have come out telling us what exactly the cause of the explosion was."

"You guys are just reading too much into that. This has to be investigated as best they can and with limited resources. They might not ever figure it out. Did you think of that?"

"No," responded Marc. "You just have to be a spoiler, don't you?" More light laughter followed. "But I can tell you this for sure, some of the crew are wondering if there could be another 'accident.' It's a bit unsettling, don't you think?"

"Listen, even if what you say is true, you need to keep it to yourself," said Sylvia with due seriousness. "If someone did this, you don't want to be telling him you know. Get it?"

"Or her, for that matter," added Stan. "And, Sylvia, where were you last Sunday night?"

"I'm not saying!" she laughed. "But I am saying you need to keep these rumors to yourselves."

"Good point."

"I hadn't thought of that."

"No, you didn't. And that's why I will be celebrating an award while you two are sitting in the audience."

"If things go as planned, I can buy the whole front row and then some!" said Marc.

"Alright, then," said Sylvia, "let's wrap this baby up and get back to the base. I'm getting hungry."

"Sounds good. Stan, could you hold that cover plate in place while I..." Marc said but stopped as bright flashes coming from near the Venturous caught his eye and he looked up. "What the hell was that?"

Sylvia and Stan had to turn but saw what appeared to be five quick flashes. Four of the flashes came from the ground just meters away from the Venturous, one came from the container of iron ore. With that flash, the container shattered at one corner. Some of the iron ore burst into dust, a small drizzle of molten ore dripped down and out of the container.

"Meteorites," yelled Stan.

"It's a shower," hollered Marc.

"Pan pan, Command, meteor shower," shouted Sylvia informing the Command Center, her emergency preparedness training kicking in.

Despite what the moviemakers would like you to believe, no person can see a meteorite fall to the surface where there is no atmosphere, not even a multitude of them. They move too fast for the human eye, like looking for a bullet that's been shot from a gun, only faster. But the consequences of the impacts – those can be seen.

There was no telling where this shower was coming from or how many there would be, but there was no reason to believe that it was done. A shower could be quick, it could be sporadic for hours or it could go on for days.

The three of them knew there was really no place to run to. Other than the Venturous, there was no protection. The Lunar Lander was even farther away. They watched and cautiously backed away.

"This is Command. Warning noted. Stand clear."

❧

Hal Lindstrum was on his way to a late breakfast. He had greeted Anna Kormendy as they passed each other in the corridor going opposite directions. He looked back, waiting for her to pass through her portal, so he could go through his. No two hatches could be open at the same time.

Oh, how he disliked her for stealing all the…

The alarm sounded, not so loud in the corridor but loud enough. Over the speaker just outside the corridor, he heard, "Warning. Meteor shower. Return to the berthing areas or Command Center. Warning."

Great, a meteor shower. What else could go wrong? He thought. He saw that Kormendy was no longer in the corridor. Since the berthing areas and the Command Center were the most fortified modules on the station, he knew he needed to get to one, now. The closest was back the way he came.

He rushed, as best as can be done on the Moon, back to the corridor hatch that Kormendy had just gone through.

But he wasn't fast enough.

He heard it first. Turning back, he also saw it, dead center of the corridor, the rush of escaping air through a breach of the outer shell and the inner core. A meteorite had struck the corridor. He was in trouble.

The emergency pressurization system kicked in instantly. Under high pressure, a life-sustaining mix of oxygen and nitrogen flooded the corridor. But, so did the quick-acting air-tight hatches at both ends. These closed and sealed to isolate the corridor, a necessary precaution.

Hal had had RCSE training, rapid compromised-space exiting, but this was real, and he was beginning to panic. To open the hatch now required that he enter three digits, 2-5-8, down the center of the keypad, simple.

He turned away from the breach to face the hatch and keypad. As he did this, in his panic, Lindstrum tripped himself. He fell forward, his forehead slamming into the hatch. He fell to the ground, unconscious.

On the other side of the hatch crew were gathering in the open space of the berthing area, gathering their suitcases should it become necessary to suit up.

"Breach of Corridor Five. Breach of Corridor Five," came the new warning message over the speaker system. Those in the berthing area knew that it was one of the corridors that connected their module. William Sosa, the new exchange astronaut from Gateway, was closest to the corridor at that moment. As he walked by the corridor hatch, he thought he heard something, a thud, against the hatch.

William stepped to the hatch and peered into the corridor through the hatch window. He could see pieces of debris swirling about from the outflow and inflow of air. It appeared empty. As he was about to step away, something caught his eye just at the limits of his view at the base of the hatch. It looked like two feet!

"Hey, guys, there's someone in the corridor!" he exclaimed.

Jon Miles, Anna Kormendy and two others crowded around the hatch. Kormendy took a look down to the base of the hatch as best she could.

"I think that is Hal Lindstrum. We had passed each other in this corridor, just before the warning sounded."

As she spoke, William reviewed the small pressure indicator located on the hatch control panel adjacent to the hatch. "It's in the yellow but holding steady," he said.

Dr. Kormendy knew this was dangerous but not deadly... yet. They would have to operate quickly before the emergency system gave out. "Ok, let's do this," she ordered. "William, when the hatch opens, you're going to have to grab him quickly. Everyone, brace yourself for the sudden decompression. Jon, you reclose the hatch. Understood?"

In unison, "got it."

"Ok, open it."

Jon Miles entered the override code and the hatch began its quick slide open. As it did, there was some sense of the rush of air from the berthing area into the corridor, but not as much as they had anticipated. The emergency repressurization system was doing its job.

William leaned over and grabbed Hal, who was face down and still unconscious, under the arms and forcibly dragged him out of the corridor. Jon shut the hatch.

"We'll need to get him to the clinic. Jon, you and William will take him there." Seeing Penelope Brightling, Anna said, "Penelope, track down Dr. Reisberg and have her meet us there."

Someone in the group said out loud, "But procedure requires that we stay within the protected modules, until cleared by Command."

"Screw procedure," Anna said, "He needs medical attention, *now*."

That was good enough. Everyone did their part to help and Hal made it to the clinic. As it was, Hal came to just before getting there, but he was groggy. Dr. Reisberg was waiting for him. As Jon and William got him on the examining table, Hal started to realize where he was and what happened to him.

Jon said to him, "Hey, buddy, that was a close one. Are you OK?"

"Wha... why did you do that? You should have left me there in the corridor."

"Don't talk nonsense. We just saved your life. No charge!" said William.

"Yeah, Hal, it's good to have you back! Looks like you're going to have one hell of a bump on your forehead though!"

Hal didn't acknowledge them but was shaking his head.

Dr. Reisberg said, "He took quite a blow to the head. I think he will be fine, but I'll give him a thorough check."

Just then, over the speaker system, "This is the Command Center. Stand down from the meteorite alert but maintain caution for now."

Jon Miles said, "Good, looks like that scare is over."

Ten minutes later, Sylvia Levander and her team reentered Venturous, safe and sound. As they moved into the dressing and staging rooms to get out of their suits, they were informed of what had happened to Lindstrum. Apparently, after the first small shower of meteorites, one stray arrived about three minutes behind the main body and had been the one to hit the corridor he was in. It had just been Moon luck.

Chapter 21
Unanswered Questions

2 April 2039, 12:22 pm UTC,

MET Moon Base Station Venturous, Sea of Serenity, Moon

*I*t's just possible I came here at the worst possible time... of course, the upside is I did save someone's life!

William Sosa was sitting alone at the lunch table, pondering the past seventy-two hours. A lot had happened in that time. For someone fresh on board, it had been one bumpy road of an introduction to life on Venturous.

Since saving Hal's life – he liked to think of it that way, even if it was likely someone else would have found him – he hadn't been alone. Nearly everyone on board wanted to congratulate him on a job well done or just be near him to express their appreciation that he was now with the Venturous crew. He was particularly pleased when Eleni Dimopolous came to talk to him. He wouldn't mind talking to her some more.

So, he was surprised that he found himself alone for lunch. Must be timing. Or what was it the crew liked to say... it must be Moon luck!

Being alone didn't last long though. Commander Wedmond entered the dining area heading toward the back wall. This was where he took a position to pass on information, news, whatever, or so William had been told. And this would be the second such informational session he attended in as many days. That could not be the norm.

The crew settled in and the empty seats around him were quickly taken.

Unlike two days ago, the commander was alone as he commenced his statement to the crew. And it did seem a bit more crowded than last time. Most likely, no one was sleeping after the meteorite shower.

"If I may begin," he said, and the area turned quiet. "I have a lot of news for you, and while you probably already know it – word travels fast in our small group – I want to make it official."

"First, we did get word, so I am very pleased to announce that Susan Ly's uncle was found, he is alive and doing well, recovering from hypothermia in a Sacramento hospital."

The cheers were overwhelming. Everyone had heard, but it was a rush for the crew to openly share this news and congratulate Susan, who had been all smiles for hours. Details were minimal, but he'd been found holding on to a large truck tire, floating in the American River.

"Also, good news, Hal Lindstrum is fine. Other than a bad bump on his forehead and a bit of a headache, there were no other injuries reported." More cheers. "Our thanks go out to the quick-thinking astronauts who were able to bring him out of the corridor. I wish to particularly thank our newest crew member, William Sosa."

More cheers and more pats on the back all around.

"The meteor shower was very close. Fortunately, it was short lived and caused minimal damage that we're well equipped to manage."

Again, adulation abounded.

"OK, there is some bad news. It looks like the toolshed will be out of commission for a while. We are just not equipped to make a durable repair that any of us can rely on. And I won't risk it. We'll try to relocate equipment and tools to other locations, but we're tight for space. Any priority repairs that you have, run them by Jim Sheppard." A few moans could be heard. Most were more for effect than true displeasure. The crew had adapted to worse conditions.

"And one last thing, I have been advised by MET that, in accordance with NASA policy, which does have application under the MET contract, that NASA will be formally looking into the explosion. The Office of Inspector General has that task. I have been in contact with their SAIC and he will most likely be calling shortly to interview some of you. Needless to say, we all want to know what happened if for no other reason than to make sure it doesn't happen again." That part was certainly true. But he wanted to get their spirits back up.

Wedmond continued, "I am sure you have all heard of or perhaps read Robert Heinlein's *The Moon is a Harsh Mistress*. I draw no similarities to the storyline of that book to us, but I think it's fair to say, while we all love our jobs exploring the Moon and love being here, it seems to make best efforts sometimes to try to kick us off. I commend you all for your persistence, patience and diligent work to keep our place on this rock."

That seemed to work. "Any questions, while we're all here together?"

"Commander, what is going to happen to Bruce's body? Has that been decided yet?" asked Stan Rivers.

"That is a very good question that I have asked MET. Unfortunately, that question has not yet been answered. I suspect we will know soon.

"Anything else? OK, if there are no more questions, I believe we have a class of young high school scientists and future astronauts who are looking forward to having us carry out an experiment for their class. Let's show 'em how we do things here!"

As the group disbursed and Wedmond turned to head to the Command Center, Anna Kormendy caught up with him.

"Anna, I hear you overrode procedure to get Hal to the clinic during the meteorite shower."

"I did," she responded. "I felt that his injuries could have been life threatening and that prevailed over a marginal possibility of further penetration."

He looked at her, seeing the defiance in her eyes and stance. "Good call. I would have done the same."

She nodded and tried to hide a smile of satisfaction. They progressed on to the Command Center passing through two corridors and a storage module as the conversation continued.

"What are we doing about the toolshed?" asked Kormendy. "We are going to need that space and the equipment to fully carry out our mission."

"How is that?"

"I am sure you realize that with the iron ore refining we've been doing, and now the titanium find, not to mention the ice mining we have planned, our equipment will need to be maintained and repaired on a frequent basis."

"And not to mention the other experiments and projects we are tasked to carry out," Wedmond said to her with just a touch of sarcasm; sarcasm that Anna Kormendy missed.

"Exactly!" she nearly shouted. "We must expedite an effective repair to the toolshed."

"What do you propose, Anna? MET is fully aware of our situation. They will do what they can to get us back in operation. I assume you are not proposing to resume use of the shed when we cannot guarantee an effective repair."

She hesitated before answering. "I understand your concern for the safety of the crew. I am all for it. But I don't see why we can't use the facility while suited up."

"I think you know that answer, doctor. The space and the equipment in it, and the functions that will need to be performed are far too risky to be undertaken by our crew when fully encumbered by a spacesuit. That would be more of a risk than using the area as is."

"Yes, you are right," she reluctantly admitted. She did not like having to admit that, but she already knew that was the concern. It was time she pushed her agenda. "We need to put more pressure on MET to get the outer shell repaired. I could do that if I were made the new XO, I could…"

"Excuse me?" exclaimed Wedmond.

"I think you should move me to the XO position, so I can be more effective. I am the next logical choice for it."

They had arrived just outside the Command Center at the hatch leading into it. They had stopped there because they both knew this was becoming a private conversation and the corridors were often the only place to assure that.

"Doctor Kormendy, I think you are out of place with this. First, it is not my call, it is that of the board of directors at MET. Second, this is too soon after Bruce's death. We will have to assess our needs, capabilities and available skills and talents before going forward with a replacement." Dan's voice was steadily rising, something few people ever experienced. "And third, I am not sure that you are the right person for that responsibility."

Kormendy was taken back by his apparent rejection. Consequently, she turned defensive. "Commander Wedmond, I don't understand your reluctance. Venturous needs strong leadership. People who can make hard decisions fast. I think I have proven myself repeatedly over the months. Bruce was too soft and, I would say, indecisive…"

Wedmond cut her off, "Now you have gone too far, doctor. I will not tolerate you disparaging a good man, who I think was an outstanding second-in-command. I don't know how you were brought up, but where I come from, we do not tolerate such disrespect." Wedmond had never been quite so... irritated for longer than he could remember. "I know you two did not see eye to eye on things, but for some reason, he often sided with you. On this station, he was both liked and respected."

Kormendy was at a loss for words. Dan Wedmond had never been this outright aggressive before. She needed to rethink her situation. And to be honest, she knew that she was a victim of her youth. It was something you just don't change overnight. Growing up and as an early adult, you were either on top of the heap or you would be clawing your way either up or out.

"I apologize commander. Perhaps I am too... forward," she said with a touch of sincerity. "I am grateful for every day I am here. Believe me. Perhaps I do expect others to live with the same standards that I do."

Dan realized he was reacting out of the tangle of emotions with so much happening and not as the CO. He needed to tone down his words, now more than ever. "Look, Anna, I know you have worked hard to get here. But so has everyone else." Throwing his own thoughts about himself back at her, "You need to temper your approach and see more of the big picture."

"I understand. I am a fighter. I have always had to be." *I don't think I have ever opened up to another like this,* she thought.

"Ok, but you made it. You are a leader among some of the best people in the world. No need to show your dominance over them. You need to be helping to bring them along. I would like to see you adapt to a more tolerant approach here."

Anna had to think. In her heart, she knew Dan was right. It was something she had always known, but could never commit to while striving to reach the top... whatever that was.

"Since joining the team, I have known that I must adapt, as you say, a new approach to working with my colleagues. It is something I can and will do."

"Frankly, I think it's a bit late in life for you to change, but we'll see," said Wedmond, softening his tone. That was the kind of leader he was.

"Whatever is decided for the leadership of the Venturous crew, you need not be concerned. I will continue to work hard and to fight for our team. I commit to you."

He paused to let the words sink in. Then changing the subject, Wedmond said, "The special agent from NASA will be contacting us shortly. I need to go. But I do hope you are serious about modifying your approach to this mission."

"I am, sir."

"I believe you will."

With that, they went on to their other respective tasks.

⨾⨾⨿

Aaron Ghiassi had spent the previous night and early morning preparing for his next communication with the Venturous crew. Normally, he preferred to do questioning face-to-face. Because of the nature of this job and the extent of NASA's reach, he had often conducted interviews and interrogation sessions remotely. But never had it been quite this remote.

Back in the conference room, where he had been yesterday, it was approaching 8:30 am – about 1:30 pm for the crew on the Venturous and well after lunch. He had one of the Mission Center staff initiate his call to Commander Wedmond.

"Good morning, Mr. Ghiassi," said Dan as he came on the monitor.

"Good morning, commander," Aaron responded, "and please call me Aaron." It was his tactic to maintain a degree of informality. It tended to make people more at ease and willing to talk frankly.

After the pause, "Certainly, Aaron," he said. "I have briefed the crew as to the investigation that you are pursuing. I advised them that it is just procedure, as we discussed yesterday."

"Thank you."

Arron was getting accustomed to the transmission delay. "You should know, however, that there was a close call earlier this morning. We had a meteorite shower that resulted in a single penetration and breach of one of our corridors while someone was in it. The astronaut that was caught in the corridor is fine, but the crew is, once again, on edge."

"I was informed this morning. I am pleased to hear everyone is alright."

"Nature of the mission here I'm afraid. So, what is your plan this morning?"

"Well, I've reviewed the written and video reports that you and Dr. Kormendy, who headed up the investigation, have submitted on the incident. My plan is to get into details with the astronauts who you had conduct the investigation. Through them, I will try to identify any physical evidence that can be photographed, and if possible salvaged and sent back here to Houston."

"Good luck with that. As I said yesterday, the next return trip to Houston is several weeks away."

"Understood."

"So, how would you like to start, Aaron?"

"I would like to begin with your investigators, Luca Barolo, Linda Miramontes, Eleni Dimopolous, and Penelope Brightling, in that order. Followed by Jim Sheppard and lastly by Dr. Kormendy," stated Ghiassi.

"I will arrange it. And just a reminder, there is no privacy per se. You will be talking to us here in the Command Center which must always be manned."

"Also understood."

Ghiassi's interviews went smoothly and, because there was little that could be added, quickly. What he learned was that in the moments after the explosion the primary response by the crew was to retrieve Holmann's body and to repair the breach in the outer structural wall. That was Luca's focus at first.

Attempting to salvage debris from the explosion came later. At the direction of Dr. Kormendy, all debris was collected as part of their investigation. What there was, was currently in a storage bin in the material storage module. As Luca talked about the debris, he paused in thought.

"A thought occurred to me, Mr. Ghiassi. It is possible that some of the debris escaped the toolshed. If the pieces were small enough, they could easily have been carried out by the escaping currents of air."

"I take it, no one looked outside for debris."

"No. sir, not specifically. However, I and several others were outside the toolshed several times since then, attempting to repair the exterior shell. I never saw anything out of place. I am sorry."

"Do you think you could go out to look around?"

"Yes, of course. We must complete the repair to Corridor 5 that was damaged yesterday. I will also have to inspect all exterior walls for other damage as well. I can do it then."

The other interviews were also, essentially, unproductive, in that no new information came out. During Linda Miramontes' interview, she asked. "Are you going to get, like, fingerprints or something, from the debris we send back to Earth?" She was very curious about all this and would most likely be carrying all the debris evidence back to Gateway in a few days.

"Highly unlikely," Ghiassi answered. "Such things as fingerprints are usually obliterated in an explosion. Even if we did find any, that would not prove much since it's very likely everyone there had been in and out of the toolshed. Hopefully, we don't have to take that long to solve the problem."

Brightling was still coming off watch there at the comms station, so Jim Sheppard went next. Jim's interview was equally unrevealing. Nothing new came out of it. Of course, having been so close to the moment of explosion, his memory was, at the very least, quite shaken and sketchy.

Penelope Brightling, SpaceX's equivalent of a computer whiz, was next. Penelope, the only other person besides Wedmond to suspect that it was not an accident, was a different story. She was very anxious to talk about her findings concerning the video. Aaron was aware of her discovery, but he wanted to hear her version directly. Since the corrupted file might be recoverable, Ghiassi made arrangements for Penelope to transfer the file Earth-side by all means possible: via laser transmission, radio transmission and via a flash copy to a drive that would be sent to Earth... whenever.

Last to be interviewed was Dr. Anna Kormendy, Hungarian, employed by SpaceX. Ghiassi introduced himself. "Good morning Dr. Kormendy, I'm Aaron Ghiassi of the Office of the Inspector General for NASA. Have you been briefed on why our division is conducting this investigation?"

"Something to do with standard procedure within NASA. Frankly, I am not sure what you are going to accomplish from where you sit in Houston that our people haven't already done, but I am sure your efforts will not go unrewarded. And if you can help us resolve the cause, that would be fantastic."

Interesting, thought Ghiassi, *she is anything but subtle.* "Exactly what we want to do. Can I call you Anna?"

"No. Dr. Kormendy is appropriate." *Ahh, be less formal, be less formal,* she thought to herself.

She is going to be tough. Maybe she does have something to hide. "Ok, Dr. Kormendy, I really just have a few questions. I know that Commander Wedmond asked you to head up the investigation and it looks like you and your team did a good job given the circumstances of being on the Moon.

"I would say that's an understatement."

"I have reviewed your reports, and I have interviewed the investigating team. It looks like there was very little to work with."

"That's correct. We concluded what the components of the explosion were. Whatever it was that ignited them remains a mystery."

"I understand that Luca and Eleni recovered bits and fragments of debris. Could you identify anything from those pieces?"

"In some cases, yes, but we ruled out everything as possible ignitors. I am sure you are aware of those."

"Yes. Eleni has provided photographic documentation, which our division will analyze. What about the ammonia product? Did you ever figure out why that was in the toolshed?"

"No."

"Ok, well, just a few more questions, then. As you know there was a partial video log recovered. Although it was damaged for the period at the time of the incident, the last video file of the toolshed was taken two days before, on Friday. Were you aware of that?"

"Really? I was not aware of that. But if it was a recording taken that Friday, I am sure I am in it."

"You are. You were the last one in the toolshed... to be recorded anyway. Let me ask you, do you recall anything that seemed to be out of place that day?"

"No, not really. Although so much has happened since then, I could not tell you much about it." Then Anna paused for a moment. I do remember one thing now that you press me. I do not recall that the tool cart was out of its storage bin."

"Why is that significant do you think?" asked Aaron.

"Well, we've pretty much concluded that the explosive materials were on the cart when it happened. But if you have the video of that Friday, you can confirm that."

She does not seem to be acting like she did it. Maybe, she is just trying to misdirect me, thought Aaron. "We'll look into that. One more thing, doctor. Could you tell me what you were doing in the toolshed that day?"

"What? Why do you care? What am I now, a suspect?"

"Not at all. The question goes to ruling out anyone who might have inadvertently contributed to the explosion."

"I see. Well, I was there to prep a piece of equipment that is part of the SMEP science experiments program."

"SMEP?"

"You know what that is, don't you? It's the Student Moon-based Experiments Program, a spin-off of the old Student Spaceflight Experiments Program carried out on the ISS. We were going to conduct some experiments on acceleration and gravity for a group of high school students back on Earth. That, of course, was postponed due to the explosion. But we are resuming that today. Actually, if I had not gone there to prep it, the kids' equipment could have been destroyed!"

Ghiassi wrapped up the interview with Dr. Kormendy. He would reexamine the photos and videos, but he did not have high hopes of solving this one anytime soon. Perhaps there would be something in the debris that only a forensic team could find, but that was most likely weeks away. For now, much depended on the cybertechs from the Computer Crimes Division and their analysis of the corrupted video recording.

Before signing off, he updated Wedmond. "So, I will say that your team did conduct the best possible investigation. I did ask Luca Barolo, however, to search for possible debris outside the toolshed area. You never know what might have escaped after the explosion."

"I hadn't thought of that."

"Actually, your guy Luca thought of it. Also, I will get a tech team on the analysis of the video file. Although, I suspect they're going to want to see the actual file on the actual server there onboard. That's not likely to happen."

"I wouldn't think so," Wedmond said. "If you're done, I need to get my comms system back. I have another important call to make."

"Certainly. I am sure you will be hearing from us again in a few days. Thank you for your patience, commander."

"No need to thank me, but if you can get this solved, I will be thanking you."

After terminating the call with Ghiassi on Earth, Dan Wedmond wasted no time in making another call of significant importance. This call was to Commander Li on the Tiangong-3.

Chapter 22
It's About the Science

Who said being an astronaut on the Moon wasn't going to be fun! As the lead geophysicist on Venturous, the task of orchestrating the gravity-acceleration experiment fell to Marc Laboe. It was not just any experiment though, in fact, every astronaut and physicist already knew the outcome. But the experiment wasn't for their benefit, it was for the high school students who called themselves the Venturous Explorers and were part of SMEP. He was very pleased to be doing it.

The experiment was to measure the gravitational acceleration due to the Moon's gravity of a baseball and a lightweight papier Mache ball of the same size dropped from fifty meters as compared to that of the Earth's gravity. It would be performed live and transmitted back to a Phoenix, Arizona, high school, while simultaneously, or nearly so (accounting for the 2.4 second transmission delay), two identical balls would be dropped from the same height on Earth. The third experiment would be dropping the pair of balls simultaneously – all four balls would drop together.

Devising the means to carry out the experiment had been no easy task. Some of the ideas discussed by the students included using helium balloons to raise a platform to the desired altitude. While this was a great idea on Earth, a lighter-than-air balloon only works when there is air to rise in. Thus, this was a no-go on the moon. Same thing with the idea of using drones – no air, no fly. Erecting a fifty-meter-tall structure was suggested, but that exceeded the materials limitation for such projects at the Venturous.

Then one student came up with an idea. Since the Moon's gravity was so much less than Earth's, why not launch a platform upward using something equivalent to model rockets. The rockets would last for up to 90 seconds, long enough to conduct the ball drops, and the platform would be tethered so it would only rise to a set height, in this case fifty meters. The rockets had to be designed and built to be slow burning, carry their own oxygen and fuel and be reusable. Brilliant!

It did take a full year for the rockets to be designed, built and transported to the Venturous. But the young student who came up with the idea gained instant fame in the scientific world. And this was before they were put to the test.

Eleni set up the video system to televise the event. Assisting Laboe with the conduct of the experiment was Dr. Kormendy. From the look on her face, though not visible through her face shield, she was also pleased to be there as well.

Laboe looked into one of the two video cameras that Eleni had set up and, when queued, introduced Dr. Kormendy and himself to his young audience. He then proceeded with his prepared comments. "As you know, back there on Earth, the rate at which things fall is pretty much a constant. It's what we call gravitational acceleration, which is 9.8 meters per second per second or meters per second squared. Here on the Moon, that rate is approximately 1.6 meters per second squared or about one-sixth of that on Earth.

"What's that mean? For one, a hundred-kilogram guy like me only appears to weigh in at sixteen point five kilos. That's one part of this job that makes my mother happy. It also means that objects seem to fall to the Moon's surface slower than we're used to on Earth. For every second an object falls to Earth it increases it's speed by 9.8 meters. On the Moon, that same object, or any object, falls with a leisurely increase in speed of 1.6 meters-per-second every second.

"There is one very important difference, however. The Earth has something the Moon doesn't have – air. Air friction on the Earth will basically stop the acceleration of gravity rather quickly once it reaches terminal velocity.

"We will talk about terminal velocity later. Today we will be conducting a simultaneous drop of various objects that will demonstrate gravitational acceleration and the effect of air friction… or… terminal velocity. Are you ready Doctor Kormendy?"

"Yes, I am, Marc."

"So, let's do it!"

Marc ignited the four rockets that lifted the four corners of the platform, slowly by Earth standards. A second video camera caught the action while the first camera stayed focused on Marc and, behind him, the target base.

Back on Earth, at the students' school in Phoenix, their similar platform was elevated up to the same fifty-meter distance by a narrow scaffolding system. Now, two equivalent platform systems were in place – one on the Moon and one on Earth. In the school yard, a large monitor was set up near the base of the scaffolding simultaneously showing the two videos that were active on the Moon. A similar video camera was set to take in the full fifty-meter scaffolding, the Moon monitor showing the two views on Moon, and the Venturous Explorer students carrying out the experiment Earth-side.

Marc received word from the school. The weather conditions were perfect – no detectible wind – on a beautiful Saturday morning. The only students there on campus were the Venturous Explorers and their teachers. It was an exciting day for them, to be interacting with astronauts on the Moon. Their scaffolding, equipment, monitors and balls were ready to go. Seeing that everything was in place and time was running, Marc said, "Looks like our platform is set and we are a go for Venturous Explorers, Acceleration Test 1."

Marc hit a trigger that performed two tasks simultaneously: It released a baseball from the platform above and started a timer that displayed on the school monitors and on a small screen that Marc and Anna could see. It also sent a signal to do the same thing on the platform at the school. Marc and Anna watched as the baseball fell at a leisurely pace, increasing velocity, and hitting the target beneath the platform. When the ball finally hit, it stopped the timer. 5.59 seconds.

At the school, both the signal to drop the baseball and the moon-based videos arrived at the same time. From the perspective of the students, it appeared that the two balls were released at the exact same time.

The baseball at the school hit its target base at 2.25 seconds per the monitor, while the baseball on the Moon took 5.59 seconds.

The demonstration was impressive. But time could not be wasted. Back at the Venturous, Marc received confirmation of a successful first test and readiness for the second, "Ready for Venturous Explorers, Acceleration Test 2."

This time papier Mache balls were dropped in the same fashion. On the Moon, the same resulting time to fall was recorded – 5.59 seconds. At the school, however, the time to fall was 8.38 seconds.

As Marc received word of the results, he nodded to Kormendy. She relayed to the students, "As you can see, the friction caused by air molecules counters the acceleration due to the

Earth's gravity. The papier Mache ball was significantly slowed due to the friction caused by air. As there is no air on the Moon, there was nothing to resist the fall and the ball fell at the same rate as the much heavier baseball,"

"That was quite the demonstration, Doctor Kormendy. And now, before we lose our platform, let's do the third and final experiment, Venturous Explorers, Acceleration Test 3." For the final drop test, it would be the two balls together – one papier Mache and one a solid baseball. One set to be released simultaneously on the Moon – or at least appearing to be so – and one set of balls on the Earth. Marc pushed the trigger and, so it appeared on Earth, the four balls all fell at once. The results were as expected, although the Earth-side papier Mache ball did show a slightly different time, the effect of air friction being somewhat... variable.

The students were thrilled. They had carried out an experiment just as Galileo had done nearly four and a half centuries ago, but this time it was on a much grander scale. And they got to work with the astronauts on the Moon. It would be something they would remember for the rest of their lives. The astronauts were thrilled about it too!

∽

It was a Saturday evening for the crew of the Venturous. And just like on Earth, the crew liked to treat Saturday evenings as they might back home. They tended to relax a bit - some made their calls home if their loved ones were awake. Some read books, on-line of course. And some would do an extra workout or play challenging mind games with each other in the physiology/recreation module, but most would hang out in the dining area just to take time to socialize.

Linda Miramontes, Stan Rivers, Sylvia Levander, Omoné

Reisberg, Laurent Benet, Luca Barolo, Eleni Dimopolous, William Sosa, and a handful of the others were there, sitting around, enjoying the moment as if they were all out at a fine restaurant having dinner together. The conversation had turned to the SMEP experiments that were completed today. Eleni told them of Marc's stellar performance, with just a small amount of storytelling exaggeration for effect. They were all laughing, enjoying the moment.

"It's a shame we could not see your face out there, Marc, "Eleni said. "I thought you were going to sail off into orbit, after you finished that video for the kids! You seemed very pleased."

"Hey, it was for the kids. But if you thought I was excited," responded Marc, "did you catch Dr. Kormendy, after we got back inside? She was downright giddy. I think she might have enjoyed doing that for the students more than me!" They all laughed and agreed that would have been considered out of character for her.

Jon Miles and Penelope Brightling were among them, but not really. They were having their own conversation, paying little attention to the others. Jon would have expected Hal Lindstrum to be here on a Saturday evening, but he was most likely sleeping off his bruise on the head, not to mention his near-death experience.

Well, he was happy enough to just be talking to Penelope at the moment. Who said Brits and Northern Irish couldn't get along? Of course, since both spent much of their adult lives outside their respective countries, they simply did not relate to such absurd concepts!

They did know that the group conversation was currently on the day's acceleration experiments and of Marc Laboe and Anna Kormendy. Jon said to Penelope, "Anna certainly had a busy day today. You know she was there directing our rescue of Hal and that we took him to the clinic right away."

"She did that?" asked Penelope. In truth, she knew more than most of the crew just what a 'busy day' Anna had.

"She did. I think she's got a cool head on her shoulders. Your SpaceX folks back home, must be very pleased with her."

Penelope wanted to say more about what she knew but was ordered not to. She just wanted this whole explosion issue to go away. "Listen, Jon, it's time for my watch at the Command Center. And then I will be sleeping most of the morning, so you have a great day. I'll catch up with you tomorrow night."

"God willing, it will be an uneventful day tomorrow. We could use one. Sorry you will be sleeping through it."

"I'll be up and about by noon. There is a telemetry project I want to get working on and I could use some help. Being a Sunday, perhaps you could help me?" Penelope asked, with just a bit of smile on her lips.

"I will see you then!" Jon said very quickly.

With that, Penelope took her leave from the group, wished them a pleasant evening and headed for the Command Center to assume her watch.

She passed through the corridor hatch into the Command Center. This was the lifeblood of Venturous – its heart and brain. There were five stations with monitors and intelliboards forming an arc facing more, larger monitors. These stations were dedicated to specific functions on Venturous, but like all computerized systems, any station could act as a backup for one of the others.

For all functions and operations, Command Center crew used the intelliboards, a virtual rendition of a real keypad, or simply voiced commands, but should either of those two methods fail, classic keyboards were tucked away if needed. The room was always well lit; but in the evening and night hours, UTC time, the main LED lighting that was overhead and built into the walls could be dimmed and the color softened. It was appropriate, for most evenings and nearly all nights, the Command Center was manned only by a single Command Center officer. Penelope Brightling was one of those officers.

Two people were in the Command Center this evening when she arrived. One was the duty officer she would be relieving. The other was Commander Wedmond, conversing with someone on the monitor in front of him. As she walked by him to get to the duty officer, she greeted him. "Good evening, Commander."

"Good evening, Penelope, "he responded, looking up from his conversation. "Coming on duty, are you?"

"Yes, sir." Penelope could see he was talking to Commander Fascar. Not wanting to interrupt, she continued over to the duty officer. "Good evening, Ken. I am here to relieve you."

Ken Herron was one of ESA's astronauts specializing in electronic systems, which qualified him for the Command Center duty watch. But like Jim Sheppard, he had been on Venturous for three years and would soon be returning Earth-side and back to his native Sweden, where he would be a nationally celebrated hero – Sweden tended to do that for any of its citizens that did something that stood out. And he was ready for it. He'd been on Venturous for three years and it was beginning to show, physically and mentally.

Ken briefed Penelope, bringing her up to speed on the various systems operations that must be monitored around the clock. It did not take long. Ken left, leaving Penelope and Dan to themselves.

"We were lucky," Dan said to Marianna Fascar. "It was a very small shower as meteorite showers go, but one that just happened to strike home."

"Yes, you were fortunate under the circumstances – all repairable damage and no one seriously hurt," she said. "I think your crew call it 'Moon luck' from what I have heard."

"I don't know where that came from, but it certainly seems to apply around here, especially after recent events here."

They talked more about the status of the OIG investigation. He wasn't sure how well that was going to go, trying to conduct an investigation from 363,000 kilometers away. They also discussed upcoming events for tomorrow, such as the going away party, and the return of the Lunar Lander to Gateway with its crew, plus Linda Miramontes, on Tuesday. So far, William Sosa, who was staying in place of Linda, was working out quite well.

He realized how much he liked these calls to Marianna. It was really his only way to escape some of the burden he was carrying. Even though there was little chance of privacy on either end – almost no privacy on Gateway – he would make it a point to reach out to her more often. It made him feel good.

⁂

After the call with Fascar, Wedmond decided to call it a night. In his quarters, relaxing on his bed, Dan once again rehashed the events of the past week. So much had happened.

Who among these brilliant, hard-working, generally unassuming and socially adept astronauts, could do such a thing as kill another of the crew? he thought to himself. *And could that person do it again?*

He kept coming back to one person, Anna Kormendy. Is she the one? The problem was he just could not fully rationalize it.

He had to consider other options. Was it someone from SpaceX, someone from ESA or even someone from NASA? What was the motive? Financial gain, political gain, or perhaps to hide something? If any of these considerations were valid motives, then he had no knowledge of them and no way to narrow down suspects, let alone whittle down a motive! This was beyond frustrating.

He decided that he must start a process of assessing each of the twenty-eight remaining crewmen. Grabbing his writing tablet, he listed the crew, where they were from, and which agency or company sponsored them. He also included their affiliation with Bruce Holmann, how well they got along with him, and then any other factors such as who might have the technical expertise to even create a way to cause the explosion. Lastly, he listed who had access to the equipment in the toolshed – that was everybody. So much for that idea.

With what he had down, he took the list, containing only a modicum of data, and rank ordered the names. With what little he had, the ranking was highly subjective. Dr. Kormendy was still at the top of the list, but number two made no sense whatsoever.

As he was ordering the list, another thought struck him. *Wait, what if Bruce was not the target? What if Jim was the target, and he left too soon.* There went his list. He was so glad that special agent, Aaron Ghiassi, was taking charge.

Chapter 23

Sunday on the Moon

3 April 2039, morning UTC,
MET Moon Base Station Venturous, Sea of Serenity, Moon

*T*his is my time. There is nothing more important in my life than this time that I have to be on the Moon.

Anna Kormendy, was in the dining area, enjoying hot tea, one of the few Earth-side beverages that was sanctioned on the Venturous. While waiting for her fellow SpaceX team – that is SpaceX and Blue Origin team – she was reveling in the experience of being on the Moon, despite the recent events and setbacks. But she realized that it was time to make sure her SpaceX and Blue Origin teammates were maintaining that same eager and aggressive attitude.

Marc Laboe and Stan Rivers entered the dining area and joined her at her table. They had come as she requested. It wasn't particularly early, but Sundays were slower starts for the crew, so there were just a few others having breakfast.

"Good morning Anna," said Marc.

"Ma'am," said Stan.

"Good morning guys. Hot tea?" she asked. Both shook their heads no.

"Marc said, "We are heading out to the Posidonius Crater in a bit to set up some sonic sounding equipment near the titanium find. Would you like to join us today, perhaps?"

Anna thought about that. *That might be fun,* she thought to herself. "I think I just might do that. I could use a break from the other tasks around here. And on a Sunday, I won't be missed."

"Great," said Stan. "Getting in our suitcases and exploring this rock can be the most exciting thing around here." Neither reacted, so he added, "Unless you are dropping baseballs and paper balls for fun!" That did get some smiles. Both Marc and Anna had enjoyed that activity for the kids yesterday.

"So, what did you want to talk to us about?" asked Marc, redirecting the conversation.

"We all know Bruce's death was a tragedy. It has affected us all, some more than others. And it might cause some of the crew to not be on top of their game, as they say. If that happens, we could fall prey to more accidents with even worse consequences. Look at what happened to Hal Lindstrum for example. I know he was not operating at peak performance or he would not have *accidentally* knocked himself out and nearly kill himself."

"You are right," said Stan after giving it some thought. "Some are losing their focus. It's noticeable in small things with little consequence. But what if this funk leads to something more significant that gets overlooked or done incorrectly. We could be in big trouble and quickly. What do you think we should do?"

"I don't know if there is much we can do. I just want to make sure our side of the team stays sharp and focused on the task of staying alive and well. That's all I really had."

"Sure, we agree with you there," said Marc.

"I think one of the best ways to do that is to focus on our work. Keep at it. This includes all the planned tasks with the iron ore, lead, ice finds, the titanium, all of it."

"Got it."

"Good. That's why I am glad you are continuing with your work on the titanium find. Stay on it. And don't let the iron refining work slip either."

"No ma'am," said Stan. "What about the others? Are you going to give them the same pep talk?"

"Pep talk?" Anna thought about that. Stan was right about that. It was her job as the senior SpaceX astronaut to keep them safe. "Of course, I will be talking to the rest of our team, and any of the other crew who I think will listen."

"What about Commander Wedmond?" asked Marc. "Shouldn't he be on top of this."

"Wedmond has his own way of doing things. Everyone does. I just want to make sure my team is safe."

"But we're all the same team, when it comes down to it," said Marc.

"Agreed. As I said, I will do my best to work with everybody here. One misstep by anyone could affect us all... negatively."

Stan and Marc headed out to check out and supply Martin for the daytrip. They were pleasantly surprised that Kormendy was going to join them. Anna, in turn, was just as pleased to be invited to go along. It would be good to get away for the day.

♒

"Dr. Reisberg," Laurent Benet said as he entered the clinic. "I thought I might find you here."

"Please, call me Omoné." She was spending her Sunday morning reviewing medical files of the crew. For Omoné, this was relaxing. There were no experiments to run today, although she did have to administer some bone density tests later in the afternoon. "Have you enjoyed your stay here on Venturous?"

"Very much so," he said. "You have a good crew here. In fact, I would like to talk to you about what I have observed since my arrival. Perhaps my observations, in conjunction with yours, could be of benefit to not only the crew but with future crews."

"That is what we're here for, Laurent. To study both the

body and mind of our fellow space travelers so we can make the journey better!"

"Precisely!" Laurent said.

Laurent Benet was a bit of an enigma, at least to his family. Laurent's family history contained no one with a medical doctor's degree. His family tree was profuse with engineers. Some served in the French military, but often as engineering officers. His brothers and one sister were engineers – they were also uncommonly tall while Laurent was smaller and leaner and prematurely balding.

His mother had been a research scientist – in electronic engineering, and his father was a rail engineer who had worked all over Europe and the Middle East. The experience of travelling had put him in an optimum position to learn English early and without a French accent. Laurent was a teenager when his father was assigned as the rail engineer in charge for the now-famous Qatar Metro system, built more than twenty years ago in support of the 2022 World Cup held in Doha.

Despite that family pressure, Laurent turned to medicine. In fairness to his parents, they were still very pleased and proud of Laurent's choice. He became a very good doctor, providing service within the renowned French universal health care system.

It was a twist of fate, however, that lead him to the ESA. Through his mother's acquaintances, he met Loukas Anagnostopoulos. Loukas was looking for keen medical talent for ESA's programs. Laurent became fascinated with the concept of space medicine and the research it entailed, probably following in his mother's footsteps.

He joined ESA at twenty-nine and became immersed in its studies of human physiology in space. He lacked a psychology background to truly round out his work with ESA. So, in his spare time, he took courses in that field. As his reward, he was invited to be part of the Gateway program. What better way to study the human condition in space than to be there? Now here he was on the Moon, on Venturous, and doing what he loved.

Doctors Laurent Benet and Omoné Reisberg spent the next two hours discussing the current stressful conditions of a crew of standout human beings, what could go wrong, the signs to look for... and found, and finally, who among the crew could be overwhelmed, if at all. It was only supposition. But the two Moon-side doctors had concluded that there were at least one, and possibly three candidates for being overstressed and possibly reactant under current conditions.

☙

It was lunchtime. Sunday brunch, as the crew called it but not by any Earth-side standards, was available in the dining area. Kormendy, Laboe and Rivers were well on their way to the Posidonius Crater. Wedmond was in the Command Center polishing off his weekly reports. Sheppard and Dimopolous were in the greenhouse admiring the latest growth spurts of some of the plants. Sosa, Miramontes and Ly were in one of the research modules, exchanging information on some of the experiments and tests that he would have to take over. Levander was in one of the storage modules, now used as the makeshift toolshed, talking to Barolo about possible modifications to one of her laser-optic systems to support one of her planned experiments. Reisberg and Benet had wrapped up their discussion and had joined a few of the crew for brunch. Miles had just checked in on Lindstrum, seeing how he was feeling, before heading to brunch himself. And Brightling was getting a few hours' sleep after her night watch.

Jon joined the group that the doctors were with just as Ken Herron was vacating a seat there. Laurent Benet was telling the group of astronauts what a treat it had been to come down to the Venturous and thanked everyone for their hospitality. One of the group, Lockheed Martin's equipment specialist, Charlene Pell, asked, "Well, doctor, are you able to cure whatever it is that ails us?"

"Oh, there is no cure – you all love being on the Moon! You cannot cure that," Dr. Benet said. "However, for all other physical maladies, I think you are all quite well. You are all excellent specimens of humankind!"

"Does that include our mental health, too, doc?" someone, a crewman that Laurent did not recall her name, asked.

Dr. Benet paused just a moment to think how best to answer that question. "I think that you here are doing quite well, irrespective of this compact environment. I have no worries about any of you." That was a true statement. No one seemed to have caught on that he had intentionally narrowed the group. He looked over to Reisberg for concurrence.

Dr. Reisberg saw this and finally said, "I think that's an accurate statement, doctor."

"Well that has to be the most noncommittal committal I have ever heard." But everyone there laughed it off, moving on to other topics.

There was a discussion of the war of sorts between Iran and Saudi Arabia. Consensus had it that it was just for show and that one side wanted to get the attention of the other, for what real purpose no one at the table knew.

There was some good news out of Northern California that the rains, and the subsequent flooding, had subsided. But the damage done was immeasurable, particularly to the agricultural industry there. It was coming out in the news just how dependent the US, and much of the world, was on California for its food. The predictions were not good.

Jon Miles asked if anyone wanted to talk about the consequences of the 2020 Brexit on the UK or the rest of the world. No one was interested. This was just old news.

After a while of listening to the group attempt to solve world problems from their very remote vantage point so far away from the world, Dr. Benet thought to himself, *these special people are not just normal, they are doing very well. No concerns here.*

Despite the good company, there was only so much processed food that could be tolerated in one sitting. Another Sunday brunch had come to an end. Around 1500 UTC, the group of researchers, scientists, doctors, astronauts all, moved on to other station tasks or duties.

As Jon was cleaning up, Penelope Brightling entered the dining area. Jon was suddenly one big smile, which did not go unnoticed by Dr. Reisberg on her way out. She smiled too.

Penelope approached Jon. "Hey Jon, I am picking up the telemetry experiments on the equipment that you and Hal set up last week. I could use a hand with some adjustments and since you already have worked with it, perhaps you could come out and assist me?

"I can do that for you, lassie." Now he was sounding Irish. "Let's go get suited up!"

ॐ

Back in Darmstadt, it was already late afternoon. Loukas Anagnostopoulos thought, *where did this day go? Where did this week go?* In truth, that was the least of his worries. What he was most concerned about was where the comradery went that once defined the Moon Exploratory Team, its leadership, and its incredible staff. For some time now, he thought that perhaps its purpose had been buried in a mire of political mud.

He did not want to step on Jeff Fund's toes. That would not

improve conditions any. But he did have a very good friend whom he could call on. Someone he had known for more than thirty years in in the space business and with whom he could just have a friendly chat, maybe discuss the current world crises, or invite for a visit. And maybe that person could talk to the leadership of SpaceX – on a very conciliatory level of course – just to be sure that the adventurous, leave-caution-to-the-wind, robust approach to exploring the Moon was toned down a bit.

He had the number, and his friend swore that Loukas could use it anytime for any reason, though preferably for social reasons. It should be early to midday where his friend was. It was time to make that call.

The call was going through. "Elon," said Loukas to the image shown on his Skylake monitor. "How are you? You are looking good for an old man!"

It was Elon Musk, founder of SpaceX, now 67 and semiretired, but not completely, from his many industries that he founded after the turn of the century. "Old man! Look who's talking. If this is a social call, I question your approach, my friend."

"I am still younger than you." Then turning more solemn, Loukas said to Elon, "You always said I should call you if I had concerns for the Moon Exploratory Team program."

"I did and I meant it. What's on your mind, Loukas?"

And so, Loukas told Elon Musk exactly what was on his mind.

Chapter 24
Visitors

4 April 2039, 10:20 am UTC,
MET Moon Base Station Venturous, Sea of Serenity, Moon

The explosion, the loss of the XO, the Lunar Lander, the titanium find, the floods in California, the meteorite shower and now the Chinese. This has been one roller coaster week!

So much had happened in the space of one week. Jon Miles ran through his mind all the events that had transpired since the explosion in the toolshed just over a week ago. And now here he was, Monday morning, awaiting the arrival of the Chinese delegation from their base to the north. And they are supposedly coming to help the Venturous!

Normally, he would have been talking about these things with his close friend Hal Lindstrum. But Hal passed on the opportunity to come out to greet the Chinese. He was, most likely, still a bit out of it after what happened to him Saturday. Incredible. He just hadn't been the same since.

Along with Jon, awaiting outside for the delegation, were Jim Sheppard, as a senior representative of the Venturous, and Susan Ly. Susan was selected as part of the receiving delegation for two reasons. As the Gateway Canadarm operator, her skills might be of benefit when they and their Moon rover arrived, and she was the only Venturous astronaut who spoke a smattering of Mandarin. This latter capability was the lesser of her skills expected to be needed.

Over his comms unit to Jim and Susan, Jon voiced what many of the crew had been talking about this morning. "I've been here nearly two years, and for most of my time, I don't even think about them being on the Moon with us. They nary say hello, mates. They just keep to their side of the ridge and we keep to ours. Some of the crew think that their presence on the Moon was just rumor that was started by M-E-T to keep us on our toes."

"Yeah, right," responded Jim sarcastically. "And all the SpaceX folks think there is gold in them thar hills!"

"There isn't?" laughed Jon. As did Susan.

"We are just as guilty as they are," said Jim. "Who knows when we would have made contact with the Chinese, had it not been for our toolshed situation. In fact, Dan Wedmond told me, they contacted him after they heard about the accident."

Susan chimed in. "I have been told by some of the crew that they are surprised that this Chinese delegation is coming – we have never seen them in the ten years we have been here - but many are also very pleased. I think, down deep inside us, we all know that anyone on the Moon, in these times, is a true explorer at heart and that we have a common bond; what the Chinese call a Yuháng Yuán – a space traveler."

"Perhaps your Chinese is better than you have let on?" But before she could respond, Jim said, "Command, any word?"

After a pause, "No word, Jim. It should be soon though."

The silence that followed seemed to just make the time go by slower.

Jon asked, "It just occurred to me, how are we going to communicate with them when they do arrive?"

"Did you miss this morning's briefing, Jon?" replied Jim. "We've established a common frequency. It's set up in your comms system. Go to Channel 5 when they arrive."

"That must have been when I was getting the Canadarm

ready," he said. The Canadarm was the Moon-side equivalent of the robotic arm used on ISS, Gateway and other spacecraft. At Venturous, it was used to maneuver equipment and materials delivered to the station.

"There, I think I see something," bellowed Jon. The bright sunlight, still low but rising now for this part of the Moon, since it had just gone through First Quarter a few days ago, did reflect off anything that moved on the Moon. Something was definitely coming from the north as had been anticipated.

"Commander, they're arriving," Jim reported to Wedmond. "They appear to be about five minutes out."

"Thank you. Doctor Kormendy and I will be out there momentarily," replied Wedmond.

Wedmond and Kormendy, who had returned late yesterday evening from the Posidonius Crater, passed through the Door and joined the three crewmen already outside just as the rover from the Tiangong-3 arrived. This was a momentous occasion, and everyone knew it. In ten years, no effort had been made to reach out from either side. It could have been that not sharing a common language was a significant barrier to any attempts to communicate. Of course, politics was also a factor.

There were three taikonauts in the rover, their spacesuits not all that dissimilar to ones used by MET astronauts. And like the astronauts, they also had visor-shielded helmets such that faces could not be seen. They also appeared to have name patches on their suits, just as the MET astronauts, but they were in Chinese characters. The three stepped out of their rover and strode over to the five astronauts.

"I am Commander Li Yuen. May I ask if Commander Wedmond is with you?" came the voice of one of the taikonauts, in excellent English and almost no typical Chinese accent, followed by an outstretched hand.

Wedmond stepped forward. "I am Commander Dan Wedmond. Welcome to Venturous, Commander Li." He then introduced the other four members of the Venturous greeting committee.

Li said, "I have brought two members of my team from the Tiangong. This is my chief engineer, Yang Junlong." Yang stepped forward so that the others would know who he was. "And this Guan Nuan, chief of sciences."

"Susan Ly, perhaps you speak some Chinese?" asked Li.

"I am Canadian. My family originated in Viet Nam; however, I do speak some Mandarin, commander."

"I see."

"I am stationed on the orbiting platform Gateway," she added. "But I have been asked to assist with the unloading of your rover today."

Trailing the rover was a heavy-duty cart containing a large piece of equipment; a specialized welding machine that worked in the Moon's zero-oxygen environment. In their conversation Saturday, Li offered the use of this machine to help Wedmond and the Venturous repair the ruptured wall of the toolshed. When he accepted, he had not realized that Li meant he would come to the Venturous immediately. After packing it on their mobile cart the next day, the three taikonauts left very early UTC time undertaking the ten-hour journey to the Venturous.

"Commander, before we begin unloading our welding machine, perhaps we can use your facilities?" asked Li. "It's been a long trip."

"Of course! Please enter. We will show you to our changing area and get you some food and drink."

Wedmond, Kormendy and the three taikonauts entered the Venturous. After showing Li and his crewmen the changing area and providing them with electrolyzed reduced water and some protein bars, Yang and Guan returned to their rover, the Venturous team still standing by outside.

Commander Li removed his suit, as had Wedmond and Kormendy, and the three met in the corridor.

"Commander Li," said Wedmond, once they were together, "It is a pleasure to meet with you in person. And again, this is Doctor Anna Kormendy, senior representative of SpaceX, our corporate partner with the Moon Exploratory Team."

"A pleasure, doctor," Li said. "I am familiar with your organization's structure. It seems to be a very effective method of achieving your overall goals with the Moon."

"Thank you, commander," said Anna. "We should discuss this subject more in the near future."

Wedmond followed her comment. "On behalf of M-E-T, I wish to thank you for your assistance and for providing your welding machine. It will be a major benefit to us. If you would like to join me, I invite you to our Command Center where we can monitor the unloading of your cart. After that, we have something prepared for your arrival. Shall we?"

Wedmond and Kormendy led Li to the Command Center while occasionally pointing out spaces and features of the Venturous encountered along the way. He was also introduced to passing crewmembers. Upon arriving at the Command Center, and more introductions of the day watch, the three turned to the monitor that was already observing the retrieval effort ongoing just outside the Door.

Outside, Susan Ly could be seen manning the remote controller for the Canadarm attached to the Venturous near the level platform that served the purpose of receiving large supply containers and heavy equipment. In this instance, the welding machine was retrieved from the Chinese rover's cart and placed on a sled as close as possible to where the rupture in the maintenance and repair module existed. The remaining four astronauts/taikonauts proceeded to drag the sled with its 150-kilogram – Moon-side weight – welder the remaining twenty meters. This was no easy task even under the Moon's lower gravity simply due to the surface terrain.

The welder could stay on the sled during the operation. With the material that was available at the base station, plus some supplemental items brought by the taikonauts, Miles and Sheppard were able to commence the patch and repair of the toolshed. Despite the language barrier and the added barrier of the spacesuits, Yang and Guan were able to assist. Yang performed the actual welding task given that he was the only one in the group with the requisite training and experience.

The process took about forty minutes and was not quite like a welding job back on Earth, but it worked. There was the expected bright white arc created by the intense heat, but the astronauts' and taikonauts' visors were more than sufficient to protect their eyes. It definitely had the look of a slapped-on patchwork, but it was functionally solid and durable. Since the inner core wall had already been repaired days ago, it took only another fifteen minutes to repressurize the module and to carry out a preliminary test for integrity. No leakage detected.

Satisfied with the success of the repair, the crew dragged the welding machine back to where the Canadarm could reach it, and it was then placed back on the cart. It was a very smooth process by all concerned.

All five of the repair team returned to the Venturous, got out of their spacesuits and headed for the dining area where Commander Wedmond, Anna Kormendy and Commander Li were waiting. It would be too crowded to meet in the Command Center.

More introductions were made as others of the Venturous

crew occupied the dining area. Commander Li rose to speak to the crew, "First, on behalf of China National Space Administration and my fellow taikonauts of Tiangong-3, I wish to express our appreciation for your warm and generous welcome."

The crew were all smiles and there were a few who applauded.

"I also offer our most sincere condolences for the loss of your fellow astronaut and to anyone who might have families or friends suffering from the floods in Northern California." Heads nodded and bowed. The crew was touched by this gesture.

"We have been neighbors for far too long to not have come and meet each other. It is regrettable that it took your misfortune to bring us together. But it was both our fortunes that we of the Tiangong were able to come to your aid. I hope this will not be the last and only time we meet."

"Here, here," was heard among the crew along with other positive endorsements of Li's sentiment. There were a few more words shared and after a while, the astronauts in the dining area gathered around the taikonauts. Dr. Reisberg, Luca Barolo, and others shared a few words of thanks and even tried to ask a few questions. Of course, only Li Yuen fully understood the English and could fully respond. Although both Guan Nuan and Yang Junlong spoke some English, which was a pleasant surprise to the Venturous crew. When asked about that, Li said, "More English is taught in China than in the United States!"

The crew were very puzzled by his comment.

"It's quite true. It is required education in most of our early school systems across China. And since we have nearly four times as many young children as in the United States, I can accurately say that more English is taught in China. I do not say, however, that we were more proficient!" Everyone laughed.

"Commander, "said Anna Kormendy, "you seem to have a sense of humor."

"So I have been told."

Wedmond gave the group a few more minutes. It was going so well, he did not want to break up the gathering, but he also did not want to overwhelm his guests. He had promised them a tour of the Venturous before they made the ten-hour journey back to the Tiangong-3.

The tour of the Venturous proceeded with Wedmond and Kormendy leading, Li and his team followed, with Ly taking up the rear. When Wedmond or Kormendy talked about a module or a specific function of a piece of equipment, Susan would try to translate to Yang and Guan. If that did not work, Commander Li would translate. Li, however, was pleased with Susan's proficiency, as was Dan Wedmond. It was timely that she had been here when the taikonauts arrived, but unfortunate that she would be returning to the Gateway tomorrow.

The most visually impressive module was the Venturous greenhouse. They took their time examining the plant growth. Eleni Dimopolous had been standing by to present her work here. Commander Li talked of their Chinese style greenhouse with its special acrylic panels that enhanced solar radiation. As they were about to leave, "Commander Li said, "This is most impressive. Thank you for sharing your experiences with us. I think it most appropriate that you come to our greenhouse, Miss Dimopolous. In fact, I invite your astronauts and scientists to come to the Tiangong in the near future."

"I would be honored," replied Eleni.

Seeing the opportunity, Commander Wedmond added, "I think that would be a wonderful experience for our team. Commander Li, I see this as an opportunity to enhance our relationship here on the Moon. Our mission is to advance our knowledge and to augment the human existence. If we can find ways to work together, learn together, live together, I believe we are achieving that mission. I would like to see that we carry out endeavors together in the future."

"I agree that we should work together, be different humans on the Moon than, perhaps, our predecessors were on Earth. In the years to come, more and more people from many nations of the world will come to live here. We need to set the ground rules for our future human communities on the Moon."

Kormendy added, "I don't think it will be long before the Russians will be setting up camp here."

"I believe that the Russians won't get here for another ten years," said Li.

"Provided they can steal the technology," said Yang in Chinese and under his breath. Susan Ly heard it though and giggled. Li turned and gave Yang a stern, be-quiet, look.

Wedmond did not know what Yang Junlong said, but in response to Commander Li he responded, "Hopefully, we won't make the same mistake of shunning them, too."

The tour continued with a few more modules. Returning to the dining area, the taikonauts were provided with some supplies for their journey back. Commander Wedmond addressed Yang and said, "I knew of your father, Yang Liwei. I think you must be the first second-generation yuháng yuan."

Li translated for Yang. He smiled, bowed and said in accented English, "Commander, you know our name for universal traveler. I am honored to follow in my father's footsteps. As you say in America, they are big shoes to fill.

"Of course, when we do meet again," said Li, "which I believe will be soon, I will tell you a few funny stories about Yang Liwei. We Chinese do occasionally have a good time in space"

Commander Wedmond smiled, "No doubt in my mind. Until then."

After suiting up, the three exited Venturous, got back in their rover and headed out. They had a long trip before them, but it had been worth every bit of the effort to come to the Venturous.

Chapter 25
The Best of the Best

4 April 2039, 10:20 am CDT,
NASA Mission Control, Houston, Texas, Earth

*O**ur own congressmen do not have such impressive backgrounds
as these astronauts.***

In his Houston office within the OIG's small common area,
Aaron Ghiassi sat at his desk reviewing files on his Skylake. It
was just midmorning, Monday, yet he was quite ready to call it a
day. He had been on this case for less than seventy-two hours. In
that time, he had caught about twelve hours of sleep total over
the last three nights. Nowhere near normal for him.

He had spent the past few days gathering the personnel dos-
siers for as much of the Venturous crew that he could obtain.
Getting the ESA personnel files was not immediate. There had
been some resistance from ESA, but since most of the information the files contained was pretty much common knowledge,
and this was a very high-profile investigation, Aaron was able
to get them, even on a Sunday.

He had read most of them. He had five to go, but so far, the
scrutiny he had given to the background files had been unrevealing – across the board. And the last five were the least likely to be
hiding the culprit. Those that were married, seem to be happily so,
though there is one exception – a divorcee, but that had been nearly twenty years prior. He was very sad to read that Commander
Wedmond had lost his wife, Deneen, to cancer several years ago.

Of those who were married, nearly all had children. There was one same-sex marriage among the crew. The partner who went on to become an astronaut, had an exceptional record of performance and no evident motive to damage or kill, as was true with all of the astronauts.

There were, of course, no criminal records, for any of them. They were all high achievers long before they were even considered for this assignment to the Moon. It was very clear that screening by their respective agencies had been thorough and in depth. What could he hope to find in just a few days?

These were the best of the best.

He was about to make his first report to his boss, Robert Hamilton, whom he hadn't talked to since last Friday. He had been asked to give him an update after lunch, Washington, DC, time. That was quickly coming up.

Ghiassi decided to prep his notes and findings, as few as there were, laying out the usual motif for an investigation of this nature: Victim and his background, manner of death, suspects and their backgrounds, motive, availability or access to the method of attack, and special circumstances and conditions.

As it approached 11am there in Houston, he made the video call via his jPhone, rather than utilizing one of the bigger video conference setups in the office. Robert Hamilton answered quickly.

"Good afternoon, sir," said Ghiassi.

"Good day, Aaron, "replied Hamilton. "How's the weather there in Houston? I hear you are expecting thunderstorms there."

Aaron didn't really know. He had been indoors most of the weekend and hadn't paid much attention when going back and forth from his home in Deer Park, a fifteen- to twenty-minute drive most days, but he did not recall hearing any weather warnings.

"It's probably overrated. No one here seems concerned. Business as usual."

"Well good," the Deputy Assistant IG said. "I know you haven't had much time but give me what you got."

"As you already know, I have very little. And the interviews I had with some of the crew on Saturday revealed little more. What I can tell you is that it does appear to have been a premeditated and deliberate attack using on-station equipment and materials to create an explosion followed by an attempt to cover it up."

"Go on. Give me your facts and your theories."

"The victim, Bruce Holmann, was well respected by NASA managers here, and by the Venturous crew. He was a family man, like many there. There is nothing in his background that raises alarms.

Although there were some rifts between him and Doctor Anna Kormendy, who is there as the senior SpaceX representative. The rifts relate to management style and direction of the exploration effort. It is a possible motive, but very highly unlikely. On the other hand, it is the best motive we have."

"You have no other motive."

"There is the possibility that money was a motive."

"Money?" Hamilton seemed quite shocked. "You will have to explain that one to me."

"It's extreme, but it is conceivable that there could be lucrative contracts or bonuses for one or more of the corporate partners for bringing in valuable mineral finds."

Hamilton thought about that. "The iron ore find was big but not something that will make anyone any money. And the titanium was found after Holmann's death."

"As I said it is extreme. It's possible that someone might have wanted to divert attention away from the find. Maybe keep it hidden."

"Hmmm. I don't know. That's far-fetched."

"Agreed, but I am having an agent look into such possible arrangements. Unfortunately, that is something that could be kept hidden or even destroyed, if it were true. I am struggling to find something else."

"What about the explosion itself?" asked Hamilton, "Anything there?"

"Needless to say, a proper forensic assessment is nearly impossible, and certainly not going to occur in a timely manner. The crew that conducted the investigation initially did as best they could. In fact, it was one of them who came to the conclusion that it was not an accident. The fact that they're researchers, might have been in our favor. But they were not conducting a criminal investigation at the time and it is... a hostile environment, so to speak.

"I did discuss with one of the crew, Luca Barolo, about gathering debris, certain tools and equipment, and other items believed to be those used by the bomber, and having these items transferred to us; however, that process will most likely take weeks to months to get back to our forensic labs here on Earth."

"I hope you are able to conclude your investigation satisfactorily long before then. We cannot have a murderer loose up there," stated Hamilton. It was an unnecessary statement as Ghiassi knew very well the consequences of not finding the culprit quickly.

"There are two other possible scenarios I am exploring. One, is that Jim Sheppard was the intended target."

"Is there any credibility to that?"

"No more so than with Bruce Holmann. But again, the investigation is still in its early stage."

"What's your other scenario? I assume you saved it for last as being the most likely." Robert Hamilton knew how this worked. You always saved the best for last.

"I am also looking into the possibility that neither Bruce Holmann nor Jim Sheppard was the intended target of the bombing, but that Holmann was simply collateral damage. This theory seems to hold the most weight."

"How so?"

"Consider the timing. I believe the explosive device was set off by a timer, based on the debris found so far. The explosion occurred late in the evening, Venturous time, on a Sunday. The blast was small and, I think, meant to look like a possible accident in a space that was not heavily utilized. I think that Holmann was there working in what they call the toolshed when it was expected to be empty."

"You're suggesting then that the bomber had another purpose in mind. Any ideas on that?"

Aaron thought about it before answering. "Again, coming up with a motive has been very difficult. Bombers set off their devices for reasons ranging from revenge, to getting rid of evidence, to just making a statement.

"If it's for revenge, I have not identified a basis for such at this early stage. Nothing has come up in the background checks nor in the few interviews I have had. Same goes for getting rid of evidence. For both these scenarios, there would be better ways to do it on the Moon."

"So, you are inclined to go with making a statement then?" asked Hamilton.

"Yessir."

"And that statement is…" Hamilton asked.

"Too soon to tell, but if it was to make a statement, that statement has not been made evident. It is my plan to look into what actions would have occurred that did not, or would not have occurred but will, as a consequence of the explosion."

"OK. I am satisfied with where you are going with this. What about the video recording that was corrupted? Where do we stand with that?"

"The recording has been transferred to our cyber unit for analysis. I am not an expert in that field, but I suspect that we will have a problem since we will be analyzing a copy of a copy of the original file. The original is not accessible anymore."

"When do you expect their assessment?"

"I just gave it to them. But I asked that it be expedited due to the circumstances. I was told they had no backlog at the moment and could get right on it. Still, they could not give me a timeframe."

"Very good. I know you don't have that much, but that's understandable. Are you getting all the support you need for this, Aaron?"

"Yessir. Well, it's just me and the cyber unit right now. I could use some help on the deep dive of the background checks, though."

Alright, give me something in an email that I can work with and I will get you what you need."

A few more elements and comments concerning the investigation were passed on by Aaron to his boss, but the significant details had been provided upfront. Upon ending the call, Aaron again considered that he was in the spotlight of sorts. But he had been there before when lives were at stake. And he could not ask for a more supportive boss than Robert Hamilton.

As it was during their FBI days together, they trusted each other. Hamilton would watch his back and in exchange, Aaron would get the job done. Ghiassi did not need to worry about managing nosy bureaucrats and congressional aids haranguing him. Hamilton would take care of that. All he had to do was keep him apprised.

As for this investigation, getting some assistance on the background checks would ease the burden, but there was no doubt in his mind, this one was going to be a bear coming up with anything useful.

Chapter 26
Reaching Out

4 April 2039, afternoon CDT,
NASA Mission Control, Houston, Texas, Earth

*O*ur astronauts make better diplomats than our professional diplomats!

So thought Dr. Feskine as she discussed with Wedmond the visit by the senior members from the Chinese base station. It was a bold and, well, unauthorized move. She was very impressed. She could only wish for more men and women like Wedmond to serve in the space programs.

It was just Monday afternoon for Cheryl. A bit late in the evening for the Venturous she realized. Still, the call now to Wedmond was significant.

"We gave them the grand tour," said Dan, recapping the visit. "They all appeared unaffectedly interested and, I think, impressed. They were definitely impressed with our greenhouse and talked to Eleni Dimopolous about it and her work. They then took that moment to invite her and the rest of us to visit the Tiangong-3."

"A defining moment, I would say," said Cheryl, pausing to wait for his reply. She had long ago learned to adapt to the delay in response and no longer thought about it.

"It was very clear to me that Commander Li Yuen was making every effort to develop a relationship. Whether he reflects the desire of his superiors in CNSA or of the Chinese government,

I cannot say. But it was an opening that I would like to take advantage of again somewhere down the road... soon."

"I am in agreement with you, Dan," Feskine said. *In fact, the sooner the better,* she thought to herself during the pause.

"After that, we discussed, very lightly, the near future of human development on the Moon, and that there should be ground rules for the coming advance of people to the Moon."

"And I am in agreement with Commander Li, as well."

"There was a moment where the Russian mission was brought up, that it would be on the Moon in the next ten years. Susan Ly told me that Yang Junlong made a crack about the Russians. I would say they hold the Russians in as high regard as we do," said Dan, suppressing a grin.

"I've heard that the Chinese often have a sense of humor and don't mind expressing it on occasion. My own experiences in a formal setting were not so, but my close friends who are Chinese can be very funny."

"Well humorous or not, their sincerity in helping us was quite genuine in my opinion. As was their return offer to come visit their station. I think there is merit in a follow up."

"Do you think there was any advantage to them by coming to our station? Generally speaking, our design of the Venturous has been an open book to the world. Could they have gleaned something from their visit?" asked Feskine, pondering what ulterior motives might be in play.

"There's always that possibility, but truthfully, we have nothing to hide that is part of the Venturous. We did not share with them all our ongoing experiments and research. Nor would we do that with any other non-M-E-T entity. But there could be an advantage for us in visiting the Tiangong-3. Their layout is definitely close to the chest."

"Well, let's see if we can make that happen. You should

continue to stay in contact with their commander, Li Yuen. I will make a few calls from my end."

"I can do that."

"Oh, and commander…" said Feskine, smiling as she spoke to him, "Great job!"

Yes, Monday afternoon, and it was shaping up to be a very long week ahead for Cheryl Feskine and MET.

◊◊◊

It was not quite noon in Hawthorne; Jeff Fund was preparing to head to lunch. As he stood, ironically, Tim Buzza entered his office. Jeff was not someone to work behind a closed door, and there had been no prior notice or appointment that the Chief Executive Officer of SpaceX was coming. That was how SpaceX worked.

"Tim, good to see you," said Jeff with just a hint of surprise in his voice. "I was going to lunch. Did you need me for something, or would you care to join me?"

"Proud Bird? I know that's your favorite local spot," inquired Buzza.

"That's where I was heading. Let's go."

Proud Bird was not quite close enough to walk to… safely or quickly. It was on a very busy street adjacent to the airport. So Fund's driver dropped them off. Proud Bird was also not high end, by any means, but the food was great, and the regulars were just that, regular folk. Jeff Fund liked his high society hobnobbing and going to dinners where everyone was someone, or knew someone, or was dating someone who was a president or CEO of a high-tech firm. He fit in fine with that crowd. But for lunch, this was his kind of place.

When they entered through the old Spanish-style entryway, they were immediately greeted and shown to Jeff's preferred table, no questions asked. It looked out at the World War II war-birds mounted in the restaurant grounds and within sight of some of the airline facilities just east of LAX Runways 25 Left and Right.

The two of them sat and talked about the weather, particularly the weather disaster that hit Northern California so hard and the wake of destruction it left behind. After ordering, Buzza moved the conversation toward the goings-on with MET and Venturous.

"I had a chat with Elon this morning. He called me. It was pleasant enough; we talked about old times back when I was his VP of Launch and Test. Those were fun times when we didn't know what we were really doing, but we were doing it big time with the Falcon 9 and Falcon Heavy rockets."

"I remember. I was just getting involved with the Dragon cargo spacecraft myself."

"Elon felt compelled to remind me why we're in the space game."

"Really? I take it he had something on his mind to bring that up," said Fund.

"Oh, he is very pleased with where the company is going and with our partnership with NASA and ESA as part of the Moon Exploratory Team. The fact that we might just pull in a little extra revenue from the titanium discovery combined with the cost savings potential from the iron ore refining, the lead extraction, the utilization of polar ice, excites us all. And even the reduction on the air production and filtering costs through our phenomenal botanical greenhouse capabilities has not escaped his attention."

"Can't ask for more than that, I would say," said Jeff.

"I think it's also safe to say the company's financial success will be felt by its employees," added Buzza.

"That would be very good news and I will say it!" Jeff Fund was becoming just a tad bit excited about the prospect of reaping the rewards of his hard work. "But I suspect there is more to his message. Is he of the belief that we're not performing to our best level? Perhaps the death of Bruce Holmann has him concerned?"

Drinks and the bread tray were brought out, causing a pause in the conversation, while each took a sip of a very nice Merlot that they had ordered and to butter a piece of bread.

Continuing, Buzza said to Jeff, "He is very concerned but not in the way you might think."

"How so?" asked Jeff.

"He is confident that the person that caused the explosion that killed Bruce will be found and dealt with. That is not the issue. What concerns him most is how it got that far."

Jeff realized, in that moment, what this was about. That perhaps SpaceX – Jeff Fund – had not been doing enough to create an environment on Venturous that would preclude such an outcome. Rather, perhaps he had allowed an environment to flourish in which someone would want to do damage and kill others.

Buzza added, "He feels, and I agree, that we need to do more on our part to create a better environment on Venturous. If we don't, we will not be able to continue with this… venture. And that goes against our mission."

Jeff thought, *this is it, I'm being let go. Maybe just from MET and not from SpaceX.* "So, are you asking me to step down from MET?" he asked.

"Not at all. Is that what you think this is about? I can assure you, it's quite the contrary."

Jeff smiled but still seemed confused. "So, if that's not it, what's this meeting about?"

"What, colleagues… friends can't go out to lunch together! Actually, there is a purpose for meeting with you today. I… the company… we all want to make sure you have all the resources you need at your disposal to make sure this works. And that you are putting those resources to work."

Buzza paused to sip his wine and eat some of the food that was delivered. Fund decided to do the same, now that his heart rate had slowed.

"You have been an asset to SpaceX for many years and you have proven yourself as many times. We all have great confidence in you to continue doing so. Just because one aspect might not be going its best, doesn't mean we give up. Just look at our Falcon recoverable rocket program. We certainly didn't give up on that, and if there ever was a reason to…"

"I get the picture, Tim. And thank you for the words of encouragement. As they say in space: message received."

The lunch continued, as did the discussion, with emphasis on how SpaceX needed to go forward. The key elements would be to have a very similar conversation with Anna Kormendy, to ensure that SpaceX was fully aware of conditions that affected the quality of life on Venturous, and also assure both Cheryl Feskine and Loukas Anagnostopoulos of its unwavering support of the MET program and mission.

✺

The weather in Houston was still stormy since yesterday. There were tornado warnings further inland from Houston, but around Houston it was just crappy. Dr. Cheryl Feskine decided it was time to reach out to her fellow board members once more. Just to talk to the three of them. She did not know how it would go with Jeff Fund, but protocol required that she include him.

Cheryl initiated a video call to the two men. It did not take long for both to answer. Since this was an unplanned call, there was no assurance that she would find either or both by their video phones. "Gentlemen, I am pleased I caught you both. I hope I can have a few moments of your time?"

"I always have time for a conversation with you, my dear Doctor Feskine," said Loukas in his so typically charming manner.

"Gladly, Cheryl," responded Fund. "I was just thinking about calling you as well. Your timing is perfect."

"Thank you, I won't keep you long. I would like to discuss with you both the recent visit by the Chinese astronauts – taikonauts as they call themselves – and what transpired with their visit."

"You mean beside the successful repair of the toolshed I take it," said Fund. The two had already been fully briefed on the visit, but they were unaware of some of the details that Dan shared with Cheryl.

"Yes. I would say that more than just the toolshed has been repaired." Dr. Feskine proceeded to share with them the essence of her conversation with Dan Wedmond.

After soaking in what Cheryl had to say, Loukas burst out, in only a fashion that someone of his stature could, "Dr. Feskine, that is extraordinary! We have never really considered the Chinese presence there as anything but coincidental. This could evolve into something far more significant for both the Westerners and for the Chinese. We cannot let this… step up wither away."

"I very much agree, Cheryl," said Jeff. "This is a phenomenal opportunity that I believe SpaceX would relish the chance to expand upon. Whatever helps advance the human cause into space, we are for it."

It would be safe to say that both Loukas and Cheryl were, dumbfounded. These were words that were not expected to come from Jeff Fund. But they were not going to let this moment slip away.

"I am inclined to believe that China has been looking for an opportunity to open more channels outside of trade. Our misfortune, to put it in blunt terms, might be the opening they are looking for. Would we not do the same thing if the roles were reversed?"

"Agreed," they both said.

"So I take it you would support any effort to establish and advance a relationship with the Chinese?" asked Cheryl.

"Support it? I want to know what SpaceX can do to nurture it," replied Fund. "I am with you one hundred percent. My concern is: Will our astronauts on Venturous think it's a good idea. After all it took the misfortune of the death of one of our very best astronauts to be the catalyst of this new acquaintanceship. I don't want to move on to something that does not have the full support of the crew."

Was this the same Jeff Fund? "I am inclined to believe that they are. I have only Dan Wedmond's take on it, but it is his belief that the crew were grateful for the help provided by the taikonauts. First impressions are critical, but they might mask true character. Still, I am inclined to believe in our colleagues on the Moon."

Loukas added, "We have the best of the best, with perhaps one exception." He was alluding to the unknown killer. "I agree with you both that we cannot let this opportunity pass us by."

Jeff pondered the situation. He wanted to affirmatively show his support. "Might I suggest something? I think you should make contact with an appropriate counterpart in CNSA. I would do it myself, but this if more of a government-entity-to-government-entity sort of thing. I can only imagine what channels you might have to go through to make it happen, but do it. If you can't, we will find a way."

Wow. Who is this guy? thought Cheryl for a brief second. "No.

Although I am enthused by your support, and it encourages me to act, I agree it is best if I attempt first contact with… whomever, government-agency-to-government-agency. If I'm unsuccessful, we'll talk further." *We'll talk further anyway. I love this new Jeff Fund.*

"Jeff, Cheryl, I think this is the right thing to do. I can assure you that the ESA will back you on this course of action. You have my word on it," interjected Loukas.

The discussion continued, focused on what Cheryl Feskine would do next and how she would approach the Chinese National Space Administration. They all agreed. This was too important to waste time running it 'up the flagpole.' The two base stations would wither and blow away, even in no atmosphere, before the bureaucracies of the all the countries involved could agree on reaching out. That would not do. They would take a chance. Well, Cheryl would, but both Loukas and Jeff told her she need not worry. She wasn't going to jail. And anything after that, they could take care of. For some reason, Cheryl believed both men implicitly.

After the call ended, all three MET board members – colleagues – space explorers in their own right, felt very good about the coming week.

༺༻

Dr. Feskine knew it was still very early in China, but she had a lot to prepare for what she had just committed to do. Tapping the intercom button on her desk, she asked her assistant, "Jean, can you track down an interpreter for me; one who speaks Mandarin Chinese? If he or she is in the building, have 'em come to my office as soon as possible."

"Yes ma'am."

She then called Manuela Lusk, Mission Control's on-duty Comms Manager. "Manuela, can you do me a favor? It's a bit

∽ 236 ∽

out of the norm, but I could use your help."

"I'll try. What is it?" Manuela asked.

"Can you find me the head of the China National Space Administration, his name, title, where that person is located and, most importantly, how I can contact him or her?"

"Tall order. Give me a half-hour or so."

About five minutes later, Manuela came to Dr. Feskine's office with a list in hand.

"Well, that didn't take so long," she said.

"It was easy. I just Googled it. It took me a few more minutes to verify the info and print it out for you. Also, Jean mentioned you required a Chinese Interpreter. We have a staff engineer who can fill the role. He's assigned over at the Space Vehicle Mockup Facility and was about to leave to go home. We asked him to come see you. He'll be here in about fifteen minutes.

"Good work, Manuela. What is his name?"

"Jim Royal, ma'am."

"He speaks Chinese?" Not a name Cheryl expected, but she should have known better to ask.

Yes, ma'am. He's three-quarters Chinese, one-quarter Caucasian… on his father's side."

"I knew you know everything and everyone around here, but how did you know that?"

"Easy, he's my neighbor. We often carpool," confessed Manuela. It was not uncommon for most Johnson Space Center employees, that number in excess of three thousand and not counting the eleven thousand contractor employees, to live in the same neighborhoods around Houston.

When Jim Royal arrived, Cheryl invited him into the adjacent conference room, apologized that he would have to stay late, and proceeded to explain why his services were needed so late in the day.

Of course, he was good with staying later. In his job, he had had to work late many an evening. But this was one for the record books. He would be interpreting between English and the National Chinese that the CNSA Administrator, Wu Yanhua, was assumed to speak. There was always the possibility that he spoke Cantonese, but that was unlikely for a native of Beijing's Haidian District and for one so highly placed.

Around 7 pm, Dr. Feskine, initiated the call. Actually, Jim Royal did. The initial call was to a listed number for the administrative office of CNSA. Royal was able to converse with responders and once it became clear that a director from NASA was calling, it did not take long to reach the office of Wu Yanhua.

Jim Royal spoke to Wu's assistant. The assistant left the view of the monitor. Ten seconds later, there was the face of an older balding Chinese man on the monitor. Jim spoke to him briefly, then turned to Dr. Feskine, "Doctor, this is Wu Yanhua, Administrator for the China National Space Administration." He introduced Cheryl Feskine to Wu and then moved away so that she could be seen in the monitor.

"Administrator Wu, thank you for taking my call," said Cheryl, which Royal promptly translated.

Wu spoke, translated by Royal, "It is my pleasure to speak to you. My apologies that I cannot speak your tongue... language." Wu continued. "It has been my desire to contact your organization due to recent events on the Moon. Truly, we were uncertain who we would contact. We did not fully comprehend your organization structure. Thus, I am glad that you have reached out to our organization."

"I understand your confusion. Our Moon-based project is managed by a joint partnership of European and North American government agencies and some of our corporations that are focused on space exploration." After a pause for the translation,

Cheryl continued, "But it is we who very much needed to contact you as we must thank you and your team on the Tiangong-3 for its assistance in repairing our base station, Venturous."

"You are most welcome Dr. Feskine."

"Our Commander Wedmond, acted on his own to contact the Tiangong-3 to ask for assistance. Apparently, your Commander Li did not hesitate to respond by coming to our aid. I believe that it is very important to appreciate that these first steps have been taken by our respective crewmen to initiate conversation, something that is many years overdue. But it was something that only our Yuháng yuán were able to accomplish as they are trusting and adventurous by their nature."

"Agreed. Dr. Feskine. Commander Li acted on his own when he responded, which we are now grateful for."

"We have two very good men there on the Moon representing humanity."

The conversation continued, ending with a promise to not let this opportunity slip away. Both sides will find the means to open channels for further discussion and, perhaps, pursue cooperative endeavors together. That would yet to be determined. It might take time, but both sides had now reached out to each other successfully.

Chapter 27
Gateway

5 April 2039, midday UTC,
Orbital Platform Gateway, Stationary Orbit, Moon

*L*iving on Venturous must be the lap of luxury... compared to living on Gateway.

Commander Marianna Fascar was into her third year as the senior astronaut and leader of the Lunar Orbiting Platform-Gateway. In that time, she had sent off and received thirteen Lunar Lander missions to Venturous, almost one every two months. She had also managed three other Lunar Lander missions not connected to Venturous, but in support of other NASA, Canadian Space Agency and European Space Agency missions. And, of course they had their own research program to carry out.

It was a very good assignment to be Gateway's commander, coveted by many of her colleagues in the European astronaut corps, but the station itself was still small, cramped and offered just a modicum of privacy. In fact, she liked it when the lander was off on a mission. Half of her six-astronaut crew were typically gone, giving her and the two remaining crewmen a bit of breathing room for a few days!

Gateway – This space station was conceived to serve as an all-purpose, solar-powered communications hub, science laboratory, short-term habitation module (initially), refueling depot, and holding area for landers and other space-based equipment in cislunar, and later in lunar orbit. Conceived in 2015, there were many iterations and much input from ESA, JAXA, CSA and others as to its design and functionality. Even Roscosmos, the Russian state corporation responsible for space flight and cosmonaut training, had a say in it.

The final product was financed, contracted for and built under the auspices of CSA and NASA with the first module to reach the Moon in 2024. The final version comprised six distinct operating modules, all of which could be and ultimately have been added to. A seventh module was added in 2031.

The seven modules were the *Power and Propulsion Element.* Its function was to generate electricity for all of Gateway and its associated equipment, and to provide solar electric propulsion. There was the *European System Providing Refueling, Infrastructure and Telecommunications* module, a fancy name given to it by the ESA so they could call it the ESPRIT module. It provided xenon and hydrazine capacity, additional communications equipment, and an airlock for science research packages and coordinated experiments with Venturous.

There was also the *U.S. Utilization Module,* a small pressurized space that enabled a crew ingress on the very first mission to the Gateway assembly mission, and it provided access to exterior equipment and operations. It also functioned as a food storage and preservation module. Its importance was obvious.

Then there were the Gateway *Logistics Modules,* consisting of small units used to refuel, resupply and provide logistics functions for Gateway operations. The first logistics module included the Canadarm robotic arm used to manipulate and transfer supplies, equipment, everything, outside Gateway. This was CSA's very significant contribution, one of many, to Gateway.

Another vital component was the Gateway *Airlock Module.* This crucial module was used to conduct the early extravehicular activities outside the space station. Three years later, it was used as the docking port for the Lunar Lander.

And, while each module was of critical importance, there were the set of modules in which the astronauts lived. These were, not surprisingly, the *International Partner Habitat*, now consisting of two units, and the *U.S. Habitat* – the three habitation modules used by the six full-time crew. Occasionally, when astronauts were being transferred from Earth to Venturous, these not-so-spacious space accommodations were shared, in rotation, with the en route astronauts.

The seventh and final module, added seven years into Gateway's existence, was the *Science, Exploration and Research Container Hub,* referred to by crew as the *SEARCH Module.*

At the moment, Commander Fascar was supervising the docking operation of the Lunar Lander, which was somewhat of a misnomer since the entire process was carried out by the Lander's onboard computer. Due to the possible but unlikely event of an extremely poor docking operation, everyone was suited up. In the past seventy years of space docking, starting with the Gemini missions in the 1960's, there had never been a docking incident. These days, with computer-controlled docking, sophisticated sensors and micro controls, the chances of an incident were so remote, it was considered safer than hitching a tractor truck to a trailer. But then, why press your luck? No one wanted to have the first incident occur and not have been suited up.

It was, of course, another safe and perfect docking. After a twenty-minute shutdown procedure and the equalization of pressure between the Lander and Gateway, the Lander hatch opened.

Exiting the Lander was today's pilot, Susan Ly, followed by Dr. Laurent Benet and the new arrival, Linda Miramontes. They had already removed their helmets. Consequently, Commander Fascar could see their smiling faces, particularly Linda's as she entered the Gateway receiving area, eyes scanning, taking in her new home. To the newcomers from the Venturous, there was essentially no gravity on Gateway. Actually, there was just a little bit of gravity since Gateway was stationed in lunar orbit much closer to the surface than past Apollo missions ever did. It was just enough 'microgravity' for the human body to know were 'down' was. Not unlike a feather falling to Earth on a very calm day. Linda displayed the usual inability to maneuver as any first-timer on Gateway did.

Linda was going to miss Venturous and the crew members who had come and gone over the twenty-eight months she lived there. But Linda Miramontes had an adventurous soul. She was eager to move on to life's next challenge and still be in space.

Linda was not the first Hispanic to go into space. There had been many before her from the United States and other countries. She wasn't even the first female Hispanic in space; she was the fifth. But she was the first Hispanic to touch the Moon. To achieve that honor, for herself, her family, including grandparents who never spoke a word of English and had struggled running a small restaurant after coming to the US in the 1960's, for the high school she attended where she was so strongly influenced and encouraged by caring teachers, and for the small rural Arizona community she grew up in, few had worked as hard as she.

"Welcome to Gateway, Linda – your new home for the next eight months," said Fascar with as much enthusiasm she could muster. "I am Marianna Fascar."

"I am very pleased and excited to be here, Commander."

"Please call me Marianna. Let me introduce your two other shipmates."

Commander Fascar made the introductions and let Linda get settled in before giving her the grand tour of Gateway's seven modules and a preview of some of its ongoing experiments. Linda noticed that there were few areas on Gateway that you could go where you were not within earshot of one of the other crew members, and there were only six! This was going to be different from living on the base station.

"Linda, I hear good things about you from Dan Wedmond," Marianna said near the end of the tour. "William was a pleasure to work with, but I believe you both have similar experiences and capabilities. You were both electrical engineers for NASA. What else can you tell me? Perhaps you have hobbies, when you are Earth-side of course?"

"Sure. When I am at home, I love to fly. I own a small Cessna 174, one of the new ones. I love flying around the deserts and hills near Sedona, not far from my home. When I could, I would fly over to the California coast. That was peaceful and simply enjoyable.

"I'm impressed."

"I was studying to be a chemical engineer initially but opted to change. I still have that background. In fact, it was beneficial to the investigation of the explosion on Venturous."

"I have been in close contact with Dan Wedmond about that. I wouldn't mind getting your take on it. But first we need to brief you on the safety aspects of Gateway, and I want to go over with you our operations on Gateway, what we do here every day, and what your role will be."

"Let's do it," said Linda enthusiastically. Even though she was feeling a bit of queasiness from the near-no-gravity effect, she bucked up and focused her attention on Marianna's words.

Marianna went over quite a few of its past and current operations. She explained that gateway's primary role was to support

Venturous, but that it was also a space observation platform for experiments performed by the Venturous or that occasionally occurred simultaneously with its crew.

Susan Ly happened to be near Gateway's own mini garden and pointed out that several of the plants – and there weren't many – were growing concurrently with the same species growing on Venturous, for purposes of comparison. Gateway had also been instrumental in the laser communications experiments with the Mars 2030 Rover and will be doing the same in the upcoming Mars 2040 Rover program. Linda Miramontes was intimately familiar with that plan and anticipated working in conjunction with Sylvia Levander on that project before returning Earth-side at the end of the year.

With the tour completed and the safety and technical briefing out of the way, the two astronauts grabbed an electrolyte drink, drifted to the habitat module that Linda would occupy and continued chatting. They remained standing as it were. There was no need to sit, even if there were a place to do so. The conversation turned to events on the Venturous and the investigation into the explosion.

"Some like to think it was Dr. Kormendy because of the animosity between Bruce and herself," said Linda.

"I take it you don't think so."

"No. Dr. Kormendy is ambitious, no doubt. But I have seen few others as dedicated as she is to her work. She also does not seem like someone who would risk anything going wrong with the base station. It's like her baby."

"She appears to be the most likely suspect," said Fascar. "But as you say, why would she take such an extreme action, when so much was going for her in her favor. But then, what do we really know?"

"Exactly. I'm inclined to believe it has to be someone who would gain from the explosion… or think they would. To my mind that could be…"

"Marianna, we have a low-oxygen reading in the SEARCH module," interrupted the CSA astronaut whom Linda had just met on her arrival. "It's the third time in the last 72 hours."

To Linda, Marianna said, "We'll have to discuss this later. Right now, we have a carbon dioxide filtering experiment in our science module that keeps going awry. It's a manageable problem, but we need to act on it now. The alternative isn't that great."

"I understand. Can I help?"

"Sure. Come along. This is your further introduction to life on Gateway. We'll talk some more later."

The six astronauts converged on the SEARCH module where the filtering equipment for the experiment was housed. Their normal air scrubbers were on stand-by while the promising new microfiltering equipment was being tested. So far, it had not held up to expected designed parameters. They would have to assess where it was failing and report back to Mission Control. This had been one of William Sosa's tasks while aboard, so now it would be turned over to Linda.

Gateway had a long history of highly successful experiments, and some not so successful, such as the microfiltering trial. There were even a few times that small animals were kept on the station. Strictly for observation, and perhaps as pets, to see how animals fared in space. The problem was that while no one objected to sending man to the Moon, when it came to sending animals along with man, the animal rights activists just wouldn't have it. All animals were safely returned. In truth, though, the animals were experiencing difficulty adapting to the extreme-low-gravity environment and the nutritional adjustments that were necessary. Still, NASA had learned from the experience, and still had plans in the works for studies to try again in the future.

For now, Linda Miramontes had plenty to keep her occupied and distracted from thoughts of the life she'd left on Venturous. Distracted because it had, for the most part, been idyllic. Distracted because she really did not want to think any more that someone on Venturous could have killed Bruce Holmann.

It was a while before Marianna got back to that topic with Linda.

Chapter 28
Foundation for the Future

5 April 2039, early morning UTC,
CNSA Moon Exploratory Station Tiangong-3, Sea of Showers, Moon

I wake, and moonbeams play around my bed…
In a rare moment of solitude, Commander Li Yuen reflected on a famous poem by the Chinese poet, Li Bai, written during the Tang Dynasty, 'Quiet Night Thoughts.' It was still early morning; he had just wakened from a very good night's sleep. Station activity was just getting started.

Glittering like hoar-frost to my wandering eyes
Up towards the glorious moon I raised my head,
Then lay me down − and thoughts of home arise.

The poem could have been written for him for this moment, only he was actually was on the Moon. There was, however, nothing else more apropos that echoed how he felt right then. To be sure, Commander Li Yuen was feeling quite pleased, for himself and for his country.

He'd done what he thought was right by helping the Westerners with their repair of the station, and now it looked as if it was going to pay off. Iron ore refinement was proceeding as planned. Their greenhouse was showing phenomenal results – as good if not better than what he saw on the Venturous. Their solar power experimentation module was one of the

Tiangong-3's most active modules, particularly with the plans in place to send Shimizu's massive Lunar Solar Power panel arrays down toward the Moon's equator.

If there was a definition of the ideal Yuháng yuán – a navigator of the universe – who best represents mankind, Li wanted to believe that he was exemplifying that definition. And so, perhaps, was Dan Wedmond.

But on the Tiangong-3, there was little time for idle moments. He needed to make his way to the physical conditioning and assessment module. It was time for his weekly physical workout and examination by Doctor Weilu. It often took about sixty-five to seventy minutes, not counting showering time afterward. And then he could eat something!

Li was almost forty minutes into his routine when his second-in-command, Xi Jian, approached.

"Commander, I am sorry to interrupt. Administrator Wu would like to talk to you."

"Xi, could you tell him that I am in the middle of my programed physical assessment?" Li replied. "And ask him, if it is not urgent, could I contact him in about an hour."

"Certainly commander," responded Xi. Xi Jian was an outstanding second-in-command, so Li was confident that Xi would properly defer the call.

With the examination complete and blood work taken, Li went through the Tiangong dining module, grabbed some electrolyte water and a power bar and headed toward the Commutations module. Fortunately, he knew he had a suitable jacket there that he could throw on over his workout clothes. He kept one there simply because this was not the first time he had to step away from a sweaty work scenario to take an important call. But this was the first time the CNSA Administrator had called him. It would be important.

"Put me through to the Administrator, please," said Li to the comms manager on duty.

After a about thirty seconds, the head of CNSA, Wu Yanhua, appeared on the monitor. Commander Li had met Wu Yanhua a few times during his training and preparation for coming to Tiangong-3, but it was always the Administrator who had spoken briefly to the crews, to give them a pep talk and thank them for what they were about to do. Wu had never talked to Li directly.

Upon seeing Wu on the monitor, he understood this would be of significance. Li bowed his head and waited, knowing there would be a three- to four second gap from the time his face and image were transmitted from the Tiangong-3 to CSNA's administrative offices in Beijing.

"Good morning, Commander Li," said Wu. "My apologies for interrupting your routine." Wu also spoke with a distinct southern accent, typical of those coming from near Hong Kong, perhaps from Guangdong.

"My apologies Administrator Wu. Thank you for allowing me to complete the required program."

After a four-second pause, "Not at all. I fully understand the necessity of completing your routine."

"I assume you are contacting me about our interaction with the Gweilo station," said Li. He personally did not like the term, but knew it was a common expression among the upper echelons and did not carry a negative connotation.

Pause. "I am. I have read your reports and reviewed your discussion with the Jiuquan command center." Wu was referring to the Jiuquan Launch Site in the Gansu Province. It was one of the three launch sites for CNSA's programs, and the one that was controlling both the Tiangong-3 operations as well as the Chang'e probes on the Moon's far side. "We at CNSA. and on up the chain to the Ministry of Industry and Information Technology, are extremely pleased that you took the initiative to help the Gweilo station, Venturous. You took a risk to reach out which many have been wanting to do for some time.

"While there are a few who have said you should be chastised for taking an unauthorized action, I can assure you, they are very few and they are not being listened to. The repercussions of your actions have been only positive among our leadership."

"I am glad that you and our leaders are pleased. It just seemed to be the right thing to do." Li, internally, gave a sigh of relief, realizing now that the pressure was, apparently, off his shoulders.

Pause. "You will also be pleased to know that the leadership of the entity called 'Moon Exploratory Team' have also contacted us directly. I personally had a very pleasant and productive conversation with one of their directors in the United States. We agreed that the actions of you and your counterpart, Commander Wedmond, have brought about a positive movement to bring together all the various space agencies with a presence on the Moon for a common purpose." Administrator Wu was clearly pleased as he relayed this information to Li.

"That is wonderful news, Administrator Wu," said Li. "Perhaps there is more we can do to keep the momentum going. I see good coming from our endeavors."

Pause. "We agree with you," responded Wu. "Internally, within CNSA, we are considering options." There was a pause, but it was clear to Li that Wu had not finished. "Consensus here is that, in time, the Moon will become more inhabited, not just by us and the Westerners, but by other countries and cultures as well."

"I believe that to be true as well."

After the pause, "There is also the future exploration and

subsequent habitation of Mars to be considered. Our leadership believes that we can succeed on the Moon, on Mars and… elsewhere, only if we have good and constructive relationships with our fellow Yuháng yuán."

"I am overwhelmed with what you are telling me, Administrator. Please let me know what we of Tiangong-3 can do to further this objective."

Pause. "You just might very well be able to participate. It is still in the early stages, but it has been proposed that our two agencies implement a taikonaut-astronaut exchange program between the Tiangong-3 and the Venturous. There is quite a bit of support for that idea. You will obviously be very much a part of that program if it happens. In the meantime, continue to communicate with your counterpart on the Venturous. Foster and build upon that relationship."

"I will Administrator. I am very proud to have been a part of this future for our countrymen."

Administrator Wu continued to praise Li for his accomplishments, not forgetting the other achievements that were part of Tiangong's normal mission on the Moon. At the end of the conversation, Li was pleased, if not ecstatic about the outcome of his talk with Wu and what it meant to the future of humankind on the Moon.

∽

Anna Kormendy also received a message from her boss. It was a prerecorded video message, the format in which most of the astronauts on board received nonurgent transmissions such as instructions, reports and occasionally messages from loved ones. It came directly to her Skylake from Jeff Fund and coded for her personal viewing only. It was not uncommon to receive such coded messages. She had received two such video messages from SpaceX executives in the past few months. But this was unusual coming from Fund.

In her berthing area, she found a place to sit down, and insert her ear pods. Once her Skylake verified her by retinal scan, she started the video. Jeff Fund's face, looking a bit tired – or was that just her perception – popped up and commenced speaking.

"Hello Anna. I hope you are still enjoying your time on the Moon and doing well. I had a few messages to share with you. I thought this would be a great means to do it.

"Let me start off by saying that SpaceX – and by that I am talking from the CEO on down – are very pleased with your accomplishments on Venturous. You have made us all proud and grateful that you are an important part of the SpaceX family. You are living our dream!"

Jeff continued his narrative, elaborating on what she and the team had accomplished most recently concerning the titanium find and what they had been doing with lead, iron ore and even ice found there on the Moon.

"Tim Buzza, himself, wanted me to reiterate our satisfaction with what you've been able to do there.

"However, he, and all of us here, are also keenly aware of the loss of Bruce Holmann. I know you will refute it, but such a devastating loss does take its toll on you and the crew, no matter how strong you all are. You would be inhuman otherwise.

"So, consider this an overdue pep talk to let you know we are behind you and supporting you one hundred percent. And, please, pass this message on to our SpaceX and Blue Origin colleagues as well.

"Finally, and this is for your action specifically, the CEO reminded me, and asked that I remind you, to always bear in mind our mission. We exist to bring opportunity for mankind to explore space and expand our reach and presence on the Moon, Mars and elsewhere.

"We are a corporation and we do strive to make money for our company and its investors, but that is not our sole purpose. If it were, we'd probably be doing something else. My point is I want you to not be so focused on these wonderful accomplishments that you neglect the big picture.

"I know I don't have to elaborate on that. You will know what to do. Let me know if there is anything we can do to support you and the team – anytime."

Anna sat in silent contemplation. She had overcome so much to become what she was, particularly as a Hungarian-born woman: PhD, scientist, astronaut, leader of the SpaceX team. Had she lost sight of the big picture?

For a while, at least for a few minutes, Anna sat there for a time despondent, for a time feeling ashamed, for a time angry with herself. But Anna was not and had never been a defeatist. Quickly, her outlook turned around as she realized that Jeff Fund really did mean what he said, that this was a pep talk. She just needed to realign her thinking to meet the situation. She had done it before. She could do it again.

♪♪

In his office in Hawthorne, California, Jeff Fund felt instilled with a revived sense of optimism and purpose. Under his re-alignment plan, he had acted to get the right message to Anna Kormendy, and now he was on the phone with Chuck Fowler. He needed to assure himself that the ground forces were on the right track as well.

"I can't stress this enough," Jeff said to Chuck. "We are not going to let what happened to Bruce hold us back. We are going to figure out what happened, who did it and why in due time.

And then we will correct that condition and move forward. That's just what we do."

"I am glad to hear that, Jeff. I worry about our people up there, and if someone is really trying to kill others, well, it's flat out not good."

"Look at it this way. With what appears to be taking place in conjunction with the Chinese base and their other space-based operations, we have a new foundation for an exciting future ahead. We can't let anything, or anyone, undermine it."

"Ok, I'm with you. You have the backing of Blue Origin. But we have to get the murder solved soon or it won't matter what foundation we have in place."

"So true. I'll check in with the NASA OIG special agent. See where he stands and get back to you."

"Sounds good. We'll talk later," said Chuck as he hung up.

Hanging up as well, Fund saw a message pop up on his desk monitor. It was from Dr. Kormendy. It read "MRAU." Messages from the Moon were sometimes short and cryptic as a matter of policy for security reasons. This message was one he expected – Message received and understood. It was all he needed.

Chapter 29
Revealed

6 April 2039, morning EDT,
NASA Headquarters, Washington, D.C., USA, Earth

I have to get this right. Our astronauts' lives are at stake.
There was not much of a view from Karen McCombs' office window in NASA Headquarters in Washington, D.C. She was just on the third floor. But she did face the Residence Inn as opposed to the I-695, aka, the Southeast Freeway. That was a more pleasant and calming view, walking distance to the Capitol.

Usually, her job was perfunctory, at least she thought so. As Laboratory Chief of the OIG's Computer Crimes Division, she spent her time isolating, counterattacking, tracking down and identifying computer hackers. Typically, these were hacks where someone just thought it would be fun to break into NASA operations. There were those few, however, who tried to influence commercial interests of NASA procurement, or those, including some foreign countries, that would try to steal information on employees or special projects.

This time was different. She wasn't investigating a cyberattack. This time she was helping to uncover the person who created the explosion on the Venturous, killing one the astronauts! Nothing would be perfunctory about her efforts this time. Nor were they, unfortunately, wholly within her normal experiences dealing with internet security. This was a forensic examination of a corrupted file that must be restored if the killer is to be found.

Karen rubbed the sleep from her tired eyes. She'd had a copy of the file and had been working on it since she walked in her office Monday morning and was told that this was both a highly sensitive and very urgent job. Now, Wednesday morning, she had little to show for her efforts. The last two days had not been highly productive. However, she had reached out to some colleagues in the forensic side of the cyber industry and was given some promising advice on how to proceed.

It would have been better had she possessed the original file located on the Venturous server, but that wasn't going to happen anytime soon. She had to work with a copy transmitted across space and via a number of systems to get to her office. Some of her colleagues were pessimistic, telling her that there would be little anyone could do with a copy.

The good news, however, was that the file had not been deleted. Her coworkers had been able to confirm that the file had, in fact, been corrupted by an operating system virus that was focused and specific. And that virus in its code form had been isolated and transmitted to Karen as well.

Working with her on this task was one of the Computer Crimes Division's many techs who had been trying several of the restoration techniques. He entered Karen's office somewhat excited. "Karen, I think we've found an approach toward undoing the corruption," he said.

Karen looked up, "That's good news. What have you got?"

"Well, it's not a total resolution, but we have raised a video image out of the dead period. It's far too grainy, but the good news is that we can tell that there was activity in the maintenance and repair module off and on during that two-day period before the explosion on Sunday night."

The two returned to the tech's computer terminal to review what had been achieved at that point. The tech was right; the video image was extremely staticky and grainy. Karen and the tech accelerated through the video file. The process took time, even when accelerated. There was no doubt, though, that there had been activity in the toolshed over the two-day period it covered, up to the time of the explosion. They slowed the video to normal when it was evident that activity was taking place. Apparently, the toolshed was a busy place, even on a Saturday and Sunday.

"I am calling this effort 'Disentangle 27-Alpha.' I will be continuing with derivations of this code to see if I can gain any improvement."

"Good," said McCombs. "But have someone else continue with the other approaches as well. If you are not successful with your derivations, we don't want to lose time if something else we can try might work."

"Will do."

The cyber tech returned to the rather laborious process, assuring the Lab Chief that he and the other techs were giving this matter their full attention. He would contact her if there was any improvement.

McCombs hurried back to her office. It was time to give Special Agent Ghiassi an update.

❧

Aaron Ghiassi had just arrived at his office at Houston's Johnson Space Center. It was about a quarter to eight. Walking by the small kitchen, he grabbed himself his usual morning cup of coffee that someone had probably brewed during the night shift. It was not his favorite. He much preferred the Persian style coffee that he could only make at home when family was around, but he wasn't going to spend his money on Starbucks coffee, as his office colleagues did, when it wasn't up to his standard either.

Arron dropped into his chair, powered on his computer, logged in and finally took his first sip of coffee, when the video call came through from the Computer Crimes Division.

"Good morning, Agent Ghiassi," said McCombs, once she saw Ghiassi's face on the monitor. "I wasn't sure I would catch you this early."

"Good morning, Ms. McCombs," he responded as he put the cup down. "You just caught me. Any sooner, and I would still be in search of my morning coffee."

"Well good. But this might perk you up. We have made some headway into our restoration of the Venturous video. I thought you should know about it."

Aaron had not been able to make any discernable progress on this investigation so far. He really had hoped that the CCD would turn something up. "Yes, I have been awaiting your call. Please tell me what you have."

Karen McCombs spent the next several minutes briefing Ghiassi on what they had done over the last two days in order to recover the file. He felt his attention wavering in the river of techno-jargon, much of which was exceedingly over his head, but that changed when McCombs finally got to the part where there had been some success in restoring a viewable image to the video file.

After discussing this point of accomplishment, Karen presented her plan for going forward – again, far too technical for Aaron. "So, I think it is fair to say that if it can be restored, we might have something for you soon, maybe by early tomorrow."

Aaron wanted to say, 'the sooner the better,' but he knew that they were giving this matter their full attention. "Very good. Do me a favor and give me an update on where you are and if you will be able to make progress any sooner in, say, two to three hours, please. I have to give my update to Robert Hamilton before noon."

"I can do that," Karen said.

"Oh, and as another favor, minimize the techno version when you do. I have trouble following you and I know the others won't understand either."

Karen smiled, sheepishly. She understood completely. "Of course. I'll make it so that you special agent types can understand."

"Excellent! Until then…" Ghiassi disconnected the call and thought about what he was just told. There just might be a break in the case coming his way.

With some progress in sight, Ghiassi felt refreshed and a bit more motivated. He had a few more crewmen who he wanted to interview. His intention was to talk to the astronauts who were classified by their personnel files as the most highly driven of the lot. Some, who had been identified as such, he had already talked to, given that they were part of that investigation team. But there were a few others he wanted to talk to, such as Sylvia Levander and Stan Rivers. Aaron leaned back, gazing out his window toward the various space center facilities, lost in the thought of how the world had advanced technologically, but still managed to bring along some of humanity's worst qualities.

He had more questions for Jim Sheppard and Anna Kormendy, as well. His plan was to press them harder and, hopefully, get someone to open up. He thought that possibly, with a little prodding, someone might point a suspicious finger, bringing to light some motive for what happened. He still did not even have that. It was an attempt to grab at straws, but it had been a successful technique in the past.

The fact that he could not actually be face-to-face while conducting the interviews created a challenge – being in the same room with the interviewee allowed him to see body movements, gestures and other tails that a video interview might not pick up. And there was that damnable three- to four-second lag in the transmission, pretty much making it impossible for him to exert any pressure on the interviewee effectively.

He also wanted to talk to Dr. Reisberg, to get her take on the psychology of the explosion and the XO's death. Maybe she had noticed some change or difference in one of the crew.

He had put all his interview question packets together and was prepared to make that call to the Venturous. Now would be a good time – it would be afternoon for them. As he rose to go ask Kurt Vaughn to arrange a call to Venturous, ironically, it was Vaughn that came to him.

"Mr. Ghiassi," Vaughn said from the doorway. "I thought I would check on you. See that you are getting everything you need. We are all quite anxious to get this matter resolved and behind us. It's not only put a damper on the crew on the Venturous, but all of us here in Mission Control and over at ESOC in Darmstadt feel it as well."

"I understand your concern and frustration, Mr. Vaughn. Let me assure you that the OIG is doing everything in its power to get to the bottom of this matter. We all know how important it is to everyone that we find answers."

"Well, I believe you… that we will find this killer. What I am concerned about is what will happen once this person is identified? We could have a very dangerous situation on Venturous that no one is trained to handle."

Ghiassi had given thought about this matter but had not really taken that next step of planning how to subdue an astronaut on the Moon. He'd have to take this up the chain. For now, he'd have to give a little false assurance. "That matter is being considered by our headquarters. I am sure you will be briefed once a specific plan is in place."

"OK. Well, again, let me know if you require anything."

"Actually, I do. I was about to find you to arrange another video call to the Venturous. I have more questions to ask."

"Let me get that going for you. In about an hour or so? Will that work?"

"That works. Thank you."

Aaron Ghiassi had always approached any investigation that he directed methodically and with a specific goal. He was trying to apply his tactics to this case, but the limitations as to what he could do, and the lack of actionable information, had made it very difficult to progress the case. On the other hand, he seemed to have ruled out numerous scenarios as impossible, or simply just not likely, faster than usual. The highly constricted and controlled environment and limited suspect pool tightened the parameters as to what was possible.

Consequently, this brought it down to one plausible scenario but still many suspects. It would seem that an astronaut had gone irrational, become unstable. Not so irrational, however, that the person could not cover his or her tracks. In fact, mental instability had to be the only answer.

The problem with that scenario was finding that person before he or she had another 'episode.' He had to talk to Dr. Reisberg ASAP.

And he did. Kurt Vaughn came through on his promise and arranged for a video conference with the Venturous, setting up Aaron's video monitor in an adjacent conference room.

After a brief exchange of courtesies with Commander Wedmond, he spoke directly with Dr. Reisberg. She, of course, was not alone, but Wedmond made sure that Penelope was on duty in the Command Center and no one else would be entering.

"Dr. Reisberg, I am glad I could get this chance to talk to you.

Due to the transmission delays, I would like to get right to the point. I'm evaluating the possibility of a mental breakdown by one of the crew as a possible explanation for the bombing and subsequent killing of Bruce Holmann. I understand it is your responsibility to monitor crew health, both mentally and physically. I am hoping that you can identify those among the crew, if any, who you think might be suffering stress or showing a change in their normal character.

"Keep in mind, this is only an investigation in which we're tracking any and all leads. What you tell me does not necessarily reflect back on anyone who is innocent. It's only to point me in a direction. As a doctor with the ESA, you might normally be subject to the Declaration of Geneva, but that does not apply to your current position with ESA and with MET. Doctor-patient confidentiality does not apply here. Do you understand that, doctor?"

After an extended pause, Reisberg said, "I do understand. And I am weighing conscience against the need to save lives. Having said that, I am prepared to share with you my findings."

Once Aaron realized she was not continuing, he said to her, "In that case, I will ask you to proceed and I will not interrupt you."

Again, a pause. "Very well, sir. You are correct that I am tasked at all times to monitor the health and well-being of the crew of the Venturous. Additionally, I received a specific task to look for personal traits that might give cause to suspect either a deviation in the previously established character of a crewman as exemplified by current behaviors, or to identify behaviors that would not be conducive to good and safe performance. One example might be a propensity to distrust or act negatively to the presence of the Chinese nearby. That was a direction given to me by the board of directors of M-E-T, our controlling authority."

Reisberg paused, but only to collect her thoughts and quickly continued. "You must understand that there is a lot that goes on here that takes my time already. I have not been able to assess all crewmen; however, my findings to date have brought two members to my attention."

"The first of which is an ESA astronaut from Sweden, Ken Herron."

Dr. Reisberg went on to detail specific observations she had made along with responses to a somewhat standard behavioral assessment examination he had taken recently that indicated variances. She noted his reluctance to accept what the group had accepted as beneficial to the mission of Venturous. This was a reference to the discovery of refinable titanium and his reaction to it. He also tended to be more solitary as of late. This was not an issue per se, but a distinct change in his character.

Dr. Reisberg continued, noting other small variances in his behavior, reminding Ghiassi that Ken Herron had been on the Venturous for three years; that such variances could well be within expectations and, very importantly, not detrimental to his mental well-being.

"These variances in his psychological profile have raised concern, but no more than that. Under normal Earth conditions and circumstances, these subtle changes would not even get the attention of most psychologists. But we're not Earth normal here. I bring this to your attention because, in Ken's case, it's the most extreme variance among this crew. And that is not saying a lot."

Aaron clearly sensed the difficulty that Omoné was experiencing by having to provide information on the crew that might not be pertinent or relevant to finding the killer. "I understand your concern and, Dr. Reisberg, I can only assure you that this stays with me. My report will not discuss anyone that is innocent of any wrongdoing."

After a pause, "I will take you for your word, Special Agent Ghiassi."

"Thank you. Could you tell me about your second... prospective variant?"

As he asked the question, the Comms Manager, Manuela Lusk, entered the conference room. "My apologies Agent Ghiassi, but there is a call in from a Karen McCombs from Washington. She insists it is very urgent."

"Ok. I'll take it," he said to Lusk. Dr. Reisberg had already started to identify the second astronaut, but Ghiassi cut her off, "Dr. Reisberg, something very important has just come up. I will need to ask that we continue this conversation later. You have been very helpful. Thank you." Because of the transmission delay, Omoné was still talking at the same time as Ghiassi. She said the name of the other astronaut, but he did not hear it. The conference call went silent.

Picking up on the video call from Washington, Aaron said, "Ms. McCombs, you are calling me earlier than I expected. I presume you have been successful in your restoration efforts."

"We've made more progress. In simple terms, we have been able to improve image resolution and quality by enhancing what we think it should be. I'll spare you the technobabble. Keep in mind, this will never pass scrutiny as admissible evidence, but it will help your investigation. I am showing you the image now."

Karen McCombs face was replaced by a video image taken from just above the entry hatch to the toolshed. The image was still very grainy and not continuous, exhibiting occasional dead spots. One of the astronauts enters with his back to the video camera. Karen continued talking as the video is playing.

"Bottom line, we have a discernable image of one of the last astronauts who we can pick out entering the module. I must remind you, there are still several hours of video imaging to process. What we can see – what you see now – is one astronaut entering the module and placing a canister in the general location of where the explosion occurred. He is doing something with it, which we can't see because his back is to us." Aaron is watching intently, listening to Karen's narration.

"He finishes what he was doing, he stands and turns to leave." As the astronaut's face comes into view, the frame freezes. Ghiassi inhaled, exalting in that giddy rush of adrenalin. He could see it well. There was no doubt who it was!

Congratulating Karen McCombs for her and her team's efforts, he reiterated that he would still need a restoration of the final hours of the video file. Ghiassi immediately placed a call to Robert Hamilton, located in the same building as McCombs. He was about a half-hour late for his update call, but the news he had should justify it.

Hamilton answered immediately. He had not yet gone to lunch. "Aaron, I was about to give up on you. I take it you were on to something?"

"Yessir. It's not one hundred percent conclusive, but damn close.

"I'm all ears. Go on," said Hamilton.

"First, let me start by saying that having ruled out – or rather not being able to support – most motives, and having talked to some of our medical staff here in Houston, I looked very seriously at the possibility of a mental breakdown by one of the astronauts as a cause. The doctors here told me that given that some of them had been Moon-side for three years or more, it was plausible that there could be stress- or environment-induced degeneration of the mind, although years of testing had not shown substantive changes in mental capacity. But there were some instances of stress-induced changes in personality."

"There were no recorded deviations in the files of the current crew. Still, I wanted to pursue this angle, so I talked directly with Dr. Reisberg on the Venturous. Turns out she had already been instructed to look for character anomalies or variations in conjunction with other events taking place."

"She told me that there were two astronauts who showed indications of personality changes based on prior documentation of factors. One of those two was Ken Herron."

"Who was the second?" asked Hamilton.

"Unfortunately, we didn't get that far. That is when I got a call from Lab Chief Karen McCombs, Computer Crimes Division. As you know, they were attempting to restore the video file that had been corrupted. It was not a complete restoration, but hours before the explosion, Ken Herron is seen taking in a canister of what I presume to be the ammonia used in the explosion."

"Do you have a motive?"

"No. But presumably, if he is suffering from a mental breakdown, only he would know why he did it."

"And you are still not certain this is our killer?"

Aaron had to pause and acknowledge the truth. "No. I am not certain. But this the closest I have been able to come."

Hamilton asked a few more questions. One question caught Ghiassi off guard: If you kill someone on the Moon, what law had been violated?

It was hard to say what, if any, law was broken. There was the Outer Space Treaty of 1967, but that document generally applied to commercial elements or the withholding of weapons of mass destruction. Criminal acts had not been contemplated. MET's legal counsel would have to assess that aspect... and soon.

They also discussed thoughts on going forward with the investigation. They still needed a degree of certainty. But it was not like they could bring in Herron for questioning.

Hamilton would have to take these issues up the chain, and they would have to bring in the MET board of directors. This was his task going forward.

The call ended with Ghiassi tasked with getting to certainty with all due haste. At this point, admissible evidence was secondary. The urgency now was to preclude another incident and the possibility of more death on the Moon.

Chapter 30
Stars That Fall, Stars That Shine

6 April 2039, midday UTC,

MET Moon Base Station Venturous, Sea of Serenity, Moon

It's another great day to be Moon-side! Gotta love it!
The workday was basically over for Marc Laboe. He had completed another test extraction of the titanium from the most recent stockpile brought back from Posidonius Crater. The results continued to be close to phenomenal. He couldn't be more excited, and he needed to work off some adrenaline, so he changed and headed for the gym.

It was crowded there today. Only one of the treadmills was available. Everything else was taken. He stepped up onto it, taking note that Anna Kormendy was working out on the adjoining machine.

Penelope Brightling and Jon Miles were there working out together. The two were becoming inseparable and everyone could see it. Ken Herron and Charlene Pell were working out as well. Ken and Jon were using the weight replicators.

There were no free weights in the gym, of course. Under the Moon's gravity, it would take huge weights to be worth the effort, plus MET was not about to spend the amount of money in fuel it would take to get such weights to the Moon. Thus, 'weight training' was done with mechanical friction devices that generate the weight that would have been experienced on Earth through resistance.

As Marc got going, Penelope said to the group, "Have you heard about the billionaire, Jim Strafford? The guy who paid $75 million for the privilege of staying on the International Space Station as a tourist for a six-week stay."

Ken spoke up first, "Yeah, I heard about him. Clearly he has way too much money if he can foot that bill!" The group laughed.

"I just heard, while I was on comms watch, that after ten days on the ISS, he is begging to be returned to Earth. Seems he can't keep any of the food down," said Penelope. "He's not able to handle the zero-grav environment."

"Serves him right," said Herron. "We have to meet all sorts of physical and mental criteria just to get selected, spend nearly a year in training, and he thinks that anyone can do it."

Anna Kormendy added, "We are the best of the best, right? Not everyone has the physical ability to go through what we do, nor get to the level of what we have achieved."

"So true," said Jon. The others concurred.

They continued their workout in silence for several more minutes. Anna Kormendy had met her quota and wrapped up her exercise. "I'm done. See you at dinner."

Ken Herron said, "I'm right behind you, two more minutes."

"Oh, and Marc," added Kormendy, "I would like to see your titanium extraction results for today." She toweled off and headed for the corridor to the berthing area.

"Sure, right after dinner," he responded. "I think you will be quite pleased."

Anna's workout was just what she needed to get her back on track and ready to go. She was still thinking about Jeff Fund's call and how she was going to make a more positive difference on Venturous. Somewhat absentmindedly, she entered the corridor, closed the hatch behind her and walked toward the other end, looking down the whole time.

"I've been looking for you, Dr. Kormendy."

Anna was startled by the voice and looked up to see Hal Lindstrum. He looked very angry, but worse... he was holding a pointed object, one of the geologists' spikes, and he held it like someone would hold a knife in a threatening manner. And he had come within a foot of her before she could even think about what was happening.

"Hal, what are you doing?" Anna said, her voice trembling even though she knew she had to keep it under control. Hal was not behaving normally. And she wasn't sure he was listening.

"I have devoted my life to astronomy, to studying the cosmos. When I was young, I knew we would leave Earth and explore space, explore the Moon, travel to Mars. I knew it and I wanted to be a part of that. Astronomy was my way to do it."

"So, you are here on the..."

"Quiet!" Hal yelled. "You've said enough on this station, now you will hear me." Anna Kormendy was now quite scared. Instantly she realized that if Hal Lindstrum was the cause of Bruce's death, she could be next. Ken Herron had better not open that hatch. Hal might not handle it well.

"I studied astrophysics, and I was very good at it. I taught it at Cal Tech. That is when JPL took notice of me, encouraged me to be a part of the space program. It was my dream, and they were asking *me* to join them."

As Hal continued on about his career and love of space, Ken Herron did approach the hatch to the corridor. He was about to open the hatch when, out of force of habit, he checked through the portal to assure it was clear. It was not. Still, it was just Dr. Kormendy and Hal Lindstrum there. But something wasn't right. He looked again. Hal was very close to Kormendy, too close. Then he saw it, the spike in Hal's hand and it was pointed at her waist.

"Oh, shhh…" said Herron to himself. He reached over to the intercom speaker control and switched it so that he could hear what was going on. He could hear Hal… "Everything was going fine. My observation programs were progressing. We were even poised to do extended telemetry experiments with Mars and…"

"Jon, Marc, ladies, come here, quickly!" said Ken in a hushed but urgent voice. He did not want to bring Hal's attention his way.

"What is it Ken?" asked Jon.

"Just come here. It looks like Hal is holding a knife or something on Anna!"

"What?" The four stopped their workouts and came over to the hatch.

"Take a look, but don't make any fast movements. I don't think it's a good idea that he knows we can see him."

Hal was focused on Kormendy, his face looking away from the portal, but a quick movement in the portal could just catch his eye. They each took brief but slow-moving looks. The portal was big enough to let two at a time look. It was clear, this was not right.

"…ruined it for me! You and your corporation flunkies. Your greed for the minerals and ores stole my opportunity from me."

"Hal, I am so sorry. I didn't mean for it to happen. I am sorry your equipment order got delayed. But I can make it up to you…" The fear was there in Anna's voice. It was clear she was trying to calm Hal down anyway she could.

"Marc, I don't know what you and I can do, but we need to be prepared to react," whispered Herron. "Penelope, we can't risk using the intercom. Can you go to the Command Center, tell the commander what is happening and bring him here, quickly?"

"Done," Penelope responded and headed out the second corridor.

"Jon, Charlene, go around through the back route and get to the other hatch into this corridor. Don't let anyone enter. And if you can, get some of the younger guys ready to go in if necessary. Can you do that?"

"You got it, Ken. Good luck." They followed behind Penelope.

"… there is nothing you can do now. The damage is done." The voice of Hal could be heard over the speaker, seemingly becoming more agitated, more aggressive toward Anna.

"You don't know that, Hal," said Anna, pressing herself to hold her composure. "I can still make things right for you."

Seeking Commander Wedmond, Penelope learned that he was in the clinic with Dr. Reisberg, after having a very closed conversation with the MET Program Director, Kurt Vaughn. She encountered the two of them as they were leaving the clinic.

"Commander, Dr. Reisberg, Ken Herron needs you immediately in the gym. You must come quickly…"

Wedmond and Reisberg, glanced at each other quickly. "Yes, we know, let's go," Wedmond said not waiting for Brightling to finish her statement. "Penelope, contact Vaughn immediately and advise him what has happened."

"Yessir." Penelope rushed toward the Command Center, wondering just what was happening.

Wedmond and Reisberg arrived in the gym through the other connecting corridor. They saw Ken Herron and Marc Laboe at the hatch to the opposite corridor, looking in through the portal. They also heard voices over the intercom speaker.

"Ken, I want you to come sit down over here, please. Right now, please." Wedmond's voice was assertive and firm. He did not want to take any chances.

"What? What are talking about? You need to come here. Dr.

Kormendy is in danger. Hal Lindstrum is threatening her with a spike of some kind. Didn't Penelope tell you?"

For a second time, Wedmond and Reisberg glanced at each other, but this time out of confusion.

Dan Wedmond had just been briefed by the Mission Director that Ken Herron was a probable perpetrator of the explosion. Planning to confront him, Dr. Reisberg had prepared a sedative-filled syringe that she held in her hand. But this was not what Wedmond had expected of someone who supposedly committed murder. As they approached the hatch, Ken noticed the syringe and gave a quizzical look.

"What's going on? Were you expecting this?" asked Ken in reference to the syringe, as he stepped back to allow the commander room to see into the corridor. Dan did not answer him but watched and listened to Hal's tirade in the corridor. Others of the crew were slowly coming into the gym. Wedmond could see the faces of Jon Miles and William Sosa in the portal on the opposite end of the corridor.

Ken quickly updated Wedmond and Reisberg about what transpired up until they had arrived. He also told them that he had sent Jon Miles and Charlene Pell to the other hatch to secure it.

"Good thinking," he said to Ken. *We clearly got this wrong*, he thought.

Inside the corridor, it was still a tense scene. Anna Kormendy was doing her best to not provoke Hal and, if possible, to get him to calm down. She had seen the faces of Sosa and Miles in the portal. It looked like they might be signaling to her. She didn't know what, but that didn't matter. It was a little reassuring that others were aware of the danger she was facing. Hopefully, someone would be able to do something!

"Hal, I can see you are very upset and disappointed. I would be too if I were in your shoes. But we are astronauts. We train for disappointment and find a way around it."

"This is way beyond that. We train to deal with the environment. I'm not used to my own agency trying to defeat me. It's just not right. NASA is siding with MET and MET is siding with you."

"That's not true, Hal. You are only seeing your side of it." As she said those words to him, she knew instantly it was the wrong thing to say. Hal had yet to listen to anything Anna was telling him; he simply did not seem to react. She had to get through to him, but how? She needed to take a different approach.

Softening her voice to be more calming, Anna said to Hal, "I want you to listen to me. I am a woman from a part of the world that is known for holding women back. I have had to face disappointment often, but I kept going. The more I was disappointed, the harder I pressed forward."

"But I am not you. I did not grow up with disappointment. I don't have your strength."

"Then let me be your support. Let me help you get through this."

"No. It's too late. I have done a terrible thing and Bruce is dead because of it. No. You cannot help me."

Anna noticed now that the spike was not pointed at her anymore. A small sense of relief came over her.

"I tried to hide what I did. I should have told the commander right away. But I didn't. What is wrong with me?"

Slowly Hal had turned the spike toward himself. Anna, no longer in fear for her own life, was in fear of Hal taking his own. That was not going to happen. "Hal, listen to me very carefully. I have decided that I want to help you and you know that when I commit to something, I do it, right?"

Hal looked at her eyes and then down. He nodded.

"So, this is what I want you to do. What I need you to do, so that I can make my promise. We are going to walk out of here and go talk to Commander Wedmond. Get him on your side. Does that sound good?" Anna asked, putting as much sincerity in her words as she could muster.

"I don't know. It's just too late."

"It's not too late. As long as we are both standing here, on the Moon, anything can be done. You know that."

Another nod from Hal and the spike went to a more neutral position.

"OK. So, let's do this. Let's walk out of here. But to do that, you will need to put that spike down. Just leave it right here. Can you do that for me?"

Hal was very downcast. His arms were going limp and he seemed to slump over. He let go of the spike which slowly fell to the corridor floor. Anna put her arm around him and helped him walk back to the hatch leading to the gym.

As they moved, the hatch opened. Commander Wedmond came in first, followed by Ken Herron and Dr. Reisberg.

Reaching the two, Wedmond said, "Anna, let me take him from here. Hal, let's get you some help."

As he took Hal from the opposite side of Anna, she collapsed on the floor. With ease, under the Moon's low gravity, Ken Herron picked her up and carried her out.

Chapter 31
Learning the Truth

6 April 2039, midday UTC,
MET Moon Base Station Venturous, Sea of Serenity, Moon

I was so wrong about Anna... and I am so glad that I was.
Anna Kormendy had been taken to the clinic and laid out on one of the examining tables. Dr. Reisberg had examined her and concluded that she had passed out and, due to the low gravity, had gently fallen to the corridor floor with no apparent trauma. She had simply fainted.

While grateful that nothing physically had overcome Anna, Dr. Reisberg was in awe of the incredible act of courage and sharp thinking that this woman displayed. Was it out of character or an act of desperation to save herself? Unlikely. She'd seen for herself that once Hal had dropped the weapon, she stuck with him. No one acting out of self-interest would do that.

Ironically, Kormendy had gone out of her way to twice save Hal. The man who had just attempted to kill her – earlier during the meteor shower and again just now – did not go unnoticed.

Reisberg smiled to herself, feeling a great sense of pride to be a colleague and fellow astronaut with Anna Kormendy.

She stirred. Anna opened her eyes and looked around. There was a room full of people and she didn't remember being here. "Why am I in the clinic?" she asked. "And why is everybody looking at me? Am I OK?"

"You're fine, Anna," said Reisberg. "You passed out after the ordeal in the corridor with Hal. You fainted."

"That's not possible. I would not faint because of that." It was quickly coming back to her where she had last been and why. "I was in control of myself the whole time. I could not faint."

Commander Wedmond spoke up in response. "Well, I might have had something to do with it. I had the air pressure in the corridor reduced, very slowly mind you. Dr. Reisberg felt that lowering the air pressure, and thus, the oxygen, just a bit would help calm down Hal. I think it helped, but I can say without a doubt, you did have it under control. I am very impressed at how you handled it."

"I just told him what I would have wanted to hear. Where is he, by the way?"

"Hal has been sedated a bit. He is currently in my berthing area under close watch. He seems quite sedentary now, but we're not taking chances."

"So, he killed Bruce then." Anna had held firm to the belief that it had been an accident. This revelation that it had not been an accident, but rather, the act of one of the astronauts was difficult to comprehend, even now.

"We will talk more about it later when you are fully recovered. But yes, it looks as though he did it. I will be asking him about it shortly. I just wanted to assure myself that you were alright."

"And M-E-T, have you told them?"

"I have. They will be meeting amongst themselves very soon to figure out how we will proceed from here."

Wedmond was about to go, then hesitated, telling Anna, "I just want you to know that what you did was heroic. And I want to thank you… for myself and on behalf of the crew. I'll leave it to your fellow astronauts to fill you in some more." Wedmond nodded to the others in the room, then to Omoné, "Dr. Reisberg, perhaps you should come with me if you can leave your patient here."

"I think she's in good hands. I can join you."

Omoné and Dan left the small group of well-wishers who surrounded Anna – Marc Laboe, along with Penelope Brightling, Jon Miles, Ken Herron and Charlene Pell – the group who had been in the gym with her.

Marc spoke to her first, "I think you should know you are not the only hero in the room. Ken, here, had a critical part as well. He was about to enter the corridor when he saw you and Hal and realized something wasn't right. He quickly directed people to get help and make sure no one entered from the other hatch. Very quick thinking on his part."

"Really? I guess I owe you a debt of gratitude."

"Nonsense. I just did what any of us would have done. It was just Moon luck that I was there at all. The good kind. Although, I do need to talk to Penelope, who I sent to get the commander. He and Dr. Reisberg came to the gym apparently thinking I was the culprit."

The six of them continued recounting the ordeal, sometimes in a serious manner, but occasionally throwing in a bit of humor as friends will do. Anna was, in fact, enjoying the moment. She thought about it and could not remember the last time she had relished the company of others quite so much. Maybe what Dan Wedmond and Jeff Fund told here was right, but inward she had known it all along. She had just been out there on the edge for so long, pursuing a career, living a life she told herself that she alone could live. She had insulated herself from others, and, as a consequence, from the warmth of friendship. That was not going to happen again.

৶৶

Wedmond and Reisberg entered the berthing area where he had lived for nearly the last two years but was now where Hal was being kept. It was a wholly different feeling to be here under these circumstances.

"Remember," said Omoné to Dan, "Avoid confrontation. Let him feel at ease. It won't be easy."

"Right. Don't be confrontational. Got it." Dan was, of course, skeptical, but he very much wanted some answers.

William Sosa was there. He appeared to be reading a report, but Dan knew that he was there to watch over Hal. Dan had first thought to confine Hal to his own berthing area, but this was less occupied. Dan believed that was most needed right now.

"Hello Hal, how are you feeling?" asked Dr. Reisberg as she sat on a bench near where Hal lay.

Hal was clearly sedated but responsive. "You know how I feel, doctor. I would think you would have far more important questions to ask me"

Commander Wedmond stepped forward. He was very anxious to get some questions answered. But he was treading in new territory now. "Hal, we did have to sedate you, but I'm told that it is not much. Just enough to keep you calm. Are you aware of that?"

"Yesss." Hal slurred his response. It was evident in his speech as well as his slowed reactions that he was far from normal.

"Why don't you tell me what this is all about? Why did you kill Bruce Holmann?"

Reisberg made a quick coughing noise toward Dan and gave him the look that said, "Be careful how you tread!"

"It's not like that. You really don't understand." Hal was not looking at either of them. It was hard to tell if he was avoiding eye contact or just not with them.

"Tell me then. I would like to understand. Maybe if you could start with why you were… upset." Dan was doing his best to present a consoling voice now. He wanted answers while Hal was still talking. He did not want to see him close down inside.

"I will tell you. I want you to know." Hal's breathing was heavy, which slowed his words. "I have worked hard my entire life. To get to come to the Moon, to this station – I was so happy. It was all going so well at first. But slowly, over the months, my experiments, my programs were being stalled, delayed. Equipment I was promised was being held up on Earth, not getting to me. Then I saw that the companies were getting everything they wanted. I saw that my research was being kept second to whatever Kormendy and Laboe and Brightling wanted."

"Hal, why didn't you bring your concern to me. Perhaps I could have done something."

"To you? You were just going along with them, supporting their requests and their pursuits. I didn't think you would listen to me. And others thought the same way."

Hearing this very much concerned Dan. Had he overlooked the research programs of some of the scientist astronauts in supporting the activities of the SpaceX group? He would have to examine this of himself… later.

Dr. Reisberg interjected, "Hal, did you feel that you had no one you could turn to? Did you feel that you needed to do something about the inequity?"

Wedmond immediately picked up on where she was going with this line of questions.

"I could talk to Jon Miles. He would listen, but he was OK with how things were going. When the metallurgy lab module was moved up on the schedule to be delivered and my space telescope equipment got pushed back, I was very upset. I decided to do something about it. I wanted to get MET's attention and refocus them on my work, our work, not just this money-making mining operation."

"How did you think you were going to that?" asked Wedmond.

"I thought if I could take out Martin, the Moon rover, at least for a while. Then priorities with MET would have to change. If there was no rover, there could be no iron ore extraction. No extraction, no need for the metallurgy lab. And a new rover was not scheduled to come for almost another year. I would be gone by then."

"Go on."

"Repair parts would be expedited. I knew that. But I thought I could still delay the lab and get my equipment while I was still assigned here. I knew that the gearbox was in the toolshed. I also knew that everything I needed to make a small explosive device was there in the shed. Except for the ammonia. I had to get that there. It just seemed logical that I could create an explosion that would look like an accident, destroy the gearbox, and no one would suspect that the gearbox was being destroyed."

"But your explosion killed Bruce. Why did you do that?"

Again, Dr. Reisberg gave Wedmond the look, but Dan was compelled to find out what happened. Hal was still willing to talk.

"That wasn't supposed to happen. He wasn't supposed to be there. No one was. I set it on a timer to go off before midnight on Sunday. No one was supposed to get hurt."

"So, you didn't want to hurt anybody. Yet both Bruce and Jim Sheppard had been working there. What if you had damaged the integrity of the station by destroying the toolshed. You could have caused more deaths."

"No. You're wrong. I knew that it was going to be a small blast. Just enough to destroy the gearbox, maybe some other equipment and tools."

Dan saw that Hal was very logical in what he did, but not very rational. Hal did not see that even if he had no intention of hurting anyone, his bomb could have imparted severe damage to the station. And this was despite having killed one of his fellow astronauts. He wanted to pursue this more with him but thought the better of it. He decided to ask other questions that needed answers. "What about the video record, Hal? I assume you did something to that as well."

"Of course, I did something. You're not so smart, you know. Why are you asking me about that?"

"The video file cannot be deleted. I believe you found a way to corrupt it, instead. Am I correct?"

"Yes, yes, yes. It could not be deleted. And if I had simply deleted it, you would have been suspicious right away. I was able to create a program that could damage the file image. It was very easy to do. All I needed was for someone like Penelope to go examine the file. The second she did, the software I placed immediately corrupted the existing file. Unless there was suspicion, it would have been assumed that it was just a fluke accident."

Dan decided it was best not to let him know that Penelope had been suspicious that the file had been intentionally attacked and that it had since been, somewhat, restored. But he needed to know about Ken Herron's involvement. How did he get that into the questioning? "Hal, can you tell me if anyone was helping you in any way? Did someone help you create the bomb?"

"No. No one helped me. At least not that they knew it. I had to get the ammonia to the toolshed without causing suspicion. I had Herron drop it off there for me. I told him that it was needed to flush out the hydraulic lines and that Bruce had requested it.

He was very happy to help. If you are looking for a conspirator, forget it. I did it alone."

Well that cleared up a very important concern. Interesting, though, that Hal had the presence of mind to not let anyone else get blamed for his actions.

"Look, I didn't want anyone to get hurt. I was just so frustrated with how things were going. I just wanted to do something. I am sorry about what happened to Bruce. I am glad that everyone knows now."

Dr. Reisberg said, "Hal, I think you should get some rest, now. I will be back to check on you. Will that be OK with you?"

"Sure, I am not going anywhere."

⁂

Commander Wedmond needed to get a report back to Houston and MET as soon as he could. Before doing so, he needed to confer with Dr. Reisberg about Hal's condition. They sat down in the dining area, each drinking a cup of wannabe coffee.

"Tell me what you think, doctor," said Wedmond. "And keep in mind, I will need to share this with MET."

"I understand," Reisberg said. She was hesitant but proceeded anyway. "Officially, a more thorough examination is called for, but I feel very certain that Hal is suffering from a mental degeneration. I can give you my educated guess that it is stress induced. More importantly, what I cannot tell you is whether it is related to our working environment here on the Moon or if it is something that has been hidden in his character make up, or perhaps a bit of both. That might never be determined. But you might consider that he is not fully responsible for his actions, that this environment attributed to what he did."

Dan thought about that. Could being on the Moon, in these close quarters, for months at a time caused Hal to break down mentally… just enough to do what he did? Others would have to make that call.

"Dan, there are studies that have been conducted about the effects and consequences on the mind attributed to extended space flight, isolation and overcrowding in a space environment, and reduced or no gravity living conditions, all of which have been inconclusive to date. Similar studies have been conducted with submarine crews for example, but even that environment does not completely compare to being Moon-side."

"Thank you, doctor. You were very helpful in there with Hal. I will go make that call to Houston."

Chapter 32
Learning Our Lessons

7 April 2039, evening CET,
ESOC, Darmstadt, Germany, Earth

We are treading on new ground here. While we endeavor to take on challenges and do great deeds in space, this was not the situation that we thought would be our biggest challenge.

As Loukas Anagnostopoulos sat in the ESOC conference room, listening to the preliminaries of the emergency board meeting, he realized that this was the third board meeting in a period spanning less than two weeks, and the second emergency board meeting. But then, quite a bit had transpired in that time.

In his long career in the space business, he had never had to deal with such a tangled, draining state of affairs as what they were addressing today. He had seen death in space and on the ground – in this industry that was always pressing the envelope, it was unavoidable. But now, he had been witness to one astronaut taking the life of another. Perhaps that, too, was inevitable.

On cue, Kurt Vaughn got the meeting officially underway. "MET directors, managers, colleagues, we have a full agenda for this board meeting that has been called under urgent circumstances. We have a lot to cover and there will be more sessions and meetings to follow as a result. So, if I may, let's get this meeting started."

The three board members' along with the Mission Director's

faces were on the monitors around the conference room. Rumbling voices could be heard from others.

"Please proceed, Mr. Vaughn," said Loukas. Nods came from Dr. Feskine and Jeff Fund.

"Thank you. As you all have been briefed, we have come to learn who is our perpetrator of the explosion on Venturous that ultimately killed Bruce Holmann. It was Hal Lindstrum. He has admitted that he is responsible to Commander Wedmond and Dr. Reisberg. There is no reason to believe that he did this with anyone else, but as a consequence of a mental breakdown that may well be attributed to stress of being on the Moon compounded by excessive disappointment by events. He is currently sedated and being watched around the clock.

"We are meeting now to discuss how we go forward. One issue is a matter of jurisdiction and the laws applicable to this situation. We have reached out to the United Nations Office of Outer Space Affairs in Vienna, for their input, but they have declined to get involved. Regardless, our own lawyers have advised us that despite the complexity of the public-private partnership and that all our contract agreements are of a commercial nature, because the death was of one NASA astronaut attributed to another NASA astronaut, NASA can assume jurisdiction and apply US Law. This comes from an interpretation of Article VIII of the 1967 Outer Space Treaty, addressing jurisdiction over persons and property on a celestial body."

Jeff Fund took the opportune pause in Vaughn's statement to ask a question. "Kurt, are we sure about applicability?"

"In truth, there is some question that the treaty and its revisions were ever contemplated to address this type of... action. However, our lawyers tell me that as long as there is no protest, there will be no issue. Further, it could become a moot point. Hal Lindstrum is cooperating fully. We expect to return him to

Earth as we would any other astronaut. And we will address his actions once here on the ground."

The board and its participants continued to discuss the nuances of the Outer Space Treaty. It was evident that such a scenario was not a concern at the time it was developed and ratified by some 131 countries. At that time, concerns were focused on commercial development of the Moon and other celestial bodies, restrictions on the placement of weapons of mass destruction, protection of satellites, and cooperation among the space-faring powers. Also, at that time, perhaps with an excess of optimism, criminal activity was not addressed. Although Article VIII did address jurisdictional matters over a broad range of activity.

One of the conference call participants from Darmstadt, given the heavy German accent, asked if he would be charged with murder and other crimes. Vaughn responded, pointing out that it was unlikely. "You should know, given Hal's mental condition and depending upon the findings of a psychiatric evaluation once he is on Earth, it is conceivable that he might not be charged with a crime."

Vaughn's response raised a multitude of comments and questions.

After forty minutes of beating that subject to death, the issue of getting Hal Lindstrum back on Earth in a safe manner was taken on. There was not that much discussion as options were very few. He would have to be returned in a sedated state. The question, however, was whether he should be restrained in any fashion. Doing so imposed certain safety concerns during the flight and reentry to Earth. Not restraining him might impose safety concerns for the crew. The consensus was that more medical and legal input was required before a decision could be properly arrived at.

As the discussion on this matter drew to a close, Dr. Feskine moved to the next agenda item: Where do we go from here?

"This was a terrible tragedy, we all agree," she stated. "But as humans on this world… and on the Moon, we only advance if we learn from such tragic events and make best efforts to control, overcome and prevent them from occurring again in the future."

There was consensus on that. Loukas spoke up, asking Cheryl, "We would be remiss if we did not solve the problem and rise above it. I take it that you have a proposal, Dr. Feskine?"

"I see three problems, Loukas. First, there is the problem concerning the legal issues that have been revealed to us. For that I propose that we form a committee to look into the legal, international and stellar issues, the purpose of which will be to devise a proposal that will result in the creation of applicable laws and forums for resolution. Perhaps it will require a world forum that can meet and discuss this issue and effect a change in the current body of treaties and law."

General agreement to this proposal was echoed by several on the call.

"Second, there is a substantive problem with the condition of mental health of our astronauts. Something went terribly wrong and we were caught by surprise. We cannot have that if we wish to continue our exploration of the Moon and, very soon, Mars. I propose that we further study what space travel and the extended exposure to the environment of the Moon has on our astronauts, with a focus on detecting issues early on."

Again, the participants were in agreement. As these were admirable and necessary goals, no one objected.

"Third, and this is as important as the first two: Our astronauts risk their lives in a very dangerous profession. I believe we have a moral and ethical responsibility to assure that our astronauts are as safe as they can be under conditions that we can control. Further, we need to be able to respond better when tragedy does strike. I do not believe we were well prepared to handle this tragedy. For that, I put it to this board to propose a plan forward."

This latter concept provoked an in-depth and sometimes heated discussion as to what was good policy in such matters. To bring it to a head, the board decided that a third committee would be established to explore this uncharted territory, and to propose policy changes as necessary.

That left two items on the agenda. The next one, being something of a very positive nature during this two-week period of distress, was an item the board was eager to discuss.

Dr. Feskine took the meeting once again. "As you know, one of the outcomes of these events has been an improvement in the relations with our Chinese counterparts. They were instrumental in effecting repairs to the Venturous. More importantly, I think, is that together we have proposals in play that will greatly open channels of communications with the leaders of the China National Space Administration, the result of which will be more cooperation on ventures in space and on the Moon. So much so, my friends, that the CNSA Administrator has already suggested to me the idea of creating an astronaut-taikonaut exchange program there on the Moon."

The swell of excitement from this announcement was immediate and overwhelming, making the conference call impossible. Voices were drowning out voices. On the monitors, the faces of the board members were clearly delighted with this prospect. After some time, the Mission Director regained control. It was not easy.

There was no firm proposal on the table as of yet, but it had only been a week since meeting the Moon neighbors. They were a long way off from a firm plan. No matter, the concept itself was a clear step in what everyone felt was the right direction. As an action by the board, a fourth committee would be formed to follow up and pursue cooperation and communications with the Chinese.

Before ending the board meeting, Kurt had one more item on the agenda. "As a last order of business, we need to act on one more motion before the board; to select a new executive officer for Venturous. If I may add, under the circumstances, I think Commander Wedmond and his crew need to have someone in that position, and they need that person now. We cannot defer this action. We have a motion before the board. Is there any further discussion before a vote is taken?"

There was no discussion. Only the vote was needed.

"Very well. All those in favor…"

Chapter 33
Telling the World

8 April 2039, morning PDT,
Blue Origin Headquarters, Kent, Washington, Earth

*S*omedays, despite the tragedy and hardship that life brings, this is a beautiful world to be on.

Chuck Fowler was sitting very relaxed in his office in Kent, Washington. It was raining outside, as usual. Normally, from his all-glass corner office on the fourth floor, he could watch the jets landing on Runways 34R and 34L at Sea-Tac, Seattle's International Airport – even on a cloudy day. He was only a 10-minute ride away, door to door. But today, it was just too overcast.

Although he had no inclination toward rain, today he loved it. It was a very good Friday to be alive this 8th of April 2039. A very good Friday indeed. In fact, as it occurred to him, he realized it was, indeed, Good Friday!

He had just talked to Jeff Fund. Seems like he had been doing that a lot lately. But it was good news. The tragic death of Bruce Holmann had been successfully resolved. The astronaut responsible was… well, he was under control. And it looked like there were going to be fresh opportunities on the Moon going forward. Perhaps even cooperative ventures with the Chinese. Jeff had asked him to head a committee to explore such opportunities. Apparently, MET could not agree on a NASA or an ESA representative to lead the charge, so Chuck got the nod.

And that was good. He would do the right thing for MET, for the future of space travel, and just maybe for the future of Blue Origin.

He felt the urge to share the news with his colleagues there in the office. Walking out his office which was adjacent to one of the main conference rooms, he saw several of the staff gathered around watching a newscast.

"Chuck, I was just about to come get you. I think you should see this," one of the project managers stated. "We just got a heads up on a report to be released by WNN."

On the screen was the young, always-attractive, female newscaster – there never was any other kind – talking in front of a background video of the flood-ravaged regions of southern Oregon and Northern California. Fowler tuned in hearing her say, "… with the let up of the heavy rains, flood waters have re-ceded in much of the heaviest hit areas of the San Juaquin Valley. People are returning to their homes and farmlands, nearly all destroyed by the downpour and flooding. The death toll is still unknown, but government estimates are in the hundreds. Initial estimates from FEMA is that the toll in lost homes, businesses and agricultural output could be fifteen to twenty-five billion dollars. But recovery efforts are already underway despite so much of the region still soaked and underwater…"

Those in the office were still stunned by the devastation and the loss, yet they also wondered how it was going to affect them personally since so much of western America's food came from the region. Chuck was no exception to these concerns.

Not batting an eyelash, the newscaster rolled into the next topic, "At NASA headquarters in Washington, there was new word on the billionaire Jim Strafford who had paid millions for a chance to go romp with the astronauts on the International Space Station, something NASA starting doing some twenty years ago. But for Jim Stafford, it has been the tourist trip to one of those places that horror movies are made of. He has been unable to retain food while on his jaunt on the ISS over the last ten days. Now, he has demanded that NASA return him to Earth before he suffers any more from malnutrition.

"Today, his lawyers have filed a lawsuit against NASA for his pain and suffering seeking a return of his $75-million ticket to ISS along with damages for pain and suffering! NASA had this to say…"

Fowler tuned this out, not particularly interested in one man's folly. "This isn't what you wanted me to see, is it?" he asked to group.

"No. Hold on. It's coming."

"And staying in space, we have this report from our correspondent at Mission Control in Houston."

The scene turned to Kurt Vaughn at a NASA podium talking to a large group. An unseen newscaster could be heard saying, "Two weeks ago, WNN reported the death of astronaut Bruce Holmann, the second-in-command on the Moon station Venturous. Initially believed to be an accident, the Mission Director for the Moon base station program acknowledged today that the death had not been an accident. We are told now that it had been the unintentional action of another astronaut, Hal Lindstrum. We go live to that press conference."

As the news feed switched to Vaughn making a formal public statement, Chuck listened intently. While he already knew all the facts, it was something entirely different to hear it portrayed on the news to the world. He felt sad. It was evident that all his colleagues in the room felt the same way. And he knew that so did thousands of Blue Origin, Lockheed Martin, SpaceX, NASA, ESA, and for that matter everyone in the space industry on every country on Earth felt the same – they were all set back by this news.

When the newscast finished, he asked that the TV monitor be turned off. "My friends, it is a sad day for those of us in the space program. It's a sad day for the world. But this is not the first time we have suffered loss of life in space. It won't be the last. It's just that the circumstances are unlike any other.

"But know this, just as it is happening in California right now, we will rise above it and we will be better for it. It might be hard to see that right now, but all it takes is to look at our history just in the United States, over the past two hundred fifty years to know what I am saying is true. YOU have done a very good job and together we have accomplished so much. We are on the Moon. And we are there to stay. Keep that in mind, keep up the good work and I can assure you, we will be celebrating the good moments once again."

Some of the women were crying, perhaps some of the men as well. Heads were nodding and there were comments to Chuck thanking him for reminding them of the reality of what was ahead. Chuck meant every word of it too.

After spending some time with his Blue Origin team, talking more about the course ahead, Chuck Fowler now had only one important task to do today. He needed to make arrangements to get to Washington, D.C., for this coming Sunday. He had been invited to attend special services to be held for Bruce Holmann at Arlington National Cemetery. It would be another sad moment, but he very much wanted to be there.

જીૐ

On Gateway, the crew of six did not get the news channels, but they were fully aware of the situation on Venturous and that the world knew it as well. Commander Fascar, seeing the sense of depression that had come over her crew, decided it was time for a few words of encouragement. What did the Americans call it – a pep talk? She needed to talk to Dan Wedmond about these idioms.

Getting everyone together was the easy part, they were all within fifteen meters of each other.

Linda Miramontes, who had been on Venturous until her transfer to Gateway, and Dr. Laurent Benet, having visited Venturous during the Lunar Lander's last five-day run just a week ago, had both met Hal. Commander Fascar and the remaining two crewmen had not. Linda, who had known him the longest, was rocked by the revelation that Hal had created the bomb blast. But as everyone began to understand, it was not something a sane and rational man would do, and that he was, in fact, not the same person he once was. Although, coming to the realization that what Hal did was not intentional, the fact that he might be mentally unstable didn't ease the tensions of those who must deal with him.

"I want to give you the latest update from Mission Control and to go through our first briefing on handling Lindstrum when he passes though Gateway back to Earth."

"We are all ears, Commander," said one of the crew. It was another one of those American expressions she frowned at whenever she heard it.

"NASA is preparing a Delta IV Heavy and getting two astronauts prepared, with a launch to be scheduled before the end of this month. The launch vehicle will remain tied here while the Lunar Lander is sent down to bring up Hal. There will be an exchange. The two new astronauts will transport back down at the appropriate time; however, Hal will return with the launch vehicle as soon as it can be made ready to return to either Earth or the ISS."

"Wouldn't a Falcon 9 Heavy be more appropriate for this mission?" asked Miramontes.

"I am told that they are all committed to the Mars project or other projects and that the Delta IV was available the soonest."

"What about Hal? Will he be safe –and will we be safe – in his current condition?"

Dr. Benet responded to the question. "Absolutely. Dr. Reisberg has been administering a calming sedative since we learned of his condition. That will be continued. And I will personally instruct the launch vehicle astronauts how to continue to administer the drug as well as watch for any signs of change in his condition. We want to be just as careful not to over sedate him. We all know that most of the journey back to Earth is not particularly stressful, but reentry into the Earth's atmosphere has its physical and, therefore, mental challenges."

In an effort to further relieve their fears and concerns, Fascar added, "M-E-T is fully aware of the crew's mixed and uncertain feelings about Hal. They are taking actions deemed appropriate to return him to Earth as safely and humanly as possible while minimizing the risk that comes along with him. You are all professionals of the highest caliber and Hal is one of our own. What happened to him could have happened to any of us here in space." She chose not to add that it could still happen again. "Let's treat him as a brother and get him back to Earth where he can get proper help."

"Understood, commander," said a crewman.

"Hey, thanks for the pep talk," said Linda. "We'll get this done, for Bruce and for Hal."

Perhaps I... yes, nailed it, thought Marianna. I should write these idioms down someday.

Chapter 34
A Piece of the Moon… Forever

10 April 2039, morning UTC,
MET Moon Base Station Venturous, Sea of Serenity, Moon

*T**his will be a day of firsts. I am so proud to be a significant part of it.*

For a Sunday morning, it was going to be a very busy day today, and uniquely special. Sylvia Levander had been asked to prepare something interesting using her lasers and, under the circumstances, she was more than happy to comply.

Sylvia was going to put on a laser light display like no other. And it would be seen, with the right equipment, back on Earth.

She was in the electronics module assisted by Ken Herron and Stan Rivers. Normally, Marc Laboe would be assisting her, but Marc had been tasked to handle a few matters outside of Venturous.

"Sylvia, I think you are about to outdo yourself," said Stan. "This laser light show will be phenomenal.

"Guys, I used to do this stuff back in my college days. It's nothing new, just a little bit bigger and better."

The framework for the laser had been erected yesterday and was already outside of Venturous. The three astronauts now needed to get the laser and the accompanying ancillary equipment out there and hooked up. They headed to the dressing and staging rooms to suit up.

Along the way, Commander Wedmond caught them as they passed though one of the storage modules.

Sylvia said to Dan, "Commander, we're heading out to place the last of the equipment and give the setup a final check. I think you'll like what we have in store."

"I know I will. From what you've told me, I know it will be suitable for the occasion as well as memorable. Thank you, Sylvia. Do you mind if I talk to Ken for a brief moment before he suits up? It won't be long." From his gaze, Sylvia know it was more of a command than a request.

"Sure, but I will need his help to finish the installation."

"Of course. You will have him shortly."

Taking Ken aside while Sylvia and Stan went on with their equipment in tow, Dan said to Ken, "I am sure everyone is still congratulating you on your handling of the incident with Hal and Anna last week. It must be getting old by now."

"True. But there are worse things to experience... like what Dr. Kormendy had to go through."

"Good point." Then with composure and softness in his voice, Dan said, "You know that the NASA OIG told me that they suspected you might be the guy who set off the explosion. When Dr. Reisberg and I heard that there was an incident in Corridor 7 and that you were involved, we took it was confirmation that it was you."

"Yeah, what was with that? I got a little confused when I saw you focus on me."

"The OIG division that analyses computer attacks on NASA systems were trying to restore a file that Hal had managed to corrupt. A partially restored version showed that you had brought ammonia to the toolshed and placed it where it was ultimately used in the explosive device."

"Wow. Is that how it happened? I can see your concern then. I think it was that Sunday morning. I had been working with Hal on some project of his. When we finished, he asked if I wouldn't mind taking the ammonia to the toolshed as I was going that way. I thought nothing of it and told him I would."

"Makes sense but weren't you suspicious after the explosion?" asked Wedmond.

"Not at all. Remember, we were never really told what the cause of the explosion was. That was being kept under wraps as part of the investigation. All we knew was that it was an accident in the toolshed. Had I known that it was not an accident, but intentional, I am sure I would have been all over it with you."

"That's what I figured. The OIG did finally restore the file to the point that it showed Hal making the bomb later that day. I'm just sorry we had to keep so many people in the dark about it. But I am glad we could clear up that one point."

"So, I'm still in hero status then?"

"You bet. Enjoy the day, Ken."

"I will!" And off he went to join Sylvia and Stan.

Wedmond had one last person with whom he needed to clear things up. And he knew just where to find her.

As expected, Wedmond found Anna working in one of the equipment modules, intently studying some readings on a monitor.

"Anna, its Sunday, why are you here working?"

"As you know well, some of these experiments don't care what day it is. I have to check them and make required tweaks and measurements every day."

In fact, Dan Wedmond knew that all too well. "Fair enough. But we will have company today, so please be ready to receive them accordingly."

"Of course, that's why I am here *early* Sunday morning."

He paused but got to the point of his visit with her. "Anna,

I would like a few moments of your time, if you can defer what you are doing."

"Certainly, unless you are here to tell me once again what a brave thing I did. Self-preservation isn't necessarily all that brave."

"We've had that argument already. You went above and beyond self-interest. You took care of Hal when he was most in need. But that's not why I'm here. I am here to tell you that I am very sorry. I am sorry because from the time I became aware that Bruce's death was not accidental, you were considered to be a prime suspect."

"Really? Well now I know why you never told me it was not an accident. I guess I could say I am hurt by it, but I will give you the benefit of the doubt and assume you had your reasons."

She is taking this a whole lot better than I expected. But of course, that is why Anna Kormendy is who she is, thought Dan. "There were reasons, but in hindsight, they were not very good reasons. If it's any consolation, in this club of Class 1 astronauts, it was impossible to find any justification for what happened."

"I suppose the fact that I argued with him frequently tops the list."

"That was part of it."

"Well, I want you to know, this experience has also taught me a few things. I do need to realign my focus and, you should know, my bosses have told me as much. Can I ask, commander, do you still want to work with me, here?" Anna Kormendy was probably never more uncertain about her outcome as this moment. Not even when she was threatened by Hal, for in her mind then, Anna was not going to let Hal take anything from her. But Dan's answer was a surprise and a relief.

Absolutely," was Dan's response. "You have long-since proven your value to the team, and frankly, your new attitude has not gone unnoticed."

Anna smiled. In fact, her eyes were swelling just a bit.

"Having said that, I have something else to share with you, Anna. The board of directors has acted on a request that you be selected as the executive officer of Venturous for the duration of your stay here. I want you to know, I think the board has made an excellent decision. You have earned it."

"I would be honored to serve as your executive officer," Anna said humbly. Then she thought for a moment. "May I ask who made the request?"

"I did."

જીર

The Lunar Lander had arrived about mid-morning from Gateway, but it did not bring any supplies with it, nor any equipment or any new crewmen to stay on Venturous. What it transported this trip were two members from Gateway: Linda Miramontes and, for her first time on the Moon, Commander Marianna Fascar. They made the trip down this morning for one purpose, to attend the funeral and burial services for Bruce Holmann.

Bruce would be the first human to be buried on the Moon.

As a friend of Bruce's, it was appropriate that Linda return for this solemn and inimitable service that was about to be performed. As commander of Gateway, it was also appropriate that Marianna be present. Marc Laboe, who had been working with some of the crew outside of Venturous preparing for the services, stood by, waiting to greet them.

As Marc watched the two women exit the lander, he smiled to himself. Even with the two women suited up, he had no trouble identifying Linda. She moved more smoothly and surefooted, having just spent more than two years on the Moon. The commander, however, who could handle the very low gravity on Gateway as if born to it, was clearly unaccustomed to even the Moon's gravity here on the surface.

"Linda, I am glad you came back for the service." To the other, Marc said, "And you must be Commander Fascar. I am Marc Laboe, SpaceX. Welcome to the Moon."

"Thank you, Marc," said Fascar. "I am glad I could be here, despite the circumstances. Where do we go from here?"

"Linda knows the way. She'll get you inside. Commander Wedmond is expecting you. Services will not be until later this afternoon.

"Marc, it seems very bright, even with my visor. I did not expect it so bright."

"Well, that is another thing you get used to. Particularly now. We just had the full moon condition two days ago, so you are getting the brightest effect. I think for the services, though, this will be ideal. You should try being here when we're in total darkness!"

Linda led Marianna through the door into Venturous and to the dressing and staging area. Once they had both changed into Venturous standard jumpsuits, Linda took Marianna to the Command Center pointing out various features of the Venturous modules along the way. When they arrived, they found Wedmond there, apparently in communication with someone.

Once he saw Fascar and Miramontes, Wedmond quickly wrapped up his conversation and, as best he could on the Moon, rushed over to greet the two arrivals. "Linda, Marianna, welcome to Venturous. Well, in your case, Linda, welcome back."

"Thank you, commander," said Linda.

"Yes, thank you," Fascar replied with a smile and grasping his outstretched hand in both of hers. "Linda showed me some of Venturous, but I hope you can give me the full tour before I return to Gateway."

Dan grinned, eyes glistening and focused on Marianna. "I am sure that can be arranged."

Miramontes could sense that something was going on and decided to make a hasty exit. "Um, I think I will go say hello to the rest of the crew, if that's ok with you two?" She was not sure if either of them heard her.

"Of course, Linda." he replied, glancing her way. "I'll see you later at the service." He then turned back to Marianna. "I am glad you could come. The circumstances are not the best, but your presence here is very much appreciated. As is your support."

"I'm just glad I could be here... for you and for one of our own."

"I can't tell you how good it is to have someone I can talk to, and not over the damned monitor, but face to face."

The conversation continued, both astronauts clearly pleased to be in each other's company for the first time.

◌◌◌

The astronauts from Gateway were not the only guests arriving for the day's ceremony. Commander Wedmond had also extended an invitation to the commander and crew of the Tiangong-3. They had accepted and were enroute, once again making that 10-hour journey. They were due to arrive within the hour, allowing just enough time for them to have something to eat and drink before the services began.

And so, they arrived in their rover, four of them. Venturous had been advised that the four were Commander Li Yuen, Yang Junlong, Guan Nuan – the three who had visited less than a week ago, and their doctor, Weilu Son. Their second in command, Xi Jian, was required to stay with the Tiangong in Li's absence, but every communication between Li and Wedmond emphasized that Xi very much wanted to attend. Wedmond surmised that it must be considered disrespectful for Xi Jian not to attend.

Dan Wedmond regretted that he was unable to come out to greet them. His attention was still required inside. However, as her first official duty as the new Venturous Executive Officer, Dan asked Anna to take on that task.

And so, she did. Suited, and standing with LaBoe, she watched as the Tiangong's rover came to a stop. As the four exited their rover, Kormendy, along with Laboe and some of the other crew who had been preparing for the services, approached the new arrivals.

"Welcome once again, Commander Li," she assumed that the person in the lead was he. "I am Anna Kormendy, if you recall."

She had presumed correctly. "Thank you, doctor. I do recall you well. As I have been told, I also congratulate you on your promotion. I understand that it was well deserved, regardless of circumstances." Li then turned and introduced his crew.

Kormendy escorted them to the Venturous dressing and staging area. As they were entering at the Door, Kormendy said, "We regret that our one crewmember that could translate, Susan Ly, has returned to Gateway. I apologize that we do not have a translator with us today."

"Fortunately, Dr. Weilu is also fluent in English and German. I imagine he will be quite popular today. He is anxious to talk to your Commander Fascar whom he has met in past international conferences on space activity."

⋐⋑

It was a beautiful spring day at Arlington National Cemetery. Only light puffy clouds were to be seen and they were in the distance. It was approaching 11am, an hour away from the services to be held for Bruce. It was going to be a unique service in that there would be a marker for Bruce, but the service would be performed in absentia. There would, however, be a simultaneous video transmission of the services, much like the televised high school experiment, as they were conducted near Venturous in the Sea of Serenity, the Moon. It was also unique in that funeral services are not normally conducted on Sundays at ANC – this was a special situation.

Numerous dignitaries were in attendance for this very special but somber occasion, attracting the attention, of course, of the media. More importantly, Bruce's family, friends and close colleagues were present. Loukas Anagnostopoulos, Cheryl Feskine, Jeff Fund, Kurt Vaughn, Chuck Fowler and several other MET and NASA astronauts and senior staff were present. Many, whether they knew Jennifer Holmann or not, offered their condolences. Jennifer had been offered a chair but she was not ready to sit while so many people wanted to take a moment to commiserate with her. It had not been easy to accept that her husband would not be buried here on Earth, but as a wife of an astronaut and former military officer, she understood long ago that he might never be buried at all. Today, she only felt the honor that was being given to him.

Jennifer was not particularly tall, but today she stood out in the crowd that formed around her. Her hair, jet black, fell over her full-length black dress. She wore a small hat and a pair of sunglasses, hiding her swollen eyes, but the pale white skin of her face still marked her presence among the men and women around her.

After talking briefly with Jennifer, Cheryl walked over to join Loukas and the others. "I am so glad you are able to join us today, Loukas," she said.

"Thank you, Cheryl. I do not like this part of our job. I have had to attend more than a few services for fallen astronauts. It is a regrettable reminder of just how dangerous their work is."

"Agreed," said Kurt Vaughn. "I must say though; it is a privilege to be here. I don't think anyone in recent time has been so honored as Bruce will be today."

Chairs had been set up on one side of the headstone marker. On the opposite side, two 3-meter monitors were set up that would be displaying the services as they occurred Moon-side. The crowd began to take their seats as the monitors changed from a display of the golden olive branches and folded US flag seal that symbolized the cemetery, to a live scene on the Moon.

❧

Outside Venturous, twenty-five of its astronauts and the four taikonauts – distinguishable by their distinctive spacesuits and helmets – were also gathering around the site that had been set aside for Bruce's resting place. It would be a cemetery for the future, should one be needed again. It most likely would.

There was, of course, no coffin. That was not feasible. Bruce's body had been carefully treated and encased in a form-fitting shell of sorts, created from a liquid plastic material that was used for repairs and other purposes on the Venturous. There was, however, a headstone. Luca and Jon fabricated a decent looking monolith taken from the local rock. Etched in it were Bruce's name, date of birth, and the words 'Venturous Explorer, Leader, Hero taken from us 27 March 2039.'

On either side of the headstone, were two very simple vases enclosed in plexiglass. Simple was all they had. Eleni Dimopolous had selected an assortment of colorful flowers from the greenhouse – ones that would endure for some time in the airtight enclosures – and had meticulously arranged them in the vases. It was a vision of beauty in an otherwise barren environment.

As noon, UTC, approached, Commander Wedmond glanced at the much smaller monitor, and concluded that the mourners at Arlington were ready. He stepped forward toward the gravesite that would be accepting Bruce's body, and began the service acknowledging the presence of family, close friends and the many colleagues and dignitaries, alike, that came to honor Bruce's life.

"We become astronauts for the sole an explicit purpose of reaching out to explore the vast unknown of space, to discover what those on Earth can only look at, to touch the Moon and to pave the way for the generations to come. We are the first, the forerunners of our generation. And we do it without any hesitation.

"But as astronauts, we know that with this drive to explore, there is an inherent risk. We make best efforts to prepare for and mitigate these risks. But we cannot… always… be successful.

"We are here today to honor one such explorer, Bruce Holmann. Bruce was one of those few who continually pressed forward to advance our knowledge of space. As a fighter pilot, he honed his skills as both a master aviator and as leader of fellow aviators. He brought these skills with him as he ventured into space, leading several missions on the International Space Station. At all times, he knew the risks of his chosen path – during one such mission on the ISS, a meteorite penetrated the shell. His quick thinking saved his fellow crewmen on the station but at the risk of severe damage to his arm. That event set him back but did not stop him.

"Here at Venturous, Bruce was a go-getter, participating in the station's numerous activities, experiments and explorations Moon-side. As executive officer, he was a distinguished leader, both respected and admired. As an explorer, I think he would very much appreciate being laid to rest here on the Moon."

Commander Wedmond was silent for a few moments. Eulogies were then given by other members of the crew who knew Bruce well. Jim Sheppard was among them. They were touching and reflected upon his character. He had been a strong force who was going to be missed. He would be a part of what he loved. He would be a piece of the Moon… Forever.

As the service came to a close, each of the astronauts walked to the mound of Moon rocks adjacent to Bruce's body. One by one, they leaned over and took a small single rock. If they were going to leave one of their own behind, then they were also going to take a piece away.

It could be seen on the monitor that back in Arlington, seven formally dressed marines presented the traditional three-volley rifle salute. This was immediately followed by a Navy flyover of four F-21 fighters in the 'missing man' formation. Once overhead, the tail jet peeled away from the other three signifying the fallen soldier.

And then something truly spectacular occurred. As one of the servicemen commenced playing taps, Commander Wedmond gave the nod to Sylvia Levander. Sylvia turned on her laser equipment. It could not be seen on the Moon. There is no atmosphere, no particles to reflect the light, but the focused beam of light made its way to Earth, in 1.3 seconds, leaving a visible red, white and blue trail in the Earth's sky above Arlington, and touched upon the headstone marker of Bruce Holmann.

Every person in attendance at Arlington National Cemetery, as well as everyone watching the service around the world and on the Moon, were in awe. It was a tribute to a single person like no other.

Chapter 35
Home Is Still on Earth

2 July 2039, morning UTC,
MET Moon Base Station Venturous, Sea of Serenity, Moon

*L*iving on the Moon is like going away on a long vacation. You love every minute of it, but when it's over, you are ready to go home.

The Lunar Lander had landed outside Venturous two days ago for its resupply and transport run with Gateway. It was July 2nd and in a few more days, Jim Sheppard would be heading home on it. As was Ken Herron. Both have served almost forty months on Venturous.

The Lander had brought with it the new metallurgy lab module. Marc Laboe, Stan Rivers and a few others were outside aligning the module in its new location and preparing to add a new access corridor between it and the toolshed. It was the ideal location and allowed for further growth of the station.

Word had it that soon Venturous would add another to its crew list as well. Berthing for the additional astronaut would be a challenge to contend with, but with both Jim and Ken leaving, and their replacements not yet scheduled to arrive, maybe MET would add a berthing module in advance of their arrival. That would be appreciated.

One of the Gateway astronauts had also come down on this run. A Venturous astronaut would be going back in his place. Originally, it had been scheduled that Dr. Benet would have exchanged with Dr. Reisberg. She would have finished her assignment on Gateway. But MET felt that it was essential that Omoné stay at Venturous as she was best suited to monitor the crew and, if it should happen, detect any further character or personality changes.

Fresh astronauts, assigned to fill the holes left by both Bruce Holmann and Hal Lindstrum, had been rushed through training. They had arrived on the Moon 28 April 2039. That was when Hal returned to Earth on the return loop. There had been a mass sigh of relief when it was confirmed that his return took place without incident.

Other than the change in the Venturous-Gateway astronaut exchange program, which was very much justified, Jim felt that life Moon-side had just about returned to normal.

Jim Sheppard was ready to go home.

But for the moment, Jim felt ready for a cup of that wannabe coffee that MET scientists had come up with. There in the dining area, he found Dan Wedmond, with his wannabe coffee, chatting with Ken Herron, Luca Barolo and Anna Kormendy. He joined them.

"You look like you have a bit more spring in your step, even for being on the Moon." Kormendy had clearly experienced a rebirth since the events of last April and everybody loved the result.

"As if you don't know why?" responded Sheppard. "What you think Ken? You feel any lighter around here?"

"Well, if I'm not now, we both will definitely feel lighter in two days' time."

Both Ken and Jim were a bit anxious to catch that shuttle ride to Gateway and then on to Earth. It wasn't so much that they wanted to leave Venturous or the many friends they had here. It was simply that Earth was home and it was time to get back to it.

Luca added, "*Non posso capire*! I don't understand. I love it here on Venturous. I don't think I will ever want to leave."

"It's not a matter of loving or not loving what we're doing here, being on the front line of what will be the future for humanity," Ken told the group. "It's more like... it's time to let someone else do it for a while." Ken paused, thought about it and added, "Who knows, I just might come back here in the not-too-distant future, if they let me."

To that, Dan said, "Ken, I think you will be most welcome to come back."

Anna said to him, "Also, Ken, there is still Mars to explore."

"There is that!"

"We are all explorers," said Dan somberly. "To some degree, each of us wants to be out there, putting caution aside and pushing our limits, being the first to do something that's not been done before. Seeing things that no one else has seen before. That is, I think, why we are here."

"Here, here," said Ken.

"It's something to think about, Dan," said Kormendy very sincerely. "But right now, I have to check on Marc and the team. I want to get that metallurgy lab module up and running within the week. If you will excuse me."

"I've got to get back to work, too." And so, they went about their jobs, the explorers of the Moon that they were.

◌◌◌

Dan Wedmond had one more nonwork task to perform before going about his duties. He needed to contact Gateway, more specifically, Marianna Fascar. It seemed he had been doing that with some frequency in recent months. But this time, he had a goal in mind.

"Marianna, how's my guy William Sosa working out for you?"

"Wonderful, Dan. He is an asset here to the team. I think, though, you will like the new crewman we just gave up to you."

"That's good, because you will be getting another one of our great astronauts in exchange in a few days!"

They discussed a few points of essential business that goes on between Gateway and Venturous. Eventually, though, Dan had to come to the intent of his call to her.

"I haven't told you, Marianna," said Dan, "I don't think I could have made it through those two weeks back in April without your support. You might not have been down here, but you were with me the whole time. Your words of encouragement kept me going. I do owe you."

"You American men, you try so hard to play it soft," Fascar said to Dan in an exaggerated German accent but smiling all the same. "You had it under control, and you handled it very well… without my help."

"That is argumentative. And we do require the occasional shoulder to lean on, my good friend. Yours was there when I needed it."

"It was my pleasure to serve… even my shoulder," she said with satisfaction beaming in her expression.

"Tell me, how much longer will you be on Gateway, Commander?"

"I will be serving here for one more year. We do not stay on Gateway as long as you do on Venturous. It's the close quarters."

"Well, I will be here for another thirteen months, unless they let me off for good behavior."

"Excuse me?"

"Sorry, an American joke. What I want to say, though, is if you aren't doing anything in, say, fourteen months, how would you like to have dinner with me?"

"I think I would like that Dan. But in whose country, mine or yours?"

"We will have plenty of time to figure that out."

☙ℛ

This was it, the last SpaceTime call that Jim would be making… ever. He explained to his wife that there would be a process he would have to go through once he returned to Earth, but it would not be long before he would be home once again.

Six seconds.

"So how long will you be in 'debrief' before you can come home?" Lori Sheppard asked her husband over the SpaceTime video call.

"It won't be long. Two days tops and I will be back in Murrieta with you and the kids. They have to make sure I'm physically able and that there are no muscle or organ reactions to returning to Earth-side conditions. It's necessary and unavoidable. You wouldn't want me to not be able to get around just when I am getting back home, now, would you?"

Jim saw her face and felt, in that moment, how much they loved each other. It really was her love that made him what he was. But he knew one thing. He would not miss these six-second dead-zone SpaceTime calls.

Six seconds.

"No. I want you whole and happy. I'll let the kids talk to you now. Sarah. Sean. Say hello to your father. He's coming home!

Sarah jumped in first. "Dad, that's great. We're having a big party for you… I mean for Sean, for his fifth birthday. Right after you get back."

Jim realized someone had just spilled the beans. But no matter.

Sean said to his father, "Will you be bringing me a Moon rock for my birthday, daddy, like you promised?"

"I will be bringing you a Moon rock. A very special one.

List of Characters and Glossary

While I enjoyed writing this story, even I had trouble keeping track of all forty-four characters that pop up – some were there from the beginning to the end, but some are there not so frequently. My very wonderful friends who reviewed the novel all said, "You need a list of the characters!" And so, here it is, just as I had created it during the writing. My recommendation is don't study it, just refer to it if you need to recall a person who might have been involved elsewhere in the story.

In addition, I have added a glossary of items and terms that exist today, or, in the near future, that might or might not exist but are based on current science and technology.

Venturous station crew:

- *Dan Wedmond*, USA, NASA, 51 years old, senior astronaut/Venturous commander, on base for 22 months, widower with three children.
- *Jim Sheppard*, USA, NASA, 38 years old, astronaut/ Venturous engineer/ agriculture enthusiast, on base for 36 months.
- *Luca Barolo*, Italy, ESA, 47 years old, astronaut/Venturous physicist. On Venturous for three weeks, but three prior tours on ISS.
- *Dr. Omoné Reisberg*, Germany, ESA, senior astronaut/ Venturous doctor/psychiatrist, on base for 30 months, came same time as Bruce Holmann.

- *Dr. Anna Kormendy*, Hungary, SpaceX, 49 years old, Venturous lead scientist, on base for 28 months.
- *Marc Laboe,* Canada, SpaceX, 36 years old, Venturous geophysicist.
- *Eleni Dimopolous*, Greece, ESA, 41 years old, Venturous astronaut/historian/ botanist, on base for three weeks, came on with Luca.
- *Bruce Holmann*, USA, NASA, 57 years old, Venturous senior astronaut/executive officer/ mechanical engineer, on base for 30 months and multiple missions completed. Former US Air, married late, no children.
- *Hal Lindstrum*, USA, NASA, Venturous astronaut/astronomer, on base for 22 months, 36 years old.
- *Penelope Brightling*, UK, SpaceX, Venturous communications and computer tech, on base for 10 months.
- *Jon Miles*, Northern Ireland, ESA, astronaut-technician, on base for 22 months, came with Hal Lindstrum, 42 years old, is fond of Penelope.
- *Linda Miramontes*, USA (Hispanic background), NASA, Venturous electrical engineer, on base for 28 months.
- *Stan Rivers,* USA, Blue Origin, Venturous mechanical engineer, 34 years old, on base for 10 months.
- *Sylvia Levander*, USA, NASA, physicist (lasers), on base for 6 months.
- *Ken Herron*, Sweden, ESA, technician-electronics engineering, on base for 36 months along with Jim Sheppard.
- *Charlene Pell*, USA, Lockheed Martin, mechanical engineer, on base 6 months

Gateway station crew:
- *Marianna Fascar*, Germany, ESA, senior astronaut/ Gateway commander, 49 years old, from Offenbach.

- *Dr. Laurent Benet*, France, ESA, senior astronaut/Gateway doctor, 42 years old.
- *William Sosa*, USA, NASA, astronaut/Gateway electrical engineer and comms specialist/youngest member at 32 years old, rotates to Venturous.
- *Susan Ly*, Canada, CSA (Vietnamese background), astronaut/Gateway mission specialist, Canadarm operator, visiting Venturous for the 6-day exchange trip.

On Earth:
- *Lori Sheppard*, wife of Jim Sheppard in Murrieta, California.
- *Sarah Sheppard*, 10-year-old daughter of Jim and Lori Sheppard.
- *Deneen Wedmond*, USA, deceased wife of Dan Wedmond.
- *Jennifer Holmann*, wife of Bruce, married late.
- *Loukas Anagnostopoulos*, Greece, ESA Director of MET at ESOC in Darmstadt, Germany, 63 years old.
- *Dr. Cheryl Feskine, MD, PhD*, USA, NASA Director of MET at the Johnson Space Center Mission Control, Houston, 52 years old.
- *Jeff Fund*, USA, SpaceX Director of MET in Hawthorn, California.
- *Kurt Vaughn*, Germany, MET Mission Director, located at Johnson Space Center Mission Control, Houston.
- *Chuck Fowler*, USA, Blue Origin, Project Manager, out of Kent, Washington.
- *Manuela Lusk*, USA, NASA, Mission Control Center, Communications Officer.
- *Jim Royal*, USA, NASA, Engineer, Chinese interpreter.
- *Tim Buzza*, USA, SpaceX, CEO.
- *Robert Hamilton*, USA, NASA OIG, Deputy Assistant Inspector General, Washington, D.C.

- *Aaron Ghiassi*, USA, NASA OIG, SAIC, Houston, Syrian ancestry.
- *Karen McCombs*, USA NASA OIG, Lab Chief, Washington.
- *Wu Yanhua*, China, Haidian District, Beijing, CNSA, Administrator (top position).
- *Jim Strafford*, USA, billionaire, lives wherever he wants.
- Chinese Moon-based station Tiangong-3 crew:
- *Li Yuen*, China, CNSA, Commander of Chinese station, *Tiangong-3*, from Shenzhen.
- *Yang Junlong*, China, CNSA, Chief Engineer, Tiangong-3, son of Yang Liwei, first Chinese taikonaut to go into space, from Beijing.
- *Xi Jian*, China, CNSA, 2nd in Command, relative of Xi Jinping, former President of China.
- *Guan Nuan*, China, CNSA, senior female taikonaut and chief of sciences, from Shanghai, 41 years old.
- *Pedro Yoshitake*, Brazil, Shimizu Corp., senior engineer and head of Lunar Solar Power project.
- *Dr. Weilu*, China, M.D.

Other Names and Fictional Devices:
- 3DTV – The three-dimensional television system that projects near-3D-like video imaging.
- Astronaut – from the Greek meaning "star sailor"
- CNSA – China National Space Administration, formed in 1993, and under the Ministry of Industry and Information Technology
- Dyneema – Formerly known as Cuben Fiber, is the strongest fabric in the world. Technically identified as a ultra-high-molecular-weight <u>polyethylene</u>, at one thousandth of an inch in thickness, Dyneema has an extraordinarily high strength-to-weight ratio and is 15 times tougher than steel

- The door – the only portal exit to the outside from Venturous
- ESOC – European Space Operations Centre in Darmstadt, Germany
- Gateway – the US/EU Moon-orbiting platform, not affiliated with MET.
- Gweilo or gweilou – Cantonese slang for Westerners meaning light-skinned. In Mandarin it is 老外 or lâowài.
- Intelliboard – a virtual keyboard and console control for home computers.
- Jiuquan Launch Site – managing CNSA's Tiangong-3 operations. Located in the Gansu Province.
- jPhone – Next generation of phones after the iPhone.
- Luna Ring – the proposed solar panel array to be built around the Moon's equator (fact).
- Lunar Lander – the vehicle built by Lockheed Martin to traverse between Gateway and Venturous
- Martin – Moon Automated Rover/Transport, a nickname given to the rover, in operation for 8 of the 10 years at the base station.
- MET – the name for the public-private partnership is *Moon Exploration Team*, aka M-E-T. While SpaceX came up with some stellar names for the PPP, this was the best that came out of the joint efforts of the US and EU space agencies.
- Orion – space capsule used to transport astronauts to and from the Moon and other space platforms
- Taikonaut – Western term for a Chinese space traveler.
- Tiangong-3 – the name of the Chinese Moon-based station.
- Skylake – computing system and devise of the time (based on current articles).

- SMEP – Student Moon-based Experiments Program, NASA's next program after SSEP
- SpaceTime – the public video telecommunications system between Earth and Moon, space stations and lunar stations.
- SRS – the name of the US rocket used to launch large payloads
- Venturous – the MET-operated Moon base station and focal location of the story.
- Venturous Explorers – Name for students participating in SMEP.
- Yuháng yuán (universe navigator) – In China, the term is used for space traveler

Location Map

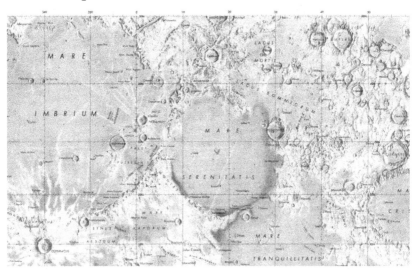

Map of Mare Serenitatis and Mare Imbrium, Moon – Location of Venturous and Tiangong-3